Deep Dark Secrets
Book One

Cozy up to a Winter mystery set in snowy Wisconsin. Who killed the local pastor with an ice auger on frozen Lake Loki? Join Frankie Champagne, baker, wine-maker and investigative reporter, as she tracks suspects, armed with delicious baked goods and old-fashioned intuition.

An engaging cozy mystery that showcases the grit of Frankie—a female entrepreneur who owns a bakery/wine bar, a vineyard, and is a budding journalist who just scooped the town's newspaper editor. I can hardly wait to read the next book in the series.

> – Laurie Buchanan, PhD,
> author of *Indelible*, the Sean McPherson Series

There's so much to love about this book. The twisty mystery, delicious recipes, and wine making in Wisconsin.

> – Diana M. Rosales

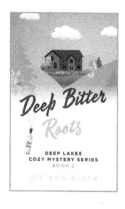

Deep Bitter Roots

Book Two

A cursed heiress, a rejected suitor, a hostile relative, a ladder-climbing doctor, a mystery cat, and two naughty aunties . . . Join Frankie Champagne: baker/vintner and part-time investigative reporter, as she unravels the granite quarry curse.

Family secrets create wonderful sparks and laugh-out-loud humor.

> – Christine DeSmet, author of the Fudge Shop
> Mystery Series and Mischief in Moonstone Series

Deep Bitter Roots brims with intrigue, old family secrets, and local color. Readers will cheer for Frankie as, while juggling the responsibilities of a baker, vintner, and journalist, she manages to out-sleuth the experts.

> – Kathleen Ernst,
> author of the Chloe Ellefson Mysteries

Deep Flakes Christmas: A Nisse Visit

Prequel

Before Frankie Champagne encountered *Deep Dark Secrets*, her main concerns were baking tasty pastries and producing flavorful wines—along with charming her mother, of course. But with the town Christmas season in jeopardy, Frankie steps up to save the day, as only someone who doesn't believe in the word impossible can do. Frankie summons her female superpowers and, with a little mysterious intervention, she might even overcome her Christmas blues in the process.

Complications abound in this delicious cassoulet of Scandinavian baked goods, fine wine, and record-breaking snowstorms. But add in a pair of delightful Norwegian Nisser, and you've got a merry tale that lifts the heart not only during the holiday season but any time of year.

> – Laurie Buchanan, PhD,
> author of *Indelible*, Sean McPherson Series

You cannot help but LOVE everything there is about Frankie, her jobs, her family, her friends and her community. I would love to visit Deep Lakes and will do so every time Ribar writes a book.

> – Cozy Mystery Book Reviews

Deep Green Envy

Joy Ann Ribar

ten16press.com - Waukesha, WI

Deep Green Envy
Copyrighted © 2021 Joy Ann Ribar
ISBN 9781645382935
Library of Congress Control Number: 2021914354
First Edition

Deep Green Envy
by Joy Ann Ribar

For information, please contact:

www.ten16press.com
Waukesha, WI

Edited by Kay Rettenmund
Cover design by Tom Heffron

Some of life's most treasured gems may not be flashy, but they are brilliant, colorful, precious, and worth a fortune. This describes my dear husband, friend, confidant, tech guru and the rock upon which I build my authorship. Here's to you John, with love.

Sign up for Joy's email newsletter!

Chapter 1

"Dogs do speak, but only to those who know how to listen."
- Orhan Pamuk

Frankie Champagne stared out the kitchen window overlooking the wide front lawn at the O'Connor sheep farm. She was accustomed to interrupted sleep, the byproduct of an overactive mind, but this particular sultry evening had been worse than normal. She wasn't certain what awakened her this time, but the orange digital clock numbers on the nightstand read 3:30 a.m., and she surrendered to the forces keeping sleep at bay.

She pressed a cold glass of ice water to her forehead, hoping it would provide relief. This was her second night at the O'Connor farm, but the air conditioning had fizzled out on her first day there. Of course, the repair company wouldn't be out until next week to fix it. Normally, Wisconsin June nights are refreshing, especially in the countryside, but the state suffered its first warm humid spell of summer, vaulting temperatures into the upper 80's with not even a whiff of a breeze. *Go figure the AC would decide to break this week*, Frankie thought.

Still, she didn't plan to let Carmen and Ryan know about the broken AC until their return from Chicago. After the wedding invitation arrived from Carmen's Chicago niece, Frankie had badgered her business partner for months to take a few days away. Carmen's brother, Andres, was her favorite. The two grew up side by side, practically twins, born 14 months apart. Frankie insisted that Carmen and her family should attend Andres's daughter's wedding, that they owed themselves some time away, time with family. Carmen and Ryan's twins, Carlos and Kyle, were asked to be ushers at the wedding. That supplied another reason for the O'Connors to go.

Frankie volunteered to stay at the sheep farm and oversee the operations while the O'Connors were away. Of course, Frankie could count on one hand her knowledge about running a sheep farm, but the farm hands knew the routines and would probably be happy to earn some extra pay while Ryan was gone. Her only real responsibility was to keep the house safe, which made her twinge since the AC was broken, and to keep track of Ryan's clipboard. The clipboard hung next to the front door in an enclosed vestibule, and served as a sign-in sheet for the hired help, pick-up services, and delivery drivers. Frankie would ensure that the schedule was being kept and deliveries made by initialing the forms.

That morning, Green-Up Fertilizer was set to pick up its monthly load of sheep manure. Frankie realized she'd need to stay put to check off the driver's load; so much for getting into Bubble and Bake by sunup to prepare for a busy summer weekend. Frankie and Carmen were business partners, running the bakery-by-day and wine-lounge-by-night operation in downtown Deep Lakes the past five plus years.

She was about to check the delivery schedule, when Sonny, the O'Connors' sheltie, beat her to the front door and emitted a low growl. An abrupt crack shattered the thick air, but as sound travels strangely in the night, Frankie couldn't be certain where it came from. Maybe the storm front that had been hanging over the area finally came unhinged, bringing the relief of rain. Frankie could hear the other farm dogs barking now, an eerie interruption to the stifling thick silence.

Sonny stood sideways against the front door like a shield, so Frankie returned to the window and peered out into the hazy darkness. The half moon attempted to cast light onto the landscape but failed, just barely illuminating the low-hanging clouds. What should she do?

Frankie waited for more sound, light, activity, something to happen. Instead, everything settled back into deep stillness. The dogs had stopped barking, but she noticed Sonny's normally tipped ears were standing up straight, and his bright eyes were focused and ready. *Ready for what, though?* Frankie wondered.

She scooted to the front bedroom she occupied and threw on her jeans and socks, opting to stay in her pajama top. She retrieved Sonny's leash, attached it effortlessly to his collar, and donned the shoes she'd left by the door.

Sonny seemed anxious to get outside, pulling Frankie down the front steps before she could check the clipboard, and immediately sticking his nose to the ground, then doing his doggy business before raising his head again, ears pricked. Frankie hushed Sonny just in case there was something lurking in the haze, and instantly regretted not grabbing a flashlight.

Sonny's sheltie sense responded to Frankie's cue to operate in stealth mode. The two moved silently, keeping close to the perimeter of the fence line along the farm's main driveway. Both stopped, their heart rates quickening as they heard tires crunching over gravel. Frankie and Sonny moved to the cover of a large oak and she squinted into the haze, willing herself to see the vehicle that was disappearing down the drive toward the main road, minus head and tail lights.

Sonny nuzzled Frankie's hand that had crept around the sheltie's mane, where Frankie squatted to make herself as small as possible behind the tree. She wasn't sure how long she stayed there, incapable of movement, holding her breath. Everything was still again, so it was time to go back to the house and get a flashlight before heading down to the sheep shed, where the phantom vehicle had materialized.

Frankie checked the time—3:45 a.m. Somehow, she decided that the time mattered. She took the flashlight from the bedroom stand and made a split-second decision to throw on a hoodie, feeling the clammy discomfort from the heavy haze seeping into her bones.

Sonny anxiously jerked on the leash Frankie held tightly. A few yards from the sheep shed, she heard the low rumble of a truck engine. Soon, the cab and box truck came into view; one headlight beamed eerily like a cyclops. Sonny was panting now and jerking harder on the leash. Frankie spoke soothingly as she patted the sheltie's side despite her own ragged breathing. Shining the light around the area, Frankie saw the open lift gate behind the hauler and walked over to it. She shined the light inside. It was empty. What's more, the manure pile, stacked on a nearby pallet, looked undisturbed.

A sense of dread overcame both human and animal. Frankie tilted the flashlight toward the cab, hoping her eyes were failing her when she saw a figure slumped over the steering wheel. Frankie's short stature was a detriment that didn't allow her to see clearly, so she climbed the two steps up to the driver's side window, flashlight in hand. She had to drop the leash to keep her balance, but Sonny perched two paws on the step, muttering his displeasure in fearful throaty growls.

What if the driver had a heart attack? Frankie could perform CPR if she had to, at least she hoped she could. She knocked on the window, in the unlikely case the driver was asleep. After all, it was too early to make a pick up, wasn't it?

She pulled firmly on the door handle, which caused the body to crumple over almost on top of her. What was that smell—a burnt odor combined with something more ghastly. She gave the driver an adrenaline-induced push, waving the flashlight wildly. Only then, Frankie saw the blood: on the headrest and down the seat back, along with other gooey globs she didn't want to think about. She shuddered as she grasped the driver's lifeless wrist to seek a pulse, but there was no pulse to find. Thank goodness she'd had the wisdom to carry her phone. She leapt from the top step to the ground, barely missing Sonny's rooted front feet, pulled out her cell and dialed 911.

"Whitman County Dispatch. This is Meg."

"Meg. This is Frankie Champagne. I need officers out at the O'Connor sheep farm. And the coroner. I think a delivery driver's been shot." Frankie's legs almost gave out on the last sentence.

Meg calmly asked for the fire number and address, then offered reassurance. "Frankie, I'm coming back on the line with you after I send out the officers. Don't hang up."

Meg Kemper had worked dispatch for over 20 years and was a pro. She didn't prod Frankie with extra questions except to ascertain if she had been hurt or was in imminent danger, but insisted they stay in contact until the department arrived.

When Frankie heard the crunch of tires on the farm drive, she told Meg the officers were there and hung up. She stood in the driveway anticipating Sheriff Alonzo

Goodman's jeep, but was surprised to see an older model pickup with a cap over the bed. Two of the O'Connor hired hands stepped out, equally surprised to see Frankie.

"What are you doin' down here by the shed this early?" a gruff voice demanded.

Frankie recognized the weathered face of Reggie Tomly, a longtime hand for the O'Connors and owner of the pickup. He was holding a dented metal lunchbox in one hand and a thermos in the other. Frankie thought he looked disheveled, like he wasn't quite awake, or maybe something had rattled him.

"I heard a noise down here, so Sonny and I came to take a look," she tried to speak with authority mixed with a folksy tone.

Dawn was breaking now, and Frankie took a good look at the other hand, a younger man they called Goat. During her tutorial of the farm, she recalled Ryan saying that Goat moved into the area during lambing that spring, looking for work.

Goat looked down at the ground, kicking at the gravel with the toe of his boot. He, too, held a lunchbox in one hand, but the other was behind his back, as if he had something secret he planned to give someone.

Nobody was saying anything but the two men looked at the manure truck with interest, especially since they could see the slumped figure in the seat with the approaching daylight. Reggie started moving toward the truck, but Frankie stepped in his path.

"The sheriff's on his way and should be here any minute," she said.

Reggie ran one rough hand through his unruly hair, then down his beard in a smooth stroke. "So, what happened?" He sounded pensive.

Frankie felt her insides shake, despite her best efforts to remain indifferent. There was no way she was going to break down in front of these two. She stiffened and mustered the persona of a tough TV cop. "Can't say. I'm sure we'll find out when the sheriff arrives," she intoned in a cool steely voice. "Why don't the two of you wait in your truck, hmm?"

Frankie couldn't fathom where this steely persona came from. It was her nature to be open and warm toward others. This chilled version of Frankie was new and scintillating; she contemplated how handy it would be for future investigative reporter assignments.

Reggie shrugged and waved his thumb at Goat toward the pickup. When Goat turned to walk, Frankie noticed his right hand was wrapped up, as if it were injured.

Just then, Alonzo's Jeep zipped up behind the pickup. He left it running with the radio on as he climbed out, Officer Green two steps behind him from the other side of the Jeep. Green was a new recruit, hired that spring to cut his policing teeth in the small town of Deep Lakes before moving on to a larger city.

Frankie was thrilled to see the two officers, rather than Donavan Pflug, who somehow managed to get under

Frankie's skin at every encounter, and vice versa. She and Alonzo had been old friends since high school, but their relationship changed after Frankie began investigating crimes for her part-time reporter's job with *Point Press*, a regional paper in Stevens Point. Alonzo's aim was always to protect Frankie, but Frankie was no longer making that aim an easy one.

"Hi, Lon." Frankie broke the ice first after observing Alonzo's grim expression.

Arms folded, he stared a foot down into Frankie's face, a half frown and puckered lips greeted her. "I really wish it hadn't been you to call this one in, Frankie," he said quietly, but matter-of-factly.

Frankie had plenty to say; she wanted to share the facts along with her initial thoughts, but her conscience kicked into gear. The inner voices that followed every move she made manifested themselves as twittering fireflies: the Golden One aka Goldie, who always erred on the side of caution and propriety, and the Pirate, who mostly nudged Frankie on to take risks. While Goldie's voice mimicked Frankie's mother, Peggy Champagne, the relaxed Pirate spoke in the sultry tone of Antonio Banderas.

Goldie spoke sharply now. "Let Alonzo take the lead and do his job, Francine. It's not your place to interfere." The word "*interfere*" drilled into Frankie's soul like a dart. But Goldie won for the moment, and Frankie waited for Lon to proceed.

To her dismay, he directed her to wait in the Jeep, sparking a negotiation.

"Please, Lon. Let me take Sonny back to the house and get him some food. He's an old dog who's feeling anxious. Let me put him inside?" Frankie tried to sound normal, as if she saw a gunshot victim every day.

"Oh, I almost forgot about the shop. I need to call Jovie and let her know I won't be in for a while I guess?" It was another question she hoped would prompt Alonzo to let her know how the investigation would proceed.

The sheriff heaved an audible sigh. He wished he'd brought one more officer along just to keep an eye on Frankie. He couldn't spare Green to stay with her; two officers were needed to conduct interviews of the hands, and of course, Frankie, too. He'd have to call the department to send at least one more officer out for sure.

"Okay," he sighed again. "But stay put in the house and wait for somebody to come take your statement. Got it?"

Frankie nodded and walked Sonny up the driveway toward the house, scheming ways to get back out to the sheep shed to talk to the hired men herself.

In the kitchen, she scooped dry food for Sonny and refilled his water dish, cell phone propped up by her chin while she stroked Sonny's silky fur.

"Hi, Frankie," Jovie picked up on the third ring, sounding cheery. "I was sure you'd be here by now. Is everything okay?"

Frankie hadn't rehearsed what she would say to Jovie, and decided to feel out the conversation, instead of leaping right to the story. "I'm going to be late and I'm not sure how late. I need to give the police a statement about an incident."

Alarms were going off in Jovie's head. "Incident? Did you have another run-in with Donavan Pflug?" All of Frankie's allies were fully aware of the ongoing feud she had with the detective.

"Oh no, nothing like that, Jovie. Pflug isn't here; at least not yet. I'll be talking with Alonzo, I think." Frankie realized she wasn't being helpful and knew she owed Jovie, a faithful employee, some logical explanation.

"There's been an accident with one of the truck drivers—the manure guy. I need to sort it out with the hired hands and Alonzo. Don't worry about anything." Frankie was satisfied with her story and hoped Jovie would be, too.

"Will you be okay at the shop without me? I'm sorry. I know it's a lot to ask . . ." Frankie did her level best not to take her employees for granted.

Jovie regained her cheerful composure. "Oh, don't worry about the bakery. Your aunt CeCe's already here, and we can manage just fine. Tess should be here in an hour. I better go though, and get things moving."

Frankie thanked her and resumed scheming. She started brewing a full pot of coffee to offer Lon, Green, and the hired hands. While the pot brewed, she retrieved

Ryan's clipboard and read the day's agenda: who was scheduled to work, what deliveries and what pick ups were expected, and anything else farm related.

Two items of interest ignited her curiosity. Reggie was not on the schedule to work. Next to his name, the word "off" appeared in capital letters. So, why was he here? The second item indicated the Green-Up Fertilizer truck was due to load manure at 5 a.m. Why was the driver over an hour early? Those questions led to an inevitable third one: Who was driving the nearly silent pickup truck without lights down the O'Connors' driveway? A cold, clammy shudder convulsed through Frankie's body. Surely, whoever was driving that truck had shot the Green-Up driver.

Chapter 2

It never troubles the wolf how many the sheep may be.
– Virgil

Frankie rummaged through Carmen's cupboards until she located travel mugs and poured out the contents of the coffee pot into three of them. She quickly reloaded the coffee maker and pressed start, then headed outside toward the shed, balancing the coffee.

Alonzo was on the phone, but still managed to give Frankie the evil eye when he spotted her heading his way. Smiling sweetly, she handed him one of the travel mugs. He nodded, produced a lopsided grin, and turned away to continue his conversation.

She supposed Lon was calling an investigative team to collect evidence from the truck and surroundings, a task that would have to be completed before the coroner came for the body. Again, she hoped she didn't have to be treated with the sneering visage of Pflug, but she knew the county only had just so many investigators.

Meanwhile, thoughts of the coroner conjured other more pleasant emotions. Garrett Iverson, a former ME, held the position of Whitman County Coroner and keeper of Frankie Champagne's heart. The two had been romantic companions for several months.

Frankie took advantage of the moment and made her way toward Officer Green, who was interviewing Goat. She walked past them, raised the coffee in offering to Green, then handed it to him, earning a warm smile in return.

When she got to the old stone building that was the sheep shed, she heaved the door, one-handed, and waited for her eyes to adjust to the half-light. Motes from the straw bedding floated around the warm air, and she disturbed at least one barn cat off its perch in the rafters above the sheep pens. On the far end she spotted Reggie raking a pen, shoveling used hay into a wagon, then pausing to peer at Frankie. He nodded in greeting; a blue bandana covered his nose and mouth to keep out the dust.

"I thought you might like some coffee?" Frankie began.

Reggie shook his head. "Naw, thanks anyway. I've got my thermos over there." He gestured to a shelf on the wall. "Sorry about being gruff earlier." He looked Frankie right in the eye when he said it. She was acquainted with Reggie only in passing over the years, but knew he was a trusted O'Connor employee. He didn't say much, but Frankie sized him up as a loner and a straight shooter. Still, she wanted to ask him at least one question.

"So, why did you seem, well, angry when you got here?" she asked.

Reggie propped the rake against the wall of the pen. She wondered why he was doing menial chores the younger hands could do, especially since he had seniority. Usually Reggie did the repair work around the farm, whether it was on equipment or fences. Cleaning pens seemed beneath him somehow.

"It was supposed to be my day off, but Coop called in. Said he had car trouble and was takin' it to get fixed this morning," Reggie spat the words out.

Frankie still didn't understand why he was angry. Sure, he had the day off. Did he have some big plans, she wondered? She couldn't recall ever seeing Reggie anywhere but the farm all the years he lived in Deep Lakes.

She pressed on. "What time did Coop call you?"

"Didn't. He called Goat. Goat called me, seeing he needed a ride to work."

Now Frankie saw the problem. Coop should have reported to Reggie, and now Reggie was feeling snubbed. "So, would Coop be the one who would load the manure truck?"

"Yeah, he and Goat or maybe Bucky. Don't matter." Reggie picked up the rake again, and turned his back on Frankie, indicating the conversation was finished.

Travel mug still in hand, Frankie left the shed in search of Jonesy, the hand who worked the overnight shift, and slept somewhere on the farm. Generally, Ryan or one of the twins slept near the sheep when the lambs were new, taking turns on overnight duty until the lambs were old enough to fend for themselves. While they were out of town, the hired hands took turns pulling the night shift.

Frankie went the long way around the shed and skirted the main barn to avoid being seen by the officers. She knew Alonzo would eventually find her and insist she return to the house until summoned. She wanted to gather what information she could, telling herself she owed it to Carmen and Ryan to be in the know.

Before opening the barn door, she saw a man standing by the pasture fence, two dogs nearby. It was Jonesy, who had worked for the O'Connors since lambing season the year before. He wore a wide-brimmed hat and when he turned in Frankie's direction, she couldn't be certain if he had noticed her, but the dogs had.

Fly, who was Sonny's partner and fellow sheltie, walked steadfastly in a pattern to protect the young sheep that were newly put to pasture. Since Frankie was still a stranger to Fly, it was the sheltie's job to maintain a barrier between her charges and any possible threat. Sitting on the ground at Jonesy's feet was JoJo, a young sheltie, commissioned to replace Sonny.

JoJo was still more pup than not, so he acknowledged Frankie with a friendly tail-wag and stood up to be petted. Jonesy immediately responded with a stern "No" reinforced with the training clicker used for communicating with the herders. Frankie instantly felt bad for the sheltie and angry with herself for being the cause of the reprimand.

"Sorry about that, Jonesy. I guess you're trying to get JoJo ready to manage the sheep, huh?" Frankie hoped her small talk would open up the focused farmhand.

Jonesy regarded Frankie with mild annoyance, wondering what she wanted. "Yep, Mr. O'Connor wants this whelp ready to go. The sooner the better."

"How's the training going?" Frankie was at least mildly interested.

"He's got a lot to learn, but he's smart. And, Fly's a great teacher. She's all business." Jonesy looked proudly at Fly, who patrolled the pasture, alert to any small movements that might spell trouble.

Following Jonesy's gaze, Frankie stared out at the expanse of pasture. The O'Connor ewes had produced a bumper crop of lambs in the past year, many of which would return a good profit at auction while others would be kept for breeding stock. When Frankie looked out at the lambs joyfully jumping around the grasses as if they had springs in their legs, she couldn't bear to think of them on the dinner table.

Her giggle at the sight of the frollicking lambs claimed Jonesy's attention. "Those lambs are so cute, pronking around the pasture, don't you think?" She showed off the new word she'd learned from Ryan to describe the bouncing action made by the lambs when they were newly pastured.

Jonesy merely cocked one eyebrow in her direction. His face remained inscrutable.

So much for idle chit-chat.

"Jonesy, I need your help. You were here all night, right?" Frankie leaned in toward the rangy figure, as if they were both in on a secret.

Jonesy removed the hat, revealing cropped wavy hair, the sides shaved off. His deep set eyes darkened with suspicion.

"You know I did. You saw the schedule. Why?" Jonesy moved a couple of steps away. "You want to know if I saw anything—anything to do with that?" He nodded toward the manure truck, which was being examined by two officers.

Frankie nodded. "Or heard anything?"

Jonesy stared at the pasture and the lambs and thumped his hat on the side of his leg before putting it back on again. "I was sleeping in the barn bunk. I didn't sleep great, probably worried about the lambs being okay and all."

Frankie waited for him to say more. Jonesy took off the hat again and boldly probed Frankie's face. "I might have heard a gun go off," he said, whacked his hat loudly with two fingers and looked at her, amused. Frankie jumped at the whack, glared at the hand, and stomped off back toward the house, anything but amused.

Chapter 3

Baking can be your therapy; let it be a salve
for difficult days and trying times.
– Kye Ameden

A few hours later, Frankie was released to go to work at Bubble and Bake. Luckily, Officer Shirley Lazzar, retired Chicago PD and part-time detective for Whitman County, was assigned to take Frankie's statement.

She and Frankie had become allies, after Shirley allowed Frankie's involvement in past criminal investigations. Shirley and husband, Tony, relocated to Deep Lakes, where they had a small vacation home, but she wasn't quite ready to give up her life's work.

"I've got too much vim and vigor to just sit around," Shirley told people. She jumped at the chance to work part-time for the short-staffed county whenever she was needed. Recently, Deep Lakes had relied on her detective work too often. So much for the usual low-key atmosphere of small town Wisconsin.

Frankie recounted all the details since she awakened in the wee hours of the morning, including the sheltie's alert behavior. Wanting to be helpful, she shared the clipboard schedule with Shirley, too.

"It was supposed to be Reggie's day off, but Coop called in with car problems. And, the Green-Up truck was supposed to pick up manure at five this morning, so why was he here before three-thirty? And, Jonesy spent last night here in the sheep barn, so you'll want to drill him. I think he's hiding something." Frankie leaned in conspiratorially toward Shirley.

Shirley laughed and shook her white cap of short permed curls. "Sheriff was worried you might be rattled after finding a gunshot victim, but I can see you're all bloodhound this morning."

"I can't promise you I'll be able to share as much information as in the past, Frankie. This could turn into a messy investigation," Shirley noted.

"So you're saying I'm out of my league here, Shirley? I know my editor is going to want me to stay close to the story. This is a big incident for our little area."

Shirley hesitated, then met Frankie's pondering gaze with a steely one. "I'll stop by the bakery this afternoon and share what I can. No promises. And, save me something good."

* * *

By the time Frankie drove down the Bubble and Bake alley on Granite Street, her body was claimed by an adrenaline rush brought on by the murder and guilty feelings from being absent at her shop. She bounded up the backstairs, darted into the kitchen, and ran head-on into Aunt CeCe.

Frankie's elderly aunt grabbed Frankie by the shoulders and took deep cleansing breaths, hoping Frankie would join her. Aunt CeCe was a free spirit, artist, nature lover, and a sister to Frankie's father, Charlie, who passed away a few years earlier.

"Calm down, dear," she said in her melodic soothing voice. "Everything's running smooth as silk here. Why don't you sit down, have a latte, and you can tell us about your morning as soon as we finish up out front."

The bakery typically sold out of goods by 9 a.m. in the tourist season, especially on the weekend when Deep Lakes was hopping. Hence, Frankie's guilt at leaving her shop short-handed.

Routinely, Bubble and Bake workers cleaned up, closed the front, then baked much of the morning for the next day. At noon, the shop reopened as a wine lounge with tastings and a small plate menu until 8 p.m., but closed early on Sundays. During the tourist season, the wine lounge was open for business four to five days a week. Fortunately, Frankie and Carmen hired seasonal employees to help out.

Aunt CeCe handed Frankie a steaming latte in a purple Bubble and Bake mug, then ran back out front. Tess and Jovie, two regular shop bakers, stood at separate stations, surrounded by flour, sugar, butter, eggs and other tools of the trade, both focused on their dough. Frankie didn't interrupt them, knowing the importance of not losing your place in following a recipe.

After a few minutes, Tess started kneading a dough ball on the counter facing her boss. Her brown skin glistened from the kitchen's heat and a few stray locks escaped her brightly printed durag. Tess kneaded dough to an inner musical rhythm that never ceased to amaze Frankie.

Jovie took another post at the same counter several feet away working her own dough ball, methodically. Jovie's long hair was tied in a messy ponytail, sticking out beneath a red bandana, and her lowered eyes focused on the task at hand. Jovie's pale skin also revealed the effects of the hot kitchen, and small beads of sweat formed on her brow as she worked.

Frankie couldn't help but smile at their work, but she also grimaced at herself for sitting here like a princess while everyone else in *her shop* was toiling away on her behalf. She launched herself off the stool and peered at the agenda board.

Saturdays were set aside to prepare quiches for the wine lounge. Tess, Jovie, and CeCe had checked off most of the items, but there were plenty of cookies to be prepared as well as fruit tarts for the winery crowd tomorrow. Since the bakery closed Sunday, the wine lounge offered cookies and tarts for the afternoon.

Frankie donned a clean apron and headed to an open station at the back counter. It was almost strawberry season and by next week she hoped to make fresh strawberry tarts with a honey glaze. But today's tart would feature rhubarb and cherries with a custard cream base and a nutty almond crust. She set to work stacking ingredients from the cooler, then chopping rhubarb on a cutting board, when Peggy Champagne strode into the kitchen pushing the bakery case.

Frankie looked up in surprise. "Oh, hello Mother. I didn't know you were here."

"Where else would I be when the shop needed extra help this morning, hm?" At 70, Frankie's mother was stunning to behold, always smartly dressed, polished and poised, even in a Bubble and Bake apron. Her frosty hair was pulled into a lovely chignon, small pearl studs graced her lobes, and her blush lipstick looked perfect. Unlike the kitchen workers, Peggy managed to appear cool and comfortable.

Frankie flushed, her guilt resumed. She was aware how her mother could make her feel confident sometimes, disappointed in herself at other times. Being the only daughter in the Champagne family of five, Frankie wrestled with the pressure she placed on herself to be the consummate daughter.

"Thanks so much for coming in, Mom. It's been quite the morning at the sheep farm. One of the truck drivers was shot and killed." There it was: Frankie blurted out the incident in stark terms. Everyone gasped and questions flew around the kitchen.

Yes, Frankie was the first on the scene and discovered the victim. No, the murderer was not in custody as far as she knew. No, she didn't see the murder weapon. Yes, Alonzo was probably still there investigating with his team. No, she hadn't talked to Garrett because he was behind police tape up to his elbows examining the truck driver's body.

"And please, all of you, do not let Carmen get wind of this." Frankie was stern. "I had to talk Alonzo out of notifying them in Chicago until tomorrow. They at least deserve a happy day with their family at the wedding."

Peggy's face softened. "That was very good of you, dear, to convince Alonzo not to call them today. I can't imagine Ryan can tell them anything worthwhile anyway. Another day shouldn't make a difference." She patted Frankie's hand.

Frankie wasn't too certain her mother was right, though. She imagined Ryan could offer plenty of details about the hired hands, and he could discuss his pick up routine with the Green-Up company as well as the drivers he knew.

Peggy noticed her daughter's knitted brow. "It seems like you have a lot of things to sort out, Frankie. Why don't you go upstairs to freshen up? We've got things under control here." Peggy sniffed meaningfully, noticing Frankie carried the sheep barn aroma into the shop.

Frankie protested since she'd just begun preparing rhubarb tarts, but Tess gave her a little shove, pointed at the stairs to her apartment above the bakery, and presented a lopsided grin. "I'm done with my dough, so will pick up where you left off."

Tess knew when Frankie contemplated the scene of a crime, she always included baking in her process, so she added, "I'll save some baking for you this afternoon, Boss."

* * *

Interlude:

Neill Starr drummed his fingers on the office desk. It was almost 10 p.m. and Sawyer was late. He should have called Starr by now. Neill fidgeted with his office computer, then hit the shutdown button. The view from his high-rise corner office was spectacular, even in the dark. Moonlight played over the ripples of water in the harbor, causing a few boats to dance.

He checked his phone again. Only five minutes had passed since the last time he'd checked. He swore loudly, rose from the office chair, and shut off his desk lamp. He would wait in the dark, for as long as necessary.

Specks of paranoia swept through his mind like chiggers making him itchy. This was it, the last hurrah. Third time's a charm, isn't that how the saying goes? His careful plans were about to pay off, and he was impatient now to finish his project. Dammit, where was Sawyer?

Unaffected by his thoughts, the burner phone buzzed in his jacket pocket.

"Yeah." A millisecond later: "It's about damn time, Sawyer."

Sawyer intoned the code word: "green-eyed," to which Starr replied, "monster."

Starr was anxious to get things rolling, agitated that he'd had to wait for Sawyer. "Follow the plan. D11. P19. C-EE 733."

Sawyer replied in staccato, "Got it."

Starr was annoyed by that somehow. "What in hell is wrong with your voice?" He drummed his fingers loudly again.

"Damn weather here is all."

Starr disconnected, exhaled a whoosh of air, only then realizing he'd been holding his breath. At least now, the last phase had been activated.

* * *

The shower revived Frankie and offered some clarity. Did she want to investigate or should she leave it to the police this time, as Shirley suggested?

Her self-inquisition nudged Pirate to life. "Of course you should investigate—safely, Cherie. After all, you have a reputation now and must uphold it, no?"

Frankie found herself nodding agreement. His sensual voice had convinced her. Besides, Goldie didn't offer a counter-argument, surprisingly. Frankie wondered how much longer she'd feel tethered to this split consciousness of hers. Maybe it was time to let them go.

She snapped out of her introspection to make a plan for the rest of the day. Besides making an appearance at the wine lounge, there was baking to do, and Shirley Lazaar to chat with. But first, she had a phone call to make.

Frankie opened her search tab on her phone for the Green-Up Fertilizer company and jotted down the number in her reporter's notebook. Instead of keeping all her notes on her phone and tablet, she decided to tear a page from the local paper editor's playbook.

Abe Arnold, owner of *The Whitman Watch,* was as old-school as they come, using a steno pad for all his notes. Internet access wasn't reliable in rural Wisconsin. After a recent fiasco, Frankie had implemented a password lock on her phone and tablet, but her tech gear often went to sleep while she paused to think. The steno pad allowed her to write and think without the interruption of punching in a password, and it couldn't be hacked. An extra copy of her notes was an insurance policy.

The Green-Up receptionist answered on the first ring. "Good morning, Green-Up Fertilizer. This is Joanne. How may I help you?"

"Yes. Hello, Joanne. I'm calling from the O'Connor sheep farm in Deep Lakes." Frankie paused to choose her words, prompting a "um-hmm" reply from the receptionist.

"A Green-Up truck arrived this morning around three-thirty for a pick-up. Can you tell me the name of the driver, and do you know why he arrived so early? The pick-up was scheduled for five a.m."

Joanne's voice faltered and became emotional. "Oh yes, it's a messy situation, I'm afraid. We've already talked to your local police, but I suppose they didn't tell you ..." She trailed off, attempting to gather her thoughts.

Frankie jumped in. "So, you know about the shooting, then?" She didn't want to say too much at once.

"Yes. But you see, that wasn't our driver who was shot, Ms. O'Connor." Frankie hadn't identified herself on purpose, so the receptionist would have good reason to speak openly with her.

Frankie was certain her gasp was audible on the phone line. "What do you mean?"

"We don't know who the driver was. The police were hoping we could identify him, but our morning maintenance guy found our driver tied up behind the dumpster with a nasty bump on his head." Joanne was talking almost as fast as Frankie's pen scrawled across the page.

"Oh that's terrible, Joanne. Can you tell me what time that was? And, does anyone know what happened?"

Joanne said the maintenance worker found Larry around 5:30 a.m., that he was conscious, tied up with duct tape and zip-tied to the leg of the dumpster. When Larry saw the maintenance man, he called out for help.

"Our man called the EMTs and police. I have a copy of Larry's statement, you know, for our worker comp files." Joanne seemed to relish in her role as an informant.

Frankie's mind was in a spin-cycle. "What was Larry doing at work so early for a five a.m. pick-up? I mean, this would have happened around two or so, right?" The drive from Green-Up to the farm was about an hour, so the driver wouldn't have to depart until four, yet he showed up two hours early when he was driving an empty truck.

"Oh, that's just Larry. He's a slow mover these days. He's getting close to retirement, you know. And, I shouldn't tell you this, but I think he's having marriage troubles, so he's been showing up early for all his shifts. Maybe even sleeping in the truck cab . . ." Joanne whispered confidentially.

She continued in a normal tone. "Let me just look at this statement. Okay . . . Larry said he was climbing into the truck cab around two when he was hit from behind, dragged to the back dumpster, bound and tied up. The thug took his keys and drove off in the truck."

"Did Larry recognize the man? Did the *thug* say anything?" Frankie asked.

"Let me see. Oh, here it is. The man was wearing uniform pants, brown work boots, a black hooded sweatshirt, black face mask, and dark leather work gloves.

Larry doesn't remember him saying anything at all. Larry couldn't be much help in identifying the guy."

Frankie thanked Joanne for her help, signed off, and speedily filled in her notes. Then she transferred all the information onto her tablet in a fresh file folder she named "O'Connor farm shooting."

Frankie's stomach reminded her she'd had a coffee at the farm and latte at the shop as her sole source of nourishment, so she explored the refrigerator and snagged an apple, which she ate greedily while making an instant oatmeal packet in the microwave.

Her thoughts turned to her daughter Violet, home from UW-Stevens Point for the summer and working as a lab intern at Frankie's winery, Bountiful Fruits. Frankie would have to carefully convey the day's events to her fragile daughter over dinner tonight.

She scraped the last of the cinnamon oatmeal topped with almond-coconut milk from her bowl, and was ready to head back to the shop kitchen to bake and think. Her buzzing phone stopped her. It was Magda, her *Point Press* editor. News traveled north faster than Frankie realized.

"Good morning, Magda. Are you calling about the shooting?" Frankie thought she could make points by anticipating Magda's purpose.

"Yes. The question is: Why haven't you called in? Are you on it already?" Magda was in a dark mood for some reason.

"Well . . . first, I had to give the police a statement, and then, I had to come to work at Bubble and Bake, that full-time business I own." She tried not to sound defiant, but at the same time, wanted to remind Magda that her *Point Press* gig was part-time and sporadic.

Magda softened a hair, but as always, stuck to business. She was climbing the ladder in the journalism world and wanted to get the jump on all big stories. A small town rural shooting was huge. "What do you mean you had to give a statement?"

Frankie explained why she was on the scene and what she had discovered there.

Magda blew out a low whistle. "Wow, that must have been something." Empathy was quickly replaced by ambition. "This is great, Frankie! You're on the inside of the story. You know things other reporters will never know, and you have the perfect reason for snooping around and asking questions."

Yep, that was Magda alright in true form; the story always came first. "I sure hope you have some time this weekend. You're going to need to hop to it before the O'Connors get back home tomorrow. Keep me posted." Magda was done, for now.

Sighing heavily, Frankie jumped off the tall kitchen stool and took her bowl to the sink to rinse out. Her phone buzzed again. This time it was the welcoming ID of Garrett Iverson.

"Good morning, Mr. Coroner. It is still morning, isn't it?" Frankie smiled brightly in spite of her present situation.

"It is, barely though. How are you Miss Francine? You've had quite a shock." Garrett's warm voice was like melted butter on a scone.

"I'm doing okay, fine really, Garrett. How about you? I can't imagine it's very pleasant digging around a gunshot victim before breakfast." Frankie wondered if she was becoming desensitized to death after all she'd seen in the past year or so.

"Not my preferred morning activity for sure. Look, I'm taking a short break but then I have a lot of work this afternoon and probably a late day with reports to fill out. I just wanted to make sure you're okay, and to tell you that I'll see you later at the O'Connor farm where I'm spending the night. Before you argue with me, forget it. There's no way you're staying out there alone. I'll bring dinner with me. Call you later."

Frankie had no intention of protesting. She was happy she wouldn't be spending the night alone at the farm. Garrett inadvertently conveyed some important information about the case: the police obviously didn't have anyone in custody for the murder. Frankie wondered if they even had a prime suspect. Then she wondered some more: *Whom did she suspect?*

Chapter 4

Fishing is marvelous . . . there is the irresistible urge to
tangle with the mysterious and unknown,
to rely on intuition and hunches.
– Katharine Weber

The sweet fragrance of the shop kitchen lulled Frankie as she worked the afternoon away, making delicate tea cookies, perfect for summer picnics and wine lounge customers. She paused occasionally while she mixed sugar, butter, flour, and special ingredients to jot down questions about each farm hand and a reminder to study the clipboard schedule with more scrutiny.

Aunt CeCe and Peggy manned the wine lounge for the afternoon, running into the kitchen periodically to prepare a quiche order or arrange a fruit, veggie, and cheese plate for customers. Neither one said much, indicating business was booming out front, and they didn't have time for chit-chat. All of that was fine with Frankie.

Tess would return Monday afternoon to bake pans of cinnamon buns and other pastries. Sunday and half of Monday amounted to a weekend off for Tess. Jovie would be back for the evening shift to run tastings with Frankie while summer helpers, Cherry Parker and Tara Mabry, would serve tables. Frankie was trying to calculate when she would find time to speak to Violet and how late it would be before she could meet Garrett at the O'Connors' for their promised dinner.

She sighed. Summer tourist season wasn't even in full swing yet. Many people flocked from Chicago to Deep Lakes just before July 4th, beginning a steady stream through Labor Day weekend. Tourists were coveted customers, and the locals competed heavily for their business. A successful Bubble and Bake summer was her number one priority. Income earned now would sustain the shop through the long, lean winter months. *Buckle up, Buttercup*, she thought, *and prepare to be exhausted on the daily!*

Around 4 p.m., Aunt CeCe sashayed into the kitchen with a slice of quiche and set it under Frankie's nose. Frankie smiled sweetly at her aunt, who almost always seemed to be in high spirits. She paused to take in CeCe's garb of the day. The green eyed free spirit was decorative in a loose yellow sundress that flowed to her ankles. A print of island women swayed across the fabric with baskets on their heads, filled with grace and joy. CeCe wore her hair long, done up in braids intertwined with beads that matched her personality to a T.

"I know you're concentrating, but a customer changed her mind about the quiche, so I brought it for you. Don't want it to go to waste." CeCe winked and did a little twirl by the swinging doors.

"Oh, and you might want to take a break from all that." She waved her finger in a circular motion as if casting a spell. "Officer Shirley just came in, and she looks like she could use a drink and some company."

The oven timer read two minutes left for the cookies, so Frankie proceeded to slice a large portion of rhubarb-cherry tart and place it on a white china plate trimmed in bluebells. Then she removed the trays from the ovens, set them to cool, and carried cookie dough to the cooler to finish up later. The kitchen was much too warm to leave dough sitting out.

The wine lounge was filled with chatter and laughter when Frankie strode out balancing two plates, the tart for Shirley in one hand and her quiche chunk in the other. Two groups occupied the tasting bar, keeping Peggy busy pouring samples and describing the properties of each wine.

A young chic-looking mixed gender set made themselves at home in a large alcove near the empty fireplace. Frankie was pleased to see three open bottles sitting on the nearby low table shared among the five of them. A large cheese and fruit platter perched on one end; a veggie and dip platter occupied the other. They nibbled leisurely, speaking in hushed voices,; then erupting in choruses of laughter. By their smart fashion and flawless hair, Frankie guessed they were urbanites enjoying a getaway to the bucolic "north."

The tables by the window were also filled with customers. Aunt CeCe was regaling a middle-aged couple with wine descriptions that floated out like poetry. Since CeCe arrived at Bubble and Back working her charms, business was thriving.

Cece raised her head in Frankie's direction, as if reading her thoughts, winked and gestured gracefully around the far corner where Shirley sat in one of the shop's low two-seater sofas, this one adorned with bright yellow and lime green swirls on a turquoise background. Frankie insisted on using happy colors, candlelight, and essential oils as part of her hygge atmosphere at the shop. Frankie's Scandinavian roots were represented in the baking she learned from her grandma, Sophie, who taught her the most important ingredient was the love she added to every dish she made.

Frankie's hygge mindset flavored the lounge, which was dotted with small alcoves and shelves housing books and games; an invitation to relax and stay awhile. Some nooks held carved nisser living a life under toadstools with other woodland creatures, all made by Frankie's father.

Still wearing her uniform that managed to look pressed and fresh, Shirley sipped a glass of white wine while looking over her police notes, methodically deciding what she would share with Frankie. Passing up the two floor cushions, Frankie pulled over a café chair after depositing the bakery plates on the sofa table.

Shirley raised her white curly crown to examine the tart.

"Looks like I picked the right wine to go with this beauty," she indicated the tart with a satisfied expression. "Where's your glass, Frankie? I hate to drink alone." Shirley let out a low chortle, and Frankie realized the conversation was about to get real. Even Shirley couldn't hide the gravity of the investigation.

Frankie came back to the nook with the remainder of the bottle of Sweet Tia, Shirley's choice, and poured herself a half a glass. The apricot chardonnay was crafted to honor Frankie's Aunt CeCe and Carmen's Tia Pepita, celebrating their artistry at Bubble and Bake. Since the aunts also conjured a good deal of mischief, perhaps Naughty Tias would have been a better name.

"Tasty," Shirley indicated both the tart and the wine. "Sweets for a sour conversation." Again with the short chortle. "Fire away, Frankie."

With a small shrug, Frankie picked up her pen, opened her notebook, and quietly addressed the questions she thought were most likely to receive answers first.

"Who's the victim?"

It was Shirley's turn to shrug. "We don't know. He didn't have an ID of any kind. No cell phone either."

"So, the killer doesn't want the ID known for some reason. Must be premeditated." Frankie vocalized her insights as she penned them.

"Did you find the weapon?"

"Not so far," Shirley said between bites. "There's a couple officers still searching the farm. But we're guessing the killer took it with him and the shell casings, too. We should know soon what we're looking for."

Frankie knew what that meant. There must not be an exit wound on the victim. After Garrett extracted the bullet, the police would identify the weapon. Still, she didn't want to assume anything.

"Was there an exit wound, Shirley? And, how do you think the shooting happened?"

"I'm impressed you thought of that, Frankie." Shirley gave her an admiring glance and nodded as Frankie conveyed she'd grown up with brothers who hunted deer, so she had some gun knowledge.

Shirley drained her wine glass and poured a second. Staring forlornly at her empty plate, she suggested, "How about you bring me something else to chow on and I'll tell you what I think."

Frankie was back in a flash with a large slice of asiago and spinach quiche, the same variety she just ate while Shirley had gazed on in envy. Shirley lingered on the first bite before resuming their conversation.

"I think the shooter was waiting for the driver, maybe hiding, came out of the dark, shot him through the windshield. Two shots were fired. The first one took out a headlight. Could have been a warning shot or a misfire. Close range, so he or she doesn't have to be a marksman." Shirley waited for that to sink in and took another bite.

Frankie admonished herself for failing to notice the bullet hole in the truck windshield. Then again, it was just nearing dawn and foggy out to boot. She was alarmed that she hadn't heard two shots and wondered if the first one happened while she slept. *Some protector of the farm she turned out to be.*

"Do you have any leads on the truck I saw leaving the farm?" This was a weak question at best.

"Do you know how many people in this county drive pickups?"

Yes, Frankie was well aware that pickup trucks were as common as mosquitos in summer, not just in Whitman County, but the whole state of Wisconsin for that matter. Without a license plate number or any other specifics, the pickup truck was probably a dead end.

"Did you find out anything useful from the farmhands?" Frankie's question landed in the cautionary category of least likely to be answered during an ongoing investigation, but she had to ask. Any reputable reporter would do the same.

Shirley took a long slug of wine, pursed her lips, and gave Frankie a hard stare. "You know, all the time I worked in Chicago, I hated talking to reporters. Most of them didn't care about the victim or the cops. Nope, they only cared about the story, about the race to be first on the scene, first on the screen, first to snag a juicy tidbit that nobody else knew."

Frankie withered on the inside. Was this the kind

of reporter she was? She knew the answer. She wasn't. She cared about the truth and about justice. Still, didn't she feel exhilarated when she discovered clues to a case? Didn't she ride the thrilling waves of trailing suspects and uncovering secrets?

"What makes you different from those reporters, Frankie, is that you listen. You care about the case before the story. You respect the experts, and you're careful. Don't change the way you operate because you could get hurt, understand?"

Like a school kid, Frankie nodded obediently.

"Okay, so ask me a question." Shirley drained her wine glass and poured a smaller amount this time. Frankie hadn't seen Shirley drink while in uniform, but she imagined the detective was done for the day and would head home from the wine lounge.

Shirley's tone indicated Frankie would have to ask pointed questions, not go fishing in the land of generalities. Time to get sharp. "Who was supposed to be loading that manure truck today?"

Shirley relaxed and smiled a little. "Coop and Bucky." She used the names the hands were known by, assuming Frankie would know them, too. She did.

"But neither one of them showed up this morning, Shirley. Coop called in with car trouble and I don't know what happened to Bucky . . . wait, do you suspect Bucky?"

Shirley tossed back the contents of her glass. "Let's say he's become a person of interest. He showed up for work after you left, saw the sheriff department vehicles, and hightailed it out of there. When we find that little turd, he's going to answer some questions."

"Didn't you chase after him?"

Shirley groaned. "We were all occupied, talking to the other hands. So, he got away—for now." Shirley picked up her papers and pulled her keys out of her pants pocket.

Frankie pondered whether or not she was okay to drive, but Shirley seemed perfectly impervious to the wine. Still, Frankie watched her walk to the door, satisfied Shirley was good to go, and she thanked her for the shared information.

Shirley left with a parting shot. "By the way, Bucky was driving a dark pickup truck."

Chapter 5

It's not only children who grow. Parents do, too. As much as we watch to see what our children do with their lives, they are watching us see what we do with ours.
– Joyce Maynard

Violet shuddered when Frankie conveyed the morning's event at the O'Connor farm. As soon as her daughter trotted through the back door, Frankie nabbed her and stated their need to talk. Violet had been fragile since she'd left the shelter of home and entered the world of college, and even though she'd just finished her sophomore year and turned 21, Frankie was still the protective parent.

"You're not going back there to spend the night tonight, are you Mom?" Violet's frosty blue eyes opened widely and her voice spoke with a tremor.

Frankie squeezed her daughter's hand in reassurance. "It's going to be fine. Garrett is coming out to spend the night. He won't let me stay there alone." She noticed Violet's pale cheeks and her fidgeting hands playing with the salt and pepper shakers on the counter. Her mind seemed miles away; it was time to change the subject.

Frankie smiled brightly. "It's Saturday night, you must have plans, huh?"

Violet pressed her lips tightly, her brows knitted together, caught up in some knotty thoughts. "Tara's working, but Paige, Haley, and I are going out to Cruzer's around eight. There's a country band playing from Milwaukee ..."

The summer population in Deep Lakes rose with the warm temperatures as Lakes Hope, Joy, and Loki served up a paradise of fishing, boating, and paddle boarding. The shuttered campgrounds and inns sprang to life, beckoning young people on college break to fill a wide range of jobs. The pristine lake community attracted people from every walk of life and every state in the country, plus a number of foreigners. Some came to work. Many came to play. Even more came to do both.

Frankie remembered her own younger days when the sleepy town woke up, and the prospect of summer romance occupied her mind. There were summers she'd been reckless: telling lies to her parents, staying out too late, choosing rebels for company. Somehow she'd managed to come out of it unscathed. Now she was on the outside of wild summer, looking in from a parent's magnifying glass. Had she been as naive back then as Violet was now?

Violet's friends, Paige and Haley, were new to Frankie. Haley moved to Deep Lakes for the summer to work at Mischief Resort on Lake Loki. She tended bar at Up To

No Good on the resort property and made bank in tips. Small wonder since she dressed in tight shorts up to her nether regions and revealing crop tops. Frankie took note of Haley's *uniform* on a couple of occasions when the girls got together.

Paige, on the other hand, lived and worked in Green Lake. She and Violet had taken a couple of classes together at Stevens Point and became fast friends. Paige, too, worked in tourism, serving at a pub and grill hot spot, The Mainsail. Her uniform was a sassy version of a sailor suit with a short flared skirt, but not as short as Haley's cutoffs at least.

Tara completed the quartet of girlfriends, and had grown up with Violet. The two had been rivals in high school, vying for music solos and theater parts. Now, however, the two had grown up and set aside the rivalry. They hung out together during school vacations.

Frankie basked in a bit of priggishness that *their* wine lounge servers did not dress provocatively. She and Carmen insisted on either a knee length dark skirt, black pants or capris and a white shirt. The no-iron button-downs sported the Bubble and Bake logo—a colorful wine glass with a donut perched on its rim. Their servers made excellent tips without seductive garb.

Any employee who worked in the kitchen or behind the bakery case wore brightly colored aprons with the shop logo. Bubble and Bake tees and wine glasses were also for sale in the merchandise area next to racks of wine from Frankie's vineyard.

Frankie snapped out of her retrospection in the middle of Violet's relating some story about Paige and a customer at The Mainsail. She hadn't registered a smidge her daughter had said in the past couple of minutes, but now nodded enthusiastically as if hanging on every word. She felt guilty for trying to fake out her daughter when all she wanted was for Violet to be open with her. Frankie shifted the conversation again, unaware of her controlling behavior.

"Can I ask how things are going at the wine lab for you?" Violet had been interning there for almost a month and Frankie vowed neither to interfere nor ask too many work-related questions. She was thrilled when her daughter, a microbiology student, had asserted her wishes to learn about wine-making as her required internship for the university. It's never easy to work for one's parents, and Frankie was only too happy to turn over training to her trusted lab techs, Nelson and Zane.

"Things are great, Mom," Violet beamed. "Nelson and Zane are as geeky as it gets. They're total wine-heads and sometimes they get way too deep into the tech stuff for me. But, I ask a lot of questions, and they're thrilled to answer them. Like little kids talking about their toys." Violet giggled, thinking about the number of details that sailed over her head. She knew she would return to college in the fall prepared for her next challenging courses, thanks to those two.

Frankie laughed out loud, decided this was a good

jumping-off spot in the conversation, and asked Violet if she had dinner plans. "You're welcome to follow me out to the O'Connors' and eat with me and Garrett after I close up the shop."

Violet shook her head of dark glossy hair and looked down her front. Her Bountiful Fruits tee had a couple spots of salad dressing from lunch on it and she was dying to get out of her hard-toed work shoes and into some sandals. "If it's okay, I'll grab a piece of quiche before I head out. I need to change out of these clothes. I'm meeting Haley and Paige at eight, remember?" Violet wore a momentary expression of disapproval.

"I thought maybe you would wait for Tara to finish up here, that's all." Frankie's voice rose a notch.

"Nope. Tara's got a date after work . . . I mean she has other plans." Violet hopped off the kitchen stool and spun to the apartment stairs behind the kitchen before Frankie could probe further.

"You better keep a closer eye on that girl, Francine." Naturally Goldie would turn up to weigh in on Frankie's alleged deficiency as a parent.

Frankie didn't have a chance to respond before Pirate put the kibosh on her planned comeback. "Let Violet be. She needs to spread her wings. Isn't that what you've wanted for her, cherie?"

Well, she didn't disagree that she'd been hoping for the time when Violet would come out of her shell and find herself. On the other hand, since Violet turned 21 a few weeks ago, she frequently went out with friends, revealing few details of her escapades to Frankie.

"Of course not, cherie. Violet is an adult. Did you tell your parents what went on during your free time? Give her some space." Pirate's deep baritone resonated to the pit of Frankie's stomach, and she found it alarmingly annoying. His words carried disturbing flashbacks to Frankie's youth and secrets she kept from her parents.

Violet was newly 21 and newly socializing with friends who were strangers to Frankie. "Sorry, Pirate. Goldie's right this time." Before Goldie could enjoy the satisfaction of being right, Frankie added, "I just don't know how to keep an eye on Violet without ruining our relationship."

* * *

It was well past five o'clock when Frankie swooped into the wine lounge and surprised her mother with a hug. "You were supposed to be off an hour ago. I'm so sorry, Mom."

Peggy wasn't accustomed to receiving hugs from her daughter as a matter of habit. Their relationship had its struggles, partly due to Peggy's infrequent displays of affection, partly due to Peggy's desire to be needed.

She gave her daughter a small shoulder pat, then stood up straighter. "I just rang up the tribe over in the fireplace alcove, and I think they're ready to leave. The two couples on this end of the bar (she gestured slightly with her head to the left), are enjoying glasses of wine. Their tasting is done. I haven't rung them up yet. The group on the other end just sat down."

Frankie smiled. Her mom was a top-notch employee, always astute and always reliable. "I'll take it from here. Go enjoy your evening." The two smiled warmly at each other, and Peggy wished her a good night.

The next three hours sailed by as a rapid succession of customers came and went for tastings. To Frankie's delight, the majority of them relaxed around the lounge with bottles and small plates, keeping Jovie, Cherry, and Tara dancing between the kitchen and shop until closing.

When Jovie sang out last call for sales at 7:50 p.m., Frankie was taken aback. She helped ring final sales, chatted with customers about their favorite wines of the night, and helped them choose bottles to take home.

Tara turned the open sign off and locked the front door behind Cherry, who was not on cleanup duty. Frankie's million dollar smile was not lost on Tara and Jovie.

"You can certainly tell it's summertime in Wisconsin!" Jovie sat down near the bar register and kicked off one shoe to rub her foot. She patted her apron pocket with a satisfying grin. Jovie was in her 30's but could race around tables like a teenager. Tall and thin, her legs were like springs, or maybe she was just content with her work. Frankie knew how blessed she was to have someone who possessed a combination of work ethic, baking skills, and personality to interact with customers.

"I'm glad you made good tips tonight. You earned them, Jovie. We're not even into full-blown summer yet, but I have to say, the past week sure is a good omen of what's to come." Frankie pulled receipts and cash from each register, rubber-banded each stack, jammed them in a bank bag labeled "Saturday", and counted out start-up cash for Sunday.

The unofficial tally of what wines sold best for the day was typical closing banter. "I'd say we have a three-way tie going with Singin' the Blues, Crown Me Pineapple and Persephone's Temptation right now," Jovie conveyed, then waited for her boss to quiz her on what grapes were used for each vintage.

Frankie knew all three wines were designed for summer. The blueberry Riesling had a slight effervescent quality and was crafted from a blend of some of her favorite varieties of white grapes, the St. Pepin and Frontenac Gris. Crown Me Pineapple, decorated with an embossed golden pineapple on the label, was a tropical-flavored pick that many customers purchased as hospitality gifts. Of course, she was quite proud of the Persephone, a pomegranate zinfandel blend that garnered awards in three Midwest-region wine competitions.

"Two weeks from now that could all change. We'll be offering our summer vintages: Strawberry Social, Midsummer Picnic, and our brand-spanking new Lemon by the Lake." The three varieties, bottled in April, sat in the dark basement of the shop, lying in wait for the summer scene. "Plus, we're almost ready to bottle two more newbies."

Tara halted the chatter when she bounced into the lounge and announced. "The kitchen is cleaned up. Anything else I need to do or can I go?"

Franked was impressed that Tara had cleaned up in 20 minutes while she and Jovie were shooting the breeze, then remembered that Tara had plans. "Yes, please, go ahead. Thanks for leading cleanup, by the way." Tara flashed a brief smile and scampered out the door.

"What about you, Jovie? Any plans tonight?" Frankie started turning off lights in the lounge, the bank bag still clutched in her hand.

"I'm meeting Lon for a late dinner, well if you call bar food at the Hat Trick, dinner, that is." Jovied chuckled. She and Lon had been dating casually for several months, and Frankie wondered if or when the relationship would turn up the heat. Lon was one of her best friends and Jovie was one of her best employees and a friend; she didn't want the relationship to go south.

"The Hat Trick has good food and drinks and not many tourists, so I'd call it a win." Frankie laughed. "I've got to get out to the farm. Garrett may already be there with dinner. I'm glad Carmen and Ryan will be back tomorrow, but I know they're going to be shocked and upset about the shooting . . ." she said with a heavy sigh.

She waved Jovie out the door, locked the bank bag in the office desk drawer, and smiled wistfully at the thought that at least tonight, Carmen and her family were partying together at her niece's wedding, oblivious that their farm was now a crime scene.

Chapter 6

*Sometimes in June, when I see unearned dividends of dew
hung on every lupine, I have doubts about the real poverty of
the sands. On solvent farmlands lupines do not even grow,
much less collect a daily rainbow of jewels.*
– Aldo Leopold

Frankie slept very little and woke up feeling hungover, although it actually had been years since she'd had a hangover. Sonny was sleeping at the end of the big bed, dutiful and protective.

"I just wonder what you know, old boy," Frankie whispered as she ruffled his mane and scratched under his chin. The sheltie closed his eyes and produced a few grateful sighs. Poor Sonny. The top-notch herder was being put out to pasture, replaced by the younger, swifter JoJo. Sonny couldn't keep pace with Fly any longer, mainly because he was losing his eyesight.

Frankie padded out to the kitchen and checked the time. Just barely five o'clock. As she lumbered to the counter, she registered a thin line of light emerging on the horizon out the kitchen window. Freshly brewed coffee registered next, a welcoming scent that could only mean Garrett was awake ahead of her.

"Good morning, Miss Francine. You look fresh as a daisy." Garrett laughed quietly and patted the sofa cushion next to him. "I've got a hot mug ready for you."

"Liar," Frankie retorted about her appearance. She knew she was looking more wilted than fresh this morning. She happily sat down next to Garrett, gave him a soft peck on the cheek, and took the coffee. "Did you get much sleep?" She indicated the corner recliner which had served as Garrett's post for the night, even though he had his choice of beds.

He yawned in response. "I was guarding, not sleeping, remember?" He gave her knee a playful squeeze. "Looks like someone's vying for my position as your protector though." Sonny followed Frankie out of the bedroom, into the kitchen, then settled on the floor at her feet.

"He's a good boy," Frankie said, rubbing her foot on Sonny's belly. "But he's no Garrett Iverson," she smiled. Her tone changed though as the coffee awakened her brain, and she began running through her task list for the day. Church, the shop, face Carmen and Ryan. But first, Frankie wanted to talk to Reggie once more.

"Hello, where are you Frankie?" Garrett waved a hand in front of her eyes.

"Oh sorry. Just thinking about what I need to do today. What's on your agenda?"

Garrett planned to return to the office, despite it

being Sunday. "I need to work on the medical findings report and log all the victim's items. Alonzo is meeting me there at seven so we can record and bag the victim's clothing for possible evidence. Lon will drive that up to Wausau Monday morning."

Garrett ran a tired hand through his thick salt-and-pepper hair. Frankie ran her own hand over his rugged face in a sweet caress. Garrett was a talented coroner, overqualified for the county position, because he had served as a medical examiner in both Duluth-Superior and Green Bay prior to choosing a quieter life in a rural area. He clasped Frankie's hand in his. "And just what kind of trouble do you plan to get into today?"

She feigned innocence. "I'm going to church first, then I have to stop at the shop to see if I'm needed. Eventually, I'm going to have to talk to Carmen and Ryan about what happened here." She didn't like the prospect, somehow feeling she'd let them down.

"It's not your fault—what happened here," Garrett said gently.

"How do you know that it isn't my fault? Maybe the killer planned the whole thing because he knew Ryan would be gone, making it easier to get away with it." She finally unbottled the ideas that had been plaguing her all night. "I mean opportunity is one of the three means of committing murder, and Ryan being gone provided that." Frankie was standing now, making dramatic hand gestures like someone presenting the facts in a courtroom.

"Take a breath, Miss Francine. Yes, opportunity is a factor but there also has to be a motive. That motive must have existed before the opportunity presented itself. And you have to consider the time of the shooting. Even if Ryan was home, he wouldn't have expected the truck or a killer to be here at three a.m."

"Three-thirty a.m.," Frankie mumbled. "Well, I can still be upset, and I will be until we get to the bottom of it."

"Just exactly what do you mean by *we*? Let Whitman County's finest handle this one. Please, Frankie. Whoever killed this guy is dangerous and armed, so don't get caught up in the investigation."

"I'm going to cover the story for *Point Press*, and if I happen to find out something along the way, well then, that's a bonus for everyone." She offered a crooked smile to Garrett's warning look, gave him a quick kiss, and headed off to shower.

On the way out to the sheep barn awhile later, Frankie paused to appreciate the morning splendor. June mornings offered the best of Wisconsin summer. The chilly temperatures promised to rise with the traveling sun. Already, the sunlight illuminated the dewy drops that provided respite to the flowers and grasses from yesterday's heat. Early birds chirped greetings, while the scent of fertile earth crept into Frankie's nostrils announcing new life. From the emerald land to the sapphire waters, Wisconsin summer was as rich as precious gems.

Frankie was shaken back to reality as she strode past the police tape and pallet of manure still stacked and waiting for pick up. The truck was gone; she imagined it parked at Whitman county garage being gone through with a fine-tooth comb for evidence.

In the rising sun, she saw a figure outlined in the far pasture with two dogs running maneuvers around the sheep. Jonesy, likely, was running one of the dog teams as they moved half the sheep to graze. After he left the dogs in charge, he would return to the barn, call the other pair of dogs, and herd the rest of the sheep to the front pasture. The O'Connor farm had five fenced-off pastures, so they could rotate grazing, and they raised two varieties of sheep— Rambouillet and Targhee—both known for quality wool and meat.

Two more farmhands were working near the manure shed. One was feeding shovels of something into a machine; the other was repairing a section of fence. Frankie couldn't tell who they were for sure, and she hadn't checked the clipboard to see who was on duty. *Guess I wouldn't make a good farm manager. I can't even remember to check the clipboard every day.*

She strode past the sheep barn to the leveled off dirt area where the hands parked. There were three pickup trucks, all dark colored. She recognized Reggie's truck but didn't know who drove the others. The newest and flashiest of the three was a sporty, black TRX with a king cab. Frankie suspected it belonged to Jonesy, who likely made the most money as a sheep and dog trainer. She would ask Ryan to be sure. A silver Jeep Wrangler rounded out the lineup. Frankie told herself that the Jeep owner wasn't off the hook for the shooting, however. Anyone could have been driving the pickup yesterday.

In the barn, Goat looked up from scooping feed into the troughs for the lambs born that spring. The lambs had graduated to eating dry grain, which they ate every morning once their mothers were released to graze. When Goat spied Frankie, he momentarily lost his balance and almost dropped the scoop.

Frankie did her best to sound upbeat and ease his mind. "Good morning, I was looking for Reggie . . ."

"He's repairing a section of fence, hoping to get it done before the O'Connors get home." Goat opened one eye wide while squinting the other, studying Frankie as if she were a predator.

Frankie nodded toward the hand that held the feed scoop. "How's your hand doing? I see you have it wrapped. Farm accident?" Frankie tried to imitate a suspicious TV tough cop.

Goat let the scoop fall back into the grain bag and hid his hand behind his back, *just like yesterday*, Frankie thought. "Naw, no, no, it wasn't no farm accident," he stammered.

When Frankie didn't respond, he scratched his chin with his left hand, trying to decide what to say next. "Anyways, I don't have to tell you nothin'." Bleating lambs signaled Goat to resume the feeding, and Frankie left, more determined than before to find out about his injured hand.

She walked the fenceline and waved to Garrett as he drove down the driveway. He stopped the truck a few feet from Frankie, opened the passenger door, and let out Sonny. The sheltie was happy to see her and to be outside in familiar territory. Frankie walked around to Garrett's side, hopped up on the running board, and leaned in the window.

She was greeted with a kiss and a warning. "Be careful. I don't like leaving you here when any one of these guys could be a killer, but I have to go. That's why I brought Sonny out. How much longer are you going to be here, Ace?" Garrett kept things light-hearted but Frankie knew he worried about her safety.

"Just a few more minutes. I have to talk to Reggie. He's right over there fixing the fence."

Garrett frowned. Frankie reassured him that she had her phone in hand and Sonny by her side. "See you tonight, Mr. G.?"

Garrett nodded and shifted the truck into gear. "I mean it, Frankie. You need to be careful."

Reggie looked up when he saw Sonny out of the corner of his eye. He took off his work hat, ran his hand through his hair, took a swig of something from a thermos, and lifted his hammer again.

"Good morning, Reggie. Look, I know you're under

the gun to get the fence fixed, but I just need to ask you something."

Reggie hammered in the two nails he'd stuck between his lips and scowled.

"It's important, Reggie." Lowering her voice, she said dramatically, "I know I can trust you." She hoped she sounded convincing because she honestly didn't know if she could trust any of the hands.

"Hurry up. What is it?"

"What happened to Goat's hand? You must know." Frankie again spoke quietly, although nobody else was around. Whoever had been loading something into the machine by the manure shed was no longer visible. But just in case he was in the shed, she kept her voice down.

Reggie cursed under his breath. "I don't want to tell you. A man's got a right to his privacy. We all kind of mind our business."

"Ah, don't ask, don't tell, huh? I see." Frankie nodded her understanding. "But, if you like Goat, you might want to help him. I mean, he could be the number one suspect right now. You know what I'm saying?"

Reggie sputtered his disbelief. "Okay. I s'pose this'll come out anyhow. I mean Mr. O'Connor or the police are gonna want to know." Reggie took off the hat again, rubbed his head, and jammed the hat back on defiantly.

"Goat likes to party on Friday nights. Sometimes he drinks too much and starts running his mouth. You know how little guys can get? Well, he got into a fight, and that's it." More nails were crimped between Reggie's lips and he moved down the fence away from Frankie. She'd been dismissed.

Frankie turned in an arc, scanning the pasture and outbuildings of the farm. Nobody was visible now except for Reggie. She wondered if they all were out of sight because they didn't want to talk to her.

"Well if that isn't a symptom of an overactive imagination, I don't know what is," the Golden One scolded. The chiding tone made Frankie giggle and Sonny pricked his ears in confusion. Clearly the sheltie didn't think Frankie was imagining anything. His fur was raised in high alert.

"Come on boy. I have to go, but I'm locking you in the house . . . where it's safe." A wisp of cool air brushed her face, making her shiver. "At least, I hope you'll be safe."

Inside, she gave Sonny a reassuring pat, loaded extra kibble into his dish, and hauled her overnight bag out the door, testing the lock to be sure it held.

* * *

Frankie looked up from her notepad in the shop kitchen, startled by a loud rap on the back door. A long black ink mark streaked across the to-do list she was making for next week. Geesh, she sure was jumpy today.

Her pulse returned to normal when she saw the familiar face of Alonzo Goodman. She waved him inside.

"Tell me why you don't have this door locked, Frankie." His face was a serious red hue.

"Well, for starters, we live in Deep Lakes. Who around here locks their doors when they're home?" Frankie meant to lighten the mood, but this was the wrong time.

"For starters, Frankie, there's a killer in the area. For seconds, the killer probably knows you were at the farm when the shooting took place and also most certainly knows where you live and work." Alonzo strutted around her perimeter, primed for a fight. He'd been friends with Frankie since they were kids, was the best man at her wedding, and took on the role of guardian after her loser husband bailed years earlier.

Frankie pushed a mug of black coffee across the counter along with a plate of cookies. "Okay, let's call a truce. I'll be more careful and lock the door when the shop isn't open." She checked the old-fashioned kitchen clock. In less than half an hour, her mom would be here to open the wine lounge. Frankie called her mother earlier to say she wouldn't be at church, claiming a headache, but truthfully, Frankie just wanted to bask in the quiet of an empty kitchen, her other sanctuary.

"So, what brings you to the shop? I know you and Garrett have a load of work on this shooting case to do." She paused to sip some water. "He told me you two were working today, bagging evidence, filling out forms." So much for the alleged glamorous life of crime-fighting.

Most of it was paperwork, as Frankie learned from the past two crime cases she was mixed up in.

Alonzo slid a sketch across the counter, before helping himself to a second cookie and gulp of coffee. "Here's the victim. Do you recognize him? Maybe saw him at the farm before the shooting?"

Frankie studied the sketch, which looked like a photograph. The man had short, dark hair and a pudgy face without any facial hair. His crooked nose looked like it had been broken once; a prominent bump decorated the top part. A scar severed his left eyebrow into two bushy pieces. He could have played a thug in *The Godfather*, Frankie thought. But she'd never seen him before.

"No, I've never seen him before yesterday. But, maybe Ryan will recognize him. How did you get this photograph anyway?" Frankie indicated the open eyes in the shot that didn't look dead like the ones she remembered from yesterday.

"We can thank Garrett for that. He's got a connection from his ME days. Sends him a picture of the dead guy and they run it through a computer to create a victim that looks alive."

"The marvels of technology." Frankie stared again at the photo, noting the open eyes were hazel, vivid and bright with life. She let out a long sigh. "What a mess."

"I have to say, Frankie, you're pretty breezy about all this. Are you sure you're alright?"

Frankie nodded, surprised by her cool attitude. But she didn't know the victim and had no personal connections to the suspects either. Still, can anyone get used to seeing dead bodies?

"I'm on my way out to Ryan's from here. Wish me luck." He put his wide-brimmed uniform hat back on, glugged the rest of the coffee, and nabbed two more cookies. Alonzo was built like a linebacker, but he had acquired some extra pounds around the middle that came and went depending on the season. Solving a murder was not conducive to dieting.

"So they're back then." Frankie hadn't heard from Carmen and wondered how angry she would be with Frankie. "Good luck, Lon. Please put in a good word for me if you can." She was only half-kidding.

* * *

Little motes of dust danced in the sunbeams in Frankie's apartment kitchen where she whiled away the afternoon making a Greek pasta salad and a creamy chicken salad with grapes and walnuts. She planned to take them as an offering to Carmen and Ryan later, after the questioning was finished. She had no idea how long Lon would be at the farm, but she didn't intend to call until she thought it was safe.

Violet had gone tubing out on Lake Loki with Tara and some other friends. Frankie noticed the change in

Violet's whole appearance since she came home for the summer. She seemed calmer, more confident and certainly looked vibrant. The sunshine agreed with her, giving her skin a warm glow.

She was coming into her natural beauty and independence, which Frankie hoped she would carry into her junior year of college. She wanted Violet to succeed now that she'd chosen a microbiology major, and she wasn't sure that a stint at the family winery was the wisest idea. Maybe Frankie should have pushed Violet toward an internship in the city, away from home. Maybe working at the vineyard was too safe, too easy.

The same thoughts kept swimming around Frankie's head as she added a lime sherbet pie to her growing repertoire of compensatory items going to the O'Connor farm. She glared at the oven clock. Could the afternoon go any slower? What else would go good with the two salads? She scribbled a sticky note to check in with Nelson and Zane this week to see how Violet was doing at Bountiful, hoping that would halt the whirlpool of nagging questions.

She slugged the contents of her water glass before adding more from the fridge. She vowed to stay hydrated all summer as a means of combating headaches she often suffered from the heat. Headaches were a new wrinkle Frankie added to her complaints of being middle-aged. She couldn't remember having many headaches when she was younger. Of course, working in a hot kitchen was a contributing factor without a solution except to drink more water.

Her upstairs apartment was also warm during the summer months, despite air conditioning, which Frankie ran sporadically, almost never enough for it to keep pace with heat and humidity. She shut the kitchen blinds to the late afternoon heat, which reminded her of the broken AC at the O'Connors'. "Crap," she said aloud to nobody. "One more reason for them to be mad at me."

Right on cue, Frankie's phone jangled on the counter and she saw Carmen as the caller. "Here we go." She blew out a stream of groaning air.

"Hi Carmen, how are you?" Frankie hoped she heard the genuine worry in her voice.

"How am I—not great. Are you coming out here so we can talk? The police just left." Carmen sounded tired, shocked, stressed. And she referred to their friend Alonzo as *the police*. Not good.

"I'm on my way. Be there in a few minutes. And Carmen? I'm really sorry." Frankie tapped the hang-up button before Carmen could say anything.

Driving up the farm lane, Frankie again noticed the emptiness outdoors. It appeared Reggie had completed the fence repairs, but neither he nor any other hands could be seen. Frankie made a point of checking to see if the trucks and jeep were still parked by the barn— they were. She wondered if Ryan had spoken to his workers, if Alonzo had shown them the police photograph of the victim.

She retrieved a large box with grips from the back end of the SUV, the lavish remedy for what Frankie imagined was her fault. She set the food down, shut the hatch, and saw Fly and JoJo raise their heads, watching every move she made from a shady spot in the front pasture.

Carmen met her at the door, eyeing the box with a knitted brow. "What's this?" She pointed to the box.

"Peace offering." Frankie shook her head, fearing she'd chosen the wrong words. "Um, I mean . . . I knew you couldn't possibly have time to cook and thought I could help out a little."

Frankie set the box on the long trestle table and began unpacking. Carmen set out plates and silverware and called the twins to get some food.

Kyle and Carlos, teen twins, came upstairs from the basement, looking around warily.

Kyle beamed a wide grin at their benefactor of food. "Thanks, Aunt Frankie. It was cool of you to bring us all this." Kyle was the splitting image of Carmen's brother, Andres, tall and handsome with thick black hair. Gregarious and charming, he was going to be a lady-killer soon.

Carlos was almost Kyle's opposite. He resembled Ryan with wavy hair and blue eyes, and he shared his dad's pride in the farm, loved tending the sheep, and loved the countryside. "Is it okay if we get some food and go back downstairs?" Carlos clearly sensed the vibe in the room and wanted to escape.

Carmen nodded at Carlos, handed each boy a soda, then opened one of the wine bottles Frankie packed at the last minute. She knew Carmen's favorites and brought one of each. When Carmen opened the red, Dark Deeds, Frankie knew Carmen's afternoon had been worse than imagined. Ryan confirmed Frankie's suspicions by waving away the offer of wine, instead opting for a double shot of Jameson in a tumbler with a little ice.

None of the three reached for any food or even a plate, but sat in silence with their drinks. Frankie waited for them to speak, no matter how much it pained her to do so. She owed them that much, she figured. Sonny had greeted her, gleefully sniffing her hand. He laid down under the table at her feet.

Frankie watched Carmen look at Ryan meaningfully, then Ryan looked down into the glass for a way to begin. This vignette played on repeatedly until Frankie felt itchy and found it difficult to sit still any longer. After an eternity, it ended.

"I'm mad as hell, Frankie, but not at you. I'm mad this happened at all, even madder that it happened when we were gone." Ryan stood up from the table, unable to contain his fury. "I thought I could trust my workers!" He swore loudly but quieted when Carmen shot him a warning look and pointed to the basement.

Ryan could be temperamental in his younger days, but he mellowed substantially after the twins were born, even more in recent years as he settled into agribusiness and was elected to the state lamb council. His temper flared now, however, and Frankie understood. Someone within his sphere had betrayed him.

"Can I ask you some questions about your men? Maybe we can put all our heads together and figure some things out?" Frankie began gently, and Ryan sat down again.

Carmen reached for her husband's hand and held it firmly against the table top. "Before we talk about anything, we're getting something to eat. We haven't eaten all day." She gave Ryan an imploring look mixed with love. "You start, honey."

Frankie breathed a long sigh of relief for the first time since yesterday. She brought out a pen and notebook, reading between bites. She relayed everything she could remember from the time the O'Connors left the farm until they returned. Even something that seemed unimportant might matter in the big scheme of things.

Next, she asked Ryan for information about each farmhand and if he had reasons to suspect anyone in particular. Ryan swore again. "They all have their flaws, Frankie. That's just it. Some are hot-heads. Some have a past." He stared at his Jameson again. "Worst part is that a couple of them are new. I mean, I don't even know anything much about them. Hands often come and go, and they don't need a resume to get hired."

Ryan pointed to Frankie's notes. His finger landed first on Coop, whom he hired from the shearing crew that came to the farm in March, then on Bucky, the part-timer who showed up looking for work just a few weeks ago. "Hell, I don't even know Jonesy that well. He's a top notch dog trainer, but he's only been here a year." Ryan rapped the table sharply with his fist.

"What about the Green-Up company? How long have you been using them?" Frankie shifted to another topic.

"About three years. One of my colleagues on the council recommended the company. As our herd grew, I wanted to do something good with the excess manure. Environmentally good, I mean."

Frankie raised her brows quizzically.

"Sheep poop makes excellent fertilizer. It dries faster than many manures because it comes in pellets instead of patties and sheep digest the contaminants that growers don't want in their fertilizer. So, it's another source of income—selling it, I mean." Ryan had veered into his agribusiness lane, comfortably offering talking points about sheep manure.

"You know it's our sheep poop that's fertilizing your vineyard every year, right?"

Frankie admitted she relied on Manny Vega, her vineyard manager, to handle those details. She redirected. "Did you know Larry, the driver who was supposed to be here yesterday?"

"Yes. He's picked up here several times, but not always. Larry doesn't strike me as anything but a mild-mannered truck driver. He picks up on time and doesn't cause problems. I told Alonzo the same thing."

"And you didn't recognize the driver who came yesterday?" Frankie refrained from using the word *victim*.

"Nope. But I kept a copy of the photograph to show to some of the other sheep farmers around here. I won't have a lamb council meeting until the end of summer now, but I'll be selling our first lambs at auction in Milwaukee in two weeks, so I'll circulate the photo there."

Two weeks? That sounded like an eternity in the crime world, because it was. The trail could grow ice cold by that time. Frankie marveled that she was thinking like a detective. And with that thought, Frankie had some work to do, including sending her editor a copy of the victim's photo.

"I need to get going. Please let me know if I can do anything at all to help." She gave Carmen a tight hug and squeezed Ryan's arm. "By the way, sorry about the AC. It went out Friday, but the repair service can't get here until tomorrow."

When she stepped outside, Carmen was hot on her heels. "Hey, you left your box."

"No, I meant to. You've got a lot to do right now. A little extra food won't hurt." Frankie smiled sympathetically, as if she were attending a wake.

"You're right. There's lots to do. Starting right now. What's your plan, Frankie? I know you're up to something." Carmen stood, hands on hips, batting her eyelashes accusingly.

Frankie giggled. "Okay, okay. I'm going to The Oasis to find out if Goat hurt his hand in a bar fight Friday night."

"Not without me, you're not. And not dressed in anything you own." Carmen smirked disapprovingly at her friend. "That's my old stomping ground. Get back in here and we'll suit up."

Chapter 7

It's not rebels that make trouble, but trouble that makes rebels.
– Ruth Messinger

The Oasis squatted on a country road that butted up against the Blackbird River. It wasn't much to look at, which suited its patrons, mainly locals and traveling biker groups. During summer and autumn, folks who owned or rented cottages on the river would stop in for takeout, pull up to the pier and be on their way again.

Built sometime in the 1960s, the one-story bar sported a high false front like an old-time saloon. Its corrugated tin roof offered endless sound effects from rain, wind, and birds nesting underneath.

Ryan began cycling when he was a teenager and proudly purchased his first Harley when he turned 21. He and Carmen traveled around the state in their younger days before the twins were born; even went to the Sturgis rally once.

After digging through the closet Carmen had planned to clean out for years, the two women were decked out in proper biker bar attire. Carmen giggled as she laid out the leather chaps and vest, heavy wallet chains, head wraps, and laced up knee-high boots that were part of her gear in the old days.

Since the two weren't riding out to the bar on a cycle, they decided not to overdo their look. Carmen donned tight black jeans trimmed in chains and studs, a black shirt with mesh inserts and low black boots.

Frankie frowned at her image in the mirror. Poured into faded jeans dripping with fringe and a tight black shirt with ladder-cut sleeves, she couldn't have felt more uncomfortable unless she was naked.

"Stop making that face Frankie, and embrace your inner renegade. You've done theater; you know how to play the part." Carmen handed Frankie some red lipstick and looked over her friend's shoulder in the mirror while she applied mascara.

Frankie didn't wear makeup except for formal events and hated lipstick because she couldn't get it to stay in place. She took the tube, horrified by the color, and painted her lips. She laughed at herself which left a red streak on her teeth.

Carmen grabbed her wrist and turned her around to face her. "Here, let me help you or we'll never get out of here." Carmen stroked black mascara on Frankie's lashes, then brushed finishing powder on both lashes and lips. "There, that should keep things in place. Take a look."

Frankie didn't recognize the stranger in the mirror. Besides makeup, Carmen had tied a black Harley-Davidson bandana around her head—flames shooting from the sides of the insignia. The look definitely subtracted years from Frankie's face. Since she was shorter than Carmen, she opted for black boots with heels so her fringed jeans wouldn't drag in the dirt. Leather straps with giant buckles flaunted her ankles and made her feel like she could kick somebody's behind if the occasion called for it.

Before heading out, the women were greeted by an audience of the three O'Connors. The twins let out a raucous catcall, and Kyle declared they were "BA." Ryan whistled approval at his wife, but insisted they both keep his number on speed dial in case they found trouble. He pulled Carmen in for a deep hug and whispered something private in her ear which made her lower her eyes and hold on tighter.

On the drive out, after a quick call to Garrett about her plan for the night, Carmen convinced Frankie to follow her lead at the bar. Sunday night at The Oasis should be pretty quiet, but since summer was prime riding season, you just couldn't tell for sure. Frankie swung into the parking lot, kicking up dry dust. Rain was on every farmer's wish list right now. There were a few motorcycles in the lot and a couple of trucks. Three other vehicles were parked behind the dumpster, probably workers.

A large banner advertised Taco Tuesdays and Wing Night Wednesdays, along with happy hour times. A neon Budweiser sign posed in one window; a light-up motorcycle flashed "bikers welcome" in the other window.

Carmen exited the SUV and adjusted her rhinestone-studded head wrap. One glance at Frankie made her stop, shake her head, and hold out her hand like a traffic cop. "Dios mío! Lose that purse, Frankie. You look like you took a wrong turn on your way to the mall."

Frankie pouted at first, then laughed out loud. She pulled her keys and wallet out of her printed Vera bag and clicked the lock. "Okay, let's do this."

Every customer looked up when the women walked into the dimly lit building, letting in the last remnants of daylight accompanied by a current of dust. The bikers looked to be traveling companions, all appeared to be middle-aged. The men nodded greetings to Carmen and Frankie, giving them a head-to-toe inspection. The two women snuggled up closer to the men and offered Carmen and Frankie requisite glares on the heels of the men's once-over.

Four other men sat on the other side of the sticky bar, definitely ten or so years younger than Carmen and Frankie. They didn't see any trouble there. The partners chose stools in the midsection of the bar away from both parties.

"Carmen Martinez, is that you? Damn, woman!" The bartender was a 50-something man with a gray handlebar mustache and long hair pulled into a ponytail under a backwards Harley cap. Large muscled arms broke out of a "Born to Ride" tank as he marched over to Carmen, large hands ready to clasp hers. Carmen's eyes widened in recognition.

"Grizz," she said warmly, holding both of his large hands, "it's been a long time."

"Too long," the hulking man said, his voice cracking with obvious emotion. "Where's that farm boy of yours?"

Carmen laughed. "At the farm, of course." She leaned over the bar and Grizz's big head joined hers. "I'm here undercover, looking for some information."

Grizz cocked one eye, his upper lip curled. Then he slapped the bar, chuckling. "First drink's on me. What'll you have?"

When Carmen ordered a Corona with lime, Frankie did the same. Grizz went to check on the other customers, brought them refills, then scooted out from the bar and fed coins into the jukebox. Soon "Bad to the Bone" poured from the speakers and Grizz pulled up a stool to sit across from the women.

"I forgot my manners. I'm Grizz, owner, bartender, and chief bottle washer at this fancy establishment. And, you are?"

"Francine Champagne. Carmen and I own *Bubble and Bake* downtown. I know what you mean by chief bottle washer. Carmen and I do all the same work as the rest of our employees." She held out her hand to shake Grizz's, but he raised it to his lips and gave it a little peck.

"It's a real pleasure, Francine. Any friend of Carmen's is a friend of mine. I don't go downtown unless I have to, but I'll come by one day and check out your place. A bar, is it?"

"Actually, a bakery by day and wine lounge by night. I also have a vineyard on Blackbird Marsh. And, please call me Frankie." She found Grizz absolutely charming in a rugged way.

Carmen cleared her throat and bumped Frankie's knee, reminding her she was supposed to be taking the lead here.

Carmen pulled up a photo on her phone and laid it on the bar for Grizz to see. "You ever see this guy in the bar?" It was an employee file photo of Goat, or Billy Grant, noted below the picture.

Grizz grunted. "That twerp comes in here most Friday nights. He don't drive so begs rides off a few regulars who live nearby. Everybody calls him Goat or a few other choice names. Why? Is he in more trouble than usual?"

Carmen crossed her arms. She didn't want to hear that the farm workers were causing trouble. "What do you mean by trouble?"

"He likes to flirt with women, but usually doesn't get anywhere. Then he drinks too much, starts to mouth off, and ends up getting kicked outta my bar, because I don't want the cops out here." Grizz took a big swig of beer from his glass.

Forgetful Frankie jumped on the information. "Was he here this past Friday night? Did he mouth off to anyone?" Carmen kicked her foot and shot her a killer look.

Grizz snorted. "I know that look, Carmen. It means business." He turned his attention to Frankie. "I remember one night years ago when Ryan and I both got juiced. Carmen had to drive us home—on the Harley." It might have happened last week; Grizz teared up from laughing so hard. "Course she couldn't get us both on the bike at the same time, so she made two trips. Never driven the Harley before in her life, but that broad has guts."

Carmen tried to look unimpressed by the reminiscence, but a smile tugged at the corners of her mouth just the same. "Yep, those were the days. I'm not sure how we made it through some of them." She cleared her throat and took a cooling drink. Back to the matter at hand.

"So what about this past Friday, two days ago? Were you here, Grizz?"

"I'm pretty much always here, especially on the weekend. We fill up fast, and it's hard to get good workers. I've got decent kitchen help, but mostly women bartenders." After seeing Carmen's hard stare, he commented, "What can I say? Women bring in the customers."

"Anyhow, Friday." He paused to gaze at the ceiling, calculating. Yeah, Goat was here, started pushing another guy around. What is it about little guys that make them want to do the dance with a big guy?" He took another swig of beer. "Before I could get across the bar, Goat shoves the guy, tries to punch him. Let's just say the other guy got him back."

"How do you mean?" Carmen leaned forward, interested.

"The guy pulled out a utility flashlight, clubbed Goat's fist. I didn't even have to throw him out. He staggered out the door, crying like a baby."

Frankie resisted the urge to ask Grizz if he called the cops, kicked the other guy out of the bar, checked to see if Goat was okay, needed a ride home, anything? She imagined the rules of polite society weren't exactly followed at The Oasis.

"Anything else you'd like to know?" Grizz wondered. He downed the rest of his beer and asked them if they wanted another drink.

Carmen answered no for both of them. "It's been a long day. Time for us to get going. Thanks for being straight with the information. It was good to see you again, Grizz." Carmen was sincere.

"Oh yeah? Same here. Don't be a stranger, Carmen. Come by on a slow day with Ryan and we'll shoot the crap. Does he still have that honey of a Harley?"

"He does. Our twins are eyeing it up, though."

"How about that. You two gonna let the twins have it then?" Grizz almost held his breath after asking.

"Not a chance." Carmen shoved some cash on the bar and winked at Grizz.

"Atta girl" and a raucous chortle followed them out the door.

Two of the young guys from the party of four were right behind Carmen and Frankie.

"What's the rush ladies? Plenty of night left to enjoy,

don't ya think?" Frankie guessed the stocky guy, dressed in a western shirt, blue jeans, and laced up crap-kickers, was maybe 30. Frankie didn't know if she should feel flattered or break down laughing.

"Sorry, not interested. Thanks, though." Frankie kept walking.

The taller guy with the sharp nose tried his luck. He might have been handsome if not for the large nose ring that looked like an animal horn. "What about you, pretty lady? Maybe you can talk your friend into having a fun night." He spoke with a refined foreign accent that didn't quite match his flannel shirt and redneck boots.

"Sorry. Like she said, we're not interested. And really, you two should look for someone your own age." Carmen couldn't resist a mock scolding.

Once buckled into the SUV, Carmen added, "I recognize that stubby guy. He's a farmhand at the Turners', just down the road from ours."

Frankie wondered if anyone referred to her short stature as "stubby." She jabbed her friend on the shoulder. "Stubby? You mean the one that propositioned me? Thanks a lot, Carmen."

Chapter 8

The fruit derived from labor is the sweetest of pleasures.
– Luc De Clapiers

Frankie's cell phone rang before her alarm clock, causing her brain to vault into high gear. What day was it? Had she missed her alarm? She fumbled for the phone and gave it a bleary-eyed perusal.

"Garrett? What's going on?" She sat up in bed, attempted to swing her legs to the side, miscalculated and almost rolled onto the floor. "Oh, oh, whoa."

"Good morning, Frankie. What's going on there? Everything okay?" Garrett sounded amused.

"What do you mean? Yes, everything's fine." Her old clock radio said 5 a.m. She let out a groan. Monday was the one day of the week Frankie slept in until 5:45. "Why are you calling so early?"

"Shoot. Monday. I'm sorry. The days are running together for me. I'll let you go back to sleep."

"It's okay. I'm awake now." This time she climbed out of bed and started for the kitchen. Coffee first. "How's the case going?"

"I was going to ask you the same thing, Ace. Sorry I

missed out last night. I heard you and Carmen were a sight to behold." Frankie imagined Garrett must be wondering what he got himself into with her as a girlfriend.

"I know you were under the gun to get that report finished, so you can move it up the chain. Are you going in early today?"

"No, just couldn't sleep. And you know how summer is. Early daylight means Freya is awake and ready to sniff squirrels." They both laughed. Frankie and Garrett had met thanks to Freya, the Norwegian elkhound who was his housemate.

"I can meet you downstairs in the Bubble and Bake kitchen with breakfast in 20 minutes, Mr. G. Whadda you say?" Frankie tingled just thinking about it.

"It's a date, Miss Francine."

Leftover shop quiche, fresh fruit and coffees consumed, Frankie and Garrett walked along Sterling Creek that gurgled behind the shop all the way down to the Blackbird River on one end, the Fox on the other. They held hands, counted the robins busily tracking worms, listened to the buzzy chirps of the red-winged blackbirds, and made idle chit-chat.

Garrett's phone dinged. He paused for a quick check, then let out a long, slow whistle.

"What's going on?" Frankie asked.

"This is going on." Garrett held up his phone which showed Frankie in full biker chick regalia from yesterday. "Wow, I'm sorry I missed this."

"Nice. You and Ryan are really something." But she made a mental note to dress up a little more inviting for their next date.

"Carmen sent that to me, not Ryan." He pulled Frankie in for a kiss before she could interject.

"How about dinner after work today? Let's go to one of the new touristy places. They're usually pretty quiet on Mondays."

"Love to," Frankie said. "I've heard rave reviews about The Taverna."

"Me, too. Greek food by the marina. Sounds wonderful. I'll pick you up at six—where?"

"Here is good. I'm working at Bountiful today, first thing. But, I'll be in the shop all afternoon."

* * *

The vineyard had taken on the lush look of summer already; every imaginable shade of green was on display from the tiny lime green grape clusters to the glossy pear-colored grape leaves. The surrounding landscape continued the palette with juniper-green pines, emerald grass, brightly feathered ferns and dark muted mosses. The short growing season in Wisconsin could be compared to watching time-lapse photography in motion. In the traditional vineyards of California, a long growing season means grape vines take their time to bud, bloom, and bear fruit. But cold climate grapes are in a hurry, rushing from spring through summer to fall for early harvest before frost ruins their chances of becoming wine.

Frankie skipped into the vineyard and absorbed its beauty in the early sunshine. She couldn't imagine anything more lovely than her grapevines, standing in trim rows, glowing in green ripples across the wire trellises. Beyond the rows, she could see the orchard trees, enclosing the vineyard into a fairy tale setting. The fruit trees were done flowering, but cloaked in their summer green, were verdant and showy. During summer, Bountiful's outbuildings were invisible below the orchard, and this effect made Frankie feel alone in her world.

Row after row she inspected the vines, coming upon Manny, the vineyard manager, in the third row of Frontenacs.

"Good morning, Frankie. This heat spell is making the vines explode, huh?" Manny gently lifted the trailing leaves to reveal hardy clusters of baby grapes.

Frankie clapped. They had been babying the Frontenac vines for five seasons and hoped to produce the first vintage from their own grapes this fall. "Excellent management on your part as always, Manny."

She sucked in a deep waft of air, purposely trying to catch the scent of sheep manure, but all she smelled was the earthy scent of mulch. "So, did all this fertilizer come from the O'Connor farm?"

Manny wiped his face with his bandana and gave her a curious grin. "Yep, we've been using composted sheep manure for the past five years, boss. You just noticed that now?"

Frankie nodded, smiling. "I just found out from Ryan that you've been picking up our fertilizer there." A tiny idea formed. "When was the last time you picked up manure?"

"Oh, no. Don't drag me into your *investigation*." Manny drew air quotes around the word. "I was there Thursday before they left for Chicago. And nothing strange was going on."

"Well, it was a long shot anyway." Frankie figured Manny didn't know the O'Connor hands well, only interacting with them a couple times a year. "Thanks, Manny. Anything strange going on with the vines or the orchard we need to worry about?"

He assured Frankie that, knock on wood, all was right with the world of Bountiful Fruits.

The two raked in the mulch manure mixture around the vines, then Manny was off to do the same around the orchard. He managed Bountiful alone most of the year except during planting and harvest. During those times, he brought in a few migrant hands that he found freelancing around the area performing seasonal work.

He had once been a migrant worker, too, so he knew the circuit as well as many of the families that arrived every spring to travel from job to job until cold weather sent them South or West again to follow other harvests. Frankie was always satisfied with her workers and tried to show them respect by using her clumsy Spanish from college.

With a sigh, Frankie traipsed out of the vineyard for the day, trading the peaceful outdoor setting for the intrigue of science in the wine lab. It was time for her to check the progress of the wines being batched and to discuss upcoming vintages with her technicians. This summer, those techies included her own daughter.

When Frankie pulled open the heavy red door that led to the lab, a cat darted inside from behind one of the bushes. "'Shoot. Cat on the loose, look out!" she called into the office.

Bountiful Fruits was home to a few outdoor kitties—great for keeping away rodents, although not always a winning situation for the local birds. Frankie tried to dismiss this fact every time the thought crept into her mind, but it wasn't so easy when she came upon a dismantled bird wing or pile of downy feathers while walking the orchard.

When she crossed the entrance into the office, Violet had already nabbed the little rogue and was holding it on her lap. Zane Casey, tech genius where wine production and computer research were concerned, was standing beside Violet, giving the cat a belly rub as it purred in approval. Meanwhile, Nelson Raye, microbiology whiz and peculiar fellow, voiced his displeasure.

"You two," he jabbed a finger at Zane and Violet. "Take that thing out of here and then put on new lab coats. I simply won't allow anything to be contaminated with cat hair or God knows what else that animal might be carrying." He put both hands on his hips and tapped his foot impatiently.

Violet snickered at Nelson then saluted him as she gathered the cat offender and shoved it back outdoors. Wearing fresh lab coats, she and Zane joined Nelson and Frankie in the tank room, where Nelson was pointing out pH measurements and sugar content on Garden Patch, a strawberry rhubarb red blend made from a few of Bountiful's own Frontenac grapes from last season, along with purchased Petite Pearl and Sabrevois.

He handed Frankie a sample and watched her perform her ritual tasting. Closing her eyes, she breathed in its bouquet and paused to jot down her findings. Then she sipped the vintage, swirled it around her mouth allowing it to linger on her tongue before swallowing. She made more notes, took a second sip, and noted the differences in flavors.

Nelson held his breath waiting for her verdict, wondering how it would compare to his and Zane's from earlier that morning. "June 18th, I think, for this one," Frankie proclaimed. Nelson and Zane high-fived each other in celebration as Violet gave a mock eye roll.

"Did you taste this wine, Violet?" Frankie indicated the Garden Patch tank.

Violet hesitated. "No. The guys arrived early and were finished by the time I got here, but I'd like to taste it now, if that's okay." She'd been tasting wine long enough to understand the methods involved, and she'd learned from one of the best: her mother. "This has an excellent balance between the tart rhubarb and the sweet strawberry. I can taste both fruits but one doesn't overpower the other. This is going to sell well, Mom."

"Excellent description, Violet." Frankie stated her approval.

They moved on past the second and third tanks where Dark Deeds was percolating full throttle. The variety had become a standard best-seller for Bountiful and was one of the first Frankie mastered. She'd been drinking Lambrusco wines for years and was determined to produce one, despite the fact the original Lambrusco grapes didn't grow anywhere in the Midwest. Once she found a supplier in Connecticut, she began experimenting with fruits. Her core group of tasters declared the sweet cherry from Washington the hands-down winner, and the recipe was etched in stone.

Violet stopped in front of the Dark Deeds tank and spoke in a teacherly voice. "I think it's worth noting that we had to add tartaric acid to tanks two and three. The wine was hazy on Friday and we determined it was likely due to pectin from the cherries."

Frankie loved to hear her daughter speak with scientific authority, but she retraced her steps to sample her beloved Dark Deeds. "Did you taste it today?" She looked at her crew. They shook their heads.

"Well, let's all give it a try then." She passed out samples gleaned from tank two's spigot. "The color is lovely." They tasted and gave it a thumbs up, then repeated sampling from tank three, which was also acceptable. "Good work all of you."

Tank four housed another new vintage, this one made from local elderberries that Frankie and Carmen had picked the past fall. She broke down in fits of laughter when she recalled the two of them, sometimes thigh-deep in marsh muck, harvesting elderberries. Both had fallen more times than they could count and returned home hours later in the waning daylight, cold and drenched, but with numerous pails of elderberries from all over the county.

Frankie's wise purchase of a fruit press repeatedly proved its value. She couldn't imagine trying to mash fruits by hand; she already had baker's ailments from kneading dough and other repetitive movements. Some ailments were alleviated after the shop purchased automated equipment, but Bubble and Bake was small potatoes and the owners couldn't justify spending money on little-used machinery. But in a winery, equipment was a necessary evil unless you were just making wine as a hobby for you and a few friends.

The Enchanted Elderberry combined the local pickings with a Michigan grower's Marechal Foch red grape, an appreciated hybrid red that could thrive in cold climates and didn't succumb to the "foxy" flavors of some red varieties. Many vineyard owners held their noses and jokingly referred to a few red grape varieties as "skunky", which provoked many vintners to learn techniques to combat musky odors and flavors from certain grapes.

Frankie and the others basked in the rich heady aroma and flavor of the new vintage. "It needs another week and then we'll see. What do the rest of you think?"

Zane said he'd happily decant a bottle and drink it over the weekend, but Nelson insisted on "completing the process accurately." Frankie found the differences in the two scientists remarkably similar to a good wine: it was all about the balance of flavors. Bountiful was blessed to employ both men with their well-matched skill sets. She also knew Violet would benefit under their tutelage.

The team left the cool tank room and reconvened in the office for a brief staff meeting. "If we bottle tanks one, two and three on or about June 18th, we'll need a definitive plan to start new vintages somewhere around the 22nd, and get summer fruits pressed as they come in."

Summer was the busiest season by far at the vineyard. Along with tending grapevines, summer fruits had to be picked from the orchard or patches as they came into season, or purchased from area farms. Frankie needed all hands on deck, meaning her scientists often doubled as machine operators, pressing fresh fruits.

Violet raised her hand amidst the litany of strawberries, cherries, peaches, plums, and apricots being chronicled by the others. She cleared her throat loudly.

"I have a wine idea that I'd like Bountiful to produce." Violet spoke imploringly, her eyes focused on the wall above their heads.

Frankie wasn't sure if she should applaud her shy daughter's bold proclamation or school her about the risk involved in producing 250 bottles of wine that might be vile. Instead, she took a deep breath and practiced uncharacteristic patience.

"I know we just can't go full bore in production without a trial run, so that's what I'm hoping we can do. We have empty carboys for experimental batches, and I think I have a good idea . . ." Violet trailed off, letting her words settle.

Frankie exhaled in relief. Her dreamy daughter must have matured greatly this past year. "Go ahead. Make your pitch."

"Well, I think the flavor profile would be perfect for autumn. We haven't done much with apples and apple wines are popular, but . . ."

"And also prevalent all over the Midwest," Nelson popped off. He didn't seem to notice the glares he received around the room, or he didn't comprehend them.

"Yes, but this wine will be different. For starters, I want to make mead, not wine. I want to use two apple varieties: Granny Smith and Ambrosia. The Granny Smith will provide a crisp tart apple taste while the Ambrosia will elevate the sweetness with its honey flavor. Both varieties are easy to find in early September. The surprise though will be the addition of butterscotch simple syrup, added during the fermentation process, and of course, local honey." Violet's pretty face held a satisfied smile.

Frankie had no intention of weighing in first, so again, she tamped down her impulsive need to respond. Instead she wore her best poker face and looked from Nelson to Zane, waiting.

Nelson massaged his forehead, pinching his brows together. "Interesting, interesting. I like the concept. I'm just wondering if it will be cloying, sickeningly sweet. We've never made mead before."

Violet looked at Zane, who was open-minded and adventurous by nature. He didn't disappoint.

"I say we try it. A caramel apple mead? I don't think it's been done. It could be cutting edge if it turns out." Zane high-fived Violet, who beamed briefly, then searched Frankie's face for the final verdict.

"I love the idea, too. It's well thought-out, Violet. The only issue I see is that you will be back at Point by September, so how can we get this experiment going now?" Frankie was practical and realistic.

"I've thought of that, too. I called around to some orchards and wholesalers. Turns out there are warehouses of apples in storage, and we can get what we need shipped in. The Ambrosia will be on the expensive side but Granny Smiths are still available in the supermarket. It's not going to taste as good as fresh-picked, but it should give us the general idea."

Nelson retreated to his computer immediately to search for mead making techniques.

Violet grabbed a paper from her desk. The calculations for the number of apples and other necessary ingredients had been recorded as part of her formal proposal. All of the numbers and costs were neatly in order.

"Well done, Violet," Frankie said, taking the paper. "I'll look at this today and let you know when to order."

Violet resisted the urge to hug her mother, but nodded her head professionally, deciding it was good practice. She also didn't want Nelson and Zane to get the false impression that her mother would play favorites in her businesses. That was not Frankie Champagne's modus operandi.

* * *

The afternoon passed quickly at Bubble and Bake. Tess was humming a melancholy tune, rolling cinnamon rolls in time with her swaying head and hips. The kitchen smells of sugar and spices lingered in the warm air.

Frankie had just finished helping Carmen unload a trove of fresh produce from area farms. The two were organizing the walk-in cooler, arguing about whether Carmen should be working today after the events of two days ago.

"I need to work, Frankie. This is what I do. I'm your business partner. I need to stick to our routine." Carmen's voice was agitated.

Frankie gave her friend a silent thumbs up, garnering a small high-five from Goldie and Pirate, who were apparently in cahoots for now.

The two women looked at the agenda for tomorrow's lineup.

"You've been a baking machine today, Tess. There's not much left for us to do."

A single tear slid down Tess's cheek. She hastily wiped it away with a floured hand and resumed winding cinnamon rolls, adding to the rows on the commercial sheet pan.

Carmen and Frankie exchanged worried looks. "What's going on Tess? Tell us."

"I don't want to bother you with my troubles," she began, more tears fell and she stepped back from the counter to avoid wetting her bakery tray. She wiped her eyes with the apron bib.

Frankie moved into Tess's place to finish the tray. "Your worries are our worries. Out with it."

Tess, an international student, was hired as an intern last Christmas and had graduated from culinary school in May. Regretfully, Frankie and Carmen would have to find a replacement intern in the fall when Tess returned to her native Ethiopia.

Tess plopped on a stool and looked down at her lap. "I can't go home," she said in her rich rhythmic voice. "I just found out this morning from my sponsor. There's civil unrest there and they are keeping international students in their countries of study." Now the tears flowed freely.

"I'm trying to call my aunts, but I cannot get through. I have to be out of my student housing by August 1st. At least the college gave me a short extension on my lease. I don't know what to do, and I'm worried about my family."

Tess's single mother died when she was two, so her three aunts raised her, insisting that all their children get the best education possible. Tess excelled in school, and her essay about returning to Ethiopia to help other girls learn a trade or get an education resonated with the international student organization. The group found a sponsor for Tess, and three years ago she arrived in Madison to begin the culinary program.

Her plan had always been to open a restaurant/bakery in her home city and employ as many of her cousins as she could. She shared many stories about poverty back home and the uncertain future for women there. She hoped her cousin Maya would be able to attend college in the U.S., too.

"Maya's application was pending last time I talked with my family. It's frustrating not knowing what's going on at home."

Frankie and Carmen wrapped their arms around Tess in a cradling fashion.

"Don't worry. We'll think of something. You can always stay with me. Violet will be going back to school in August."

"And you'll have a job here as long as you want it. Believe me, we're in no hurry to see you go, Tess." Carmen chimed in and squeezed her a little harder.

Tess smiled a little and stood up. "Would you mind if I make these muffins?" She held up a recipe that read "Teff Muffins" on it with a photo of a walnut-topped brown muffin. "They remind me of home. I brought the ingredients with me today."

Frankie and Carmen were intrigued. Tess padded to the back door where a plastic crate was parked and began pulling out a myriad of ingredients: agave nectar, coconut oil, carrots, apples, flax seeds, and two types of flour not usually seen in the Bubble and Bake kitchen.

"This is tapioca flour. I know we probably have some, but I wasn't sure. And this is teff flour. It's very popular in Ethiopia because it's from a small grain that grows well in my country. And, it's very healthy." The tiny grains reminded Frankie of grape-nuts cereal, but the flour resembled finely ground pecans.

"On one condition—you have to let Carmen and me try one."

"We've never been disappointed in any of your recipes from home, Tess. Have at it."

Tess's tune changed to a happier melody. Carmen bade them both goodbye to reconnect with the farm situation.

"If you could have heard Ryan chew out the farmhands, you would have turned purple. It wasn't pretty. I'm glad

Tia Pepita wasn't there. She's riding back from Chicago today with my brother Esteban, so I'm sure we're in for quite the night."

Carmen's aunt had a flare for the dramatic and a murder on the farm was certain to bring out the theatrical in her. It looked like Carmen was in for a long night.

"Maybe we should go back to The Oasis, huh Frankie?" Carmen winked and disappeared out the back door.

Tess and Frankie were enjoying warm teff muffins with apple chunks, raisins, and carrots in the kitchen when Alonzo, Shirley, and Garrett walked through the back door in tandem, looking like a trio of grim reapers.

"Frankie, can we talk to you in private?" Alonzo looked apologetically at Tess, who gave him a wide-eyed stare, picked up her plate and mug of tea, and hightailed it to the wine lounge.

"What's going on? Is it my mom, Violet, Aunt CeCe?" A large bubble of fear rose in Frankie's stomach and caught in her throat. "Just tell me."

Garrett sat down next to her and put a protective arm around her shoulders. "It's nothing like that. They're all fine as far as we know."

Frankie remained standing, waiting.

Alonzo looked at Shirley, eager to relinquish the task. Shirley shook her head briefly. *Why were men such chicken-hearts sometimes?*

"This is about Violet and we thought you'd appreciate hearing this from us. Did you know she was seeing Clay

Cooper?" Shirley's voice had a tinge of softness to it, something Frankie wasn't accustomed to hearing.

"And who's Clay Cooper?" Frankie drew a blank. No, she didn't know Violet was dating anyone but the name didn't ring any bells.

"One of the O'Connor farmhands."

"Oh dear." Frankie sat down heavily on the stool, thoughts flying around her head. *Why hadn't she told her she was seeing someone? Especially after the shooting, why didn't she say something? Where had she met Clay Cooper?*

"Which hand is he? I mean, I only know their nicknames."

"I believe he goes by *Coop* at the farm," Alonzo offered.

Frankie had met Coop once, the day she came to get the lowdown about the farm before Ryan and Carmen left for Chicago. She couldn't remember anything remarkable about him. There must be more to the story.

"He wasn't there the day of the murder. I remember he called in. Car trouble, I think. Anyway, Reggie had to take his shift and wasn't happy about it." Frankie racked her brain in case she missed any details.

Shirley picked up the narrative. "Yes, that's right. Well, turns out Clay has an alibi to corroborate his story. Violet. Your daughter followed him to the mechanic in Waupaca." She paused for Frankie to absorb that.

Frankie was off the stool again, pacing the kitchen. *Why would Coop call Violet at that ungodly hour? Or were*

Violet and Clay together all night, so she simply volunteered to follow him? Just how serious were they?

Garrett caught Frankie by the arm on her second lap around the counter. "Whoa, take a breather, Miss Francine." Gazing sternly at the two officers, he spoke frankly. "Maybe let's get the details out on the table here, so we can go over things."

Shirley opened a file folder labeled "Clay Cooper" and retrieved a piece of paper with Violet's name under the heading "witness statement." Frankie felt like crying. No way did she want her daughter to be involved in this murder.

"Let's see, Violet says Clay called her around one a.m. and said his car was acting up. He knew a mechanic in Waupaca and asked Violet if she would follow him there in case he broke down on the way. She picked him up shortly after the call at his residence. They arrived at the mechanic's less than an hour later, and Violet left him there. Clay said he would wait for the car." Shirley placed the statement back in the folder.

Frankie's investigator switch clicked on. "If Violet left him, say around two-thirty, how does that let him off the hook? I heard the gunshot around three-thirty."

Alonzo took over. "Yeah, we have a statement from the mechanic, too. He says Clay was there until the car was fixed around eleven a.m. He said they went to breakfast at the local diner when it opened at five-thirty while they waited for the auto parts store to open. He even had the receipt."

She looked from Lon to Shirley and back again. "You're sure about the alibi?"

Shirley nodded. "I interviewed the mechanic, then stopped at the diner. The waitress remembered them and gave a good description of both."

Frankie sighed, somewhat relieved. At least her daughter's boyfriend wasn't a murderer. Right now that seemed like a fair trade for the blow she'd been dealt. Now she needed to determine how she would approach the topic with Violet because she knew one thing for certain—she couldn't just let it go.

Chapter 9

The most important thing that parents can teach their children is how to get along without them.
- Frank A. Clark

"Why don't we take a raincheck on dinner tonight, Frankie? I know you probably want to talk to Violet ASAP." Garrett's warm caramel eyes probed her green ones, gauging her emotions. Alonzo and Shirley had taken off to leave the two of them alone at the counter.

Frankie felt like an open book and wondered when she allowed herself to become so vulnerable. Her relationship with Garrett was comfortable, like a favorite sweater, but stitched with romance and the undiscovered.

"You know me too well. I wouldn't be good company tonight, and I need to figure out how I'm going to start the conversation."

Garrett kissed her cheek gently. "Keep in mind that Violet is an adult. If you treat her like a naughty child, you're not going to get anywhere. Even if she is acting like a child." Garrett smiled.

"Wait, don't go yet. I want to ask you some questions about the case." Frankie went to her office alcove to grab her notebook, then remembered that Tess was still in the wine lounge. She found her curled up on a sofa, sound asleep, probably all cried out for the moment.

"Poor Tess. She's having a crisis of her own." Frankie filled Garrett in and indicated she wanted to help her.

"One trial at a time, Frankie. The case: What do you want to know?"

"Are there any leads on the victim's identity?"

Garrett shook his head. "The photo's only been in circulation . . . well, not even a day. And yes, we showed the photo to Violet, and she had never seen the man." Garrett added, "Of course, none of the farmhands claimed to recognize him either, so . . ."

"So, someone might be lying unless the killer wasn't connected to anyone on the O'Connor farm, which is possible. Was there anything on him or anything he wore that could be helpful in figuring out who he was?" Frankie was hoping to make some headway on the mystery.

"Nothing really. He wore run-of-the-mill work boots pretty much like any other outdoor worker. Normal uniform pants you can buy anywhere. He had on Larry's Green-Up shirt. No wallet, no phone. I'm sure the shooter took care of those items in one way or another."

Frankie jotted down the details and started to close the notebook when Garrett held up his hand.

"There is one odd thing. He had a plaid shirt sitting next to him on the seat. I'm guessing he planned to ditch the uniform shirt at some point. Might not mean anything, but the label was ripped off of it. Left a tear in the collar."

Frankie wrote, speculating at the same time. "You think the killer took time to rip the shirt tag off? Why? Describe the shirt for me."

"Plaid, long sleeves, buttons down the front, buttons on the cuffs. Two chest pockets—both were empty. Nothing special that I could see."

"Typical flannel shirt worn in this neck of the woods," she said, matter-of-factly..

"Not flannel. We sent the shirt to the lab with the victim's other things. There was blood on it, and the lab will formally identify the fabric. If we're lucky, maybe the killer even left some DNA behind."

"If we could only figure out what that driver wanted at the O'Connor farm," Frankie shook her head side to side, making her coppery bob shimmer.

"If I promise to share my ideas with you, Ace, will you promise to let the professionals work the case?"

Frankie grinned broadly. "Scout's honor," she said, fingers raised.

Garrett kissed her full on the mouth. "That's the peace sign, Frankie, but you already knew that, didn't you?"

*   *   *

By the time Frankie heard Violet's footfalls on the apartment stairs, she was ready to jump out of her own skin. She'd rehearsed several opening lines to the conversation, and now that it was go time, she wondered which one would spill out of her mouth.

"Hi Mom. What are you up to?" Violet perused the breakfast bar, saw two place settings laid out, a caprese salad platter, and a pitcher of hibiscus iced tea.

Frankie turned from the oven where she had just pulled out a garlic-rosemary focaccia. "It's been awhile since we've had supper together; I thought we could catch up." She tried a lighthearted tone, but some edginess had crept in.

Violet plopped down on the stool and dropped her office tote bag at her feet. She pulled out her phone, texted someone, then dropped it next to her plate, a noticeable frown etched on her face. "I suppose you've heard from Alonzo or someone at the sheriff's department, hmm?"

Before Frankie responded, she poured iced tea into the tall glasses, scooped up salad onto their plates, and broke apart the focaccia. "Yes, I heard" was all she said, forcing herself to exercise patience as she weighed her words.

Violet took a sip of tea. "Well, go on. Say what you need to say."

Frankie hadn't expected to hear defiance from her unassuming daughter. She rose from the stool, turned her back on Violet for the moment, and grabbed olive oil, a shaker of herb blend, and a plate from the cupboard. Meditatively, she drizzled the green oil onto the plate, then slowly sprinkled the herbs on top. She took the ingredients over to the counter, still contemplating her next words.

She raised her eyes to meet Violet's and spoke quietly. "I wish you would have told me, Violet. I would rather have heard it from you directly. Why didn't you say something?"

Violet set her fork down rather loudly and jutted her chin forward. "Because you would have made a big deal about it. About Clay, I mean. I know how suspicious you can be."

Frankie tried to process those words, looking for some guidance from her inner voices. The fireflies were still. *Was she naturally suspicious? Possibly. Did she have good reason to be? Uncertain.*

"Okay, here's the thing. I never want my children to get hurt." Frankie took a breath to steady the emotions that were gurgling within. "You're an adult, but you don't have much experience when it comes to dating . . ."

Violet cut her to the quick. "I don't need your approval, Mom. I'm old enough to make my own choices. I was going to tell you when the time was right." Violet abruptly hopped off the stool, turned her back on Frankie, and made ready to stomp off, then turned back.

She sat down and huffed noisily, staring at her plate. "This tastes really good. Can we just eat, please?" Violet's torso drooped like a wilted flower.

An angry flame started to flare inside Frankie's stomach. The conversation had turned into a battle of wills, something unexpected. Frankie was certain she would be the director of this face-off, and she had not finished speaking her mind when Violet took the reins, dismissing the subject. What was she supposed to do now—make idle chit-chat?

She nibbled a tomato, sipped tea, dabbed her lips with a napkin. The silence seemed to last forever. "Why don't you have Clay over some night for dinner? It would be nice to meet him."

Violet glared at her mother over the rim of her glass. "You've met him. At the O'Connors'. Plus, you'll give him the third degree. Like we're in high school."

Violet's pouty face reminded Frankie of a middle-schooler. She dropped the subject. "Are you doing anything special tonight?" She mistakenly thought it was a safe question.

Violet bounced off the stool. "You just don't give up, do you?" She rushed off to her bedroom and slammed the door.

Frankie's lip trembled as the flame of hurt ignited her insides. She cleaned up what was supposed to be a peaceful supper, catching her breath between little sobs. There was no way she would give her daughter the satisfaction of knowing her words had gotten to her. She could hear Violet's shower running, so she worked quickly in the kitchen, then retreated to her bedroom to avoid further contact for the night.

Later, Violet opened her own bedroom door, peeked into the living room and kitchen, then crept out quietly.

Dressed in a cute sundress, she snatched her purse from the breakfast bar, slipped on a pair of sandals by the door, and left the apartment. In her room, she had finalized last-minute plans to meet Tara and Haley at The Main Sail where Paige was finishing an afternoon shift. She needed the empathy of her girlfriends, who could relate to unreasonable parents.

Frankie heard Violet leave, and picked up her phone, a second wave of tears on the horizon.

"Hello, Mom." Immediately the warble ensued.

"What's the matter, dear?" Peggy Champagne reported for mother duty.

Frankie's recap of the afternoon report, beginning with the police visit through the awkward exchange with Violet, tumbled out amid tears of frustration and heartache.

After consoling Frankie as best as she could, Peggy imparted her parental wisdom. "I suppose you never expected that from her. She's never been one to assert herself. Poor shy Violet. I guess you can be thankful she found her voice. Don't worry, Frankie. She still needs you. Believe me, I know."

Frankie laughed to acknowledge the truth in her mother's words. Here she was, in her 40s, still needing her own mother's advice and consolation. "Thank you, Mom. I guess once a parent, always a parent, right?"

Peggy said she'd contact Violet later to invite her and Clay for a cookout at her place. "How's Wednesday night for you and Garrett?"

Frankie smiled. Violet might be able to blow off her own mother, but her grandmother was someone she couldn't say no to. Confident, Frankie called Garrett immediately to set the date.

* * *

Frankie and Garrett pulled into Peggy's driveway a little early Wednesday, hoping to arrive before Violet and Clay. Dan Fitzgerald, an old family friend and her mother's steady companion, was firing up the grill on the back deck.

Peggy greeted her daughter with a warmer-than-usual embrace. She looked like a cool breeze in her summer whites, loose cotton capris and gauzy blouse trimmed in blue cord. Peggy's shoulder-length white hair was tied back with a pretty nautical scarf.

"I brought dessert." Frankie set the whipped berry pie on the kitchen counter and placed the whipped cream topping in the fridge.

Peggy gazed at the pie and brushed an imaginary stand of hair from her forehead. "I see you made the grandmothers' pie? Maybe you're trying too hard."

Since Peggy wasn't big on baking, Frankie brushed off the remark. The berry pie came together easily for her. "It's too bad Aunt CeCe can't join us tonight, but she's hosting a Sip and Paint at Rachel's shop."

Besides being skilled at baking French macarons,

Aunt CeCe was a talented artist. She'd found her niche helping Coral Anders, the owner and artist in residence at Lovely Lavender Farm, where CeCe lived above the garage. Besides the weekend workshops there, she also offered a monthly Sip and Paint at the craft store next door to Bubble and Bake.

Peggy smiled slyly.

"Oh, I see. You picked tonight because you didn't want Aunt CeCe to come." Frankie's mother and aunt were governed by two distinctly different personalities.

Peggy briefly hugged Garrett and handed him a Spotted Cow brew. "Why don't you join Dan on the deck? He might need some grilling pointers."

"You know how Cecile is. Let's just say she'd add a few wrinkles to the evening. Anyway, how have the last couple of days been with Violet?" Peggy wanted to know.

"Great, if you like the cold shoulder, that is. We've managed to avoid seeing each other except to say good morning. I did tell her we'd be here tonight. I didn't want her to find out when she got here, or she'd be pissed off at both of us."

"Language, Francine," Peggy tsked at her daughter. She didn't like cuss words of any kind, deeming them an unnecessary manner of self-expression.

As soon as Violet and Clay arrived, Garrett handed him a beer and led him through the patio door that led to the deck. Frankie and Peggy both gave him the once-over while trying not to look obvious about it.

Clay was dressed in jeans and a casual shirt that accented his muscular frame. His tousled ash-blonde hair gave him a boyish flair and he had dimples that could be classified as irresistible. Frankie pegged him to be late 20s in age, older and more worldly than her daughter. Frankie imagined his looks, combined with his Australian background, made him an enviable catch in little Deep Lakes.

What the two women were most interested in, however, was observing his interactions with others, Violet in particular.

Frankie noticed that Clay was most relaxed conversing about fishing, hunting, and sheep ranching with Dan and Garrett. He even used some cute Aussie lingo, referring to himself as a snagger instead of a shearer and bragging he could shear 150 jumbuck a day. He touted the Merino sheep breed as the finest in the world.

Whenever Frankie or Peggy asked him questions about his home, he seemed fidgety, and Violet's eyes threw darts in their direction, although the women were trying to learn more about Australian culture from him and most questions were of the general interest type.

After dinner, Violet followed the women inside to serve dessert.

"Honestly you two, do you have to ask so many questions? It's like an interrogation out there." Violet's voice was curt.

Peggy jumped in before Frankie had a chance. "We're trying to get to know Clay and besides, it's not every day we have visitors from Australia, sweetheart. Such an interesting place to live." Frankie nodded enthusiastically to corroborate her mother's approach.

Violet's suspicion wasn't assuaged. "Clay's been in the United States for more than two years. He doesn't like to talk about his home. I don't think he had a great family life." She picked up two dessert plates and hurried out to the deck.

Peggy and Frankie exchanged exasperated looks. "I think we'll open another bottle of wine. How about Persephone's Temptation? It should blend well with dessert." Frankie agreed, feeling that a round of wine might take the edge off the evening.

During dessert, Peggy poured the pretty magenta pomegranate wine around the table. They admired how lovely it looked in the setting sun, and Frankie turned the conversation to the happy topic of Violet's proposal to make mead at the vineyard.

Violet blushed at her mother's praise, and Frankie kept her compliments to a minimum so as not to lay it on too thick. She noticed Clay's admirable reaction toward Violet, how he stroked her hand gently, how his eyes shone with genuine interest. He contributed to the conversation by asking a few questions about grape cultivation and the vintages produced in Wisconsin.

He held up the pomegranate wine. "This is nothing like any Australian wine. We're known for our shiraz, which is pretty robust and packs a wallop." Frankie admitted she hadn't tried any Australian vintages, but added it to her list.

"I s'pose you don't buy much wine since you produce it, but I can recommend a couple choice ones you can pick up in the city." They had finally found a topic where Clay seemed at ease. He jotted down three varieties on a napkin and pushed it over to Frankie with a smile.

Shortly after dessert, Violet grabbed Clay's arm and rose to leave, bidding everyone a good night. Clay seemed surprised at the sudden exit. He shook hands confidently with Dan and Garrett and thanked Peggy for the invitation, gently clasping her hand. He turned to Frankie last and offered her a disarming smile. He hesitated as if he wanted to say something, thought better of it, and gave her a small wave instead from the opposite side of the counter.

"It was nice to meet you and get to know you a little better, Clay." Frankie's voice held maternal authority mixed with sincerity. Their eyes locked for a moment. Frankie hoped hers communicated "don't mess with my daughter." An alarmed expression clicked into place on Clay's face for a flash, then vanished.

Before the foursome could scrutinize the content of the evening, Garrett's phone went off. "That was Alonzo. He has some information about the victim. We need to leave, Frankie. Sorry, Peggy and Dan. Let's do this again soon."

Chapter 10

Sometimes we put our great treasures in museums,
other times we take them for walks.
— Unknown

Walking on eggshells around people did not sit well for long with Frankie. She wanted resolution, even if it meant shoving it along at breakneck speed.

"Which is why sometimes your resolution lands like a cannonball, Francine. Stop trying to force things to happen." The Golden One had resurrected.

"What Goldie is trying to say—and saying it badly—is to wait it out. Things have a way of working themselves out. Be patient, Cherie." The silver tongued Pirate winked his light at Goldie. It appeared they were still a tag team.

Frankie dressed in the half-light of early morning, then headed to her safe haven: the shop kitchen. She could make more noise there for starters. But she admitted that baking was therapy for her. It allowed her mind to open, think methodically, and process information.

She made scone dough, which only required a short rest after a small amount of kneading. Today the bakery would offer lemon-raspberry, rhubarb-apple, and white chocolate-almond varieties. She could make these in her sleep.

Her mind fixated on the latest case information, thanks to a late-evening call from Garrett.

"We're teaming up with a Grant County detective. He's coming up tomorrow and bringing his case file along." Garrett said. "The officer got a tip from a farmer who recognized the victim, connecting our vic to an October incident involving a fertilizer pick up on a Grant County farm. Soil Solutions out of Dyersville, Iowa reported their truck was hijacked at a nearby Kwik Trip gas station. The farmer identified our guy as the driver from the October pick up."

"That's it?" Frankie scoffed. "Doesn't sound like much to go on, but maybe there will be something helpful in the case file."

"Don't be so hasty to grumble, Miss Francine. There's more," Garrett sounded amused.

"Lon picked up Bucky yesterday, thanks to Ryan and his Oasis friend, Grizz. Ryan remembered Bucky had a girlfriend, knew they frequented the biker bar, so called Grizz for help."

"Turns out the girlfriend used to tend bar at The Oasis, then moved to Shalamar to help her cousin run a restaurant. They found Bucky hiding out at her place. He claims he ran when he saw the cops at the farm because he didn't want his truck confiscated." Garrett chuckled, thinking Bucky wasn't the brightest.

"So I imagine that's the first thing Alonzo did—take the truck to look for evidence."

Garrett laughed again. "Turns out there's a bench warrant out for Bucky for driving without a valid license. No matter how you sliced that turkey, he was going to lose his truck."

"Thanks for keeping me in the loop." She wondered if Bucky would lose his job or worse, go to jail. A third possibility crept into Frankie's head. What if Bucky was the shooter?

Within an hour, the bakery crew reported for duty. Tess looked worse for wear, probably from lack of sleep. Regardless, she pulled a cheerful red and yellow print head wrap from her apron pocket and tucked it around her thick curls. She dutifully strode to the station near the back window, and dragged out more ingredients from her tote.

"The teff muffins were a hit, so I'm going to work on the orders for those, if that's okay."

"Tess, we love it that you bring the bakery you grew up with into Deep Lakes, and it makes the customers happy, too." Frankie never imagined she'd be showcasing African pastries at her primarily Scandinavian bakery. Just in the past year, Bubble and Bake's repertoire grew to feature Tia Pepita's empanadas and pan dulces or sweet breads, Aunt CeCe's macarons and croissants, and other cultural delights.

The kitchen would be buzzing today and tomorrow to prepare for the weekend traffic. This was the first time in a week the kitchen was fully staffed, and Frankie paused to acknowledge it. She still got the tingles from time to time, contemplating the good fortune of running the business she loved with a complementary partner and capable staff.

Jovie was confidently preparing cookie orders in one corner. Carmen and Tia Pepita had paired up in another corner near the stove to concoct breakfast empanadas on commercial baking sheets. This time of year, the lighter empanadas would go over better than the deep-fried versions.

In what seemed like no time, Frankie loaded the finished scones and empanadas into the bakery case for Aunt CeCe to push out front at the opening bell. Aunt CeCe was the best salesperson in the shop, hands down. She charmed the money right out of the customers' wallets and purses. Today, she looked like a summer watermelon in her patterned tunic.

Once sales were done for the morning, there was time for banter in the kitchen before Peggy and Tara arrived at noon to open the wine lounge. Most of the discussion centered around the shooting, which made Tia Pepita anxious and skittish.

Tia scooped up the visiting shop kitty, Sundae, a chubby Tortie who sported ribbons of caramel and chocolate fur. Violet had christened the cat as soon as she picked her up at Dr. Sadie's, the local vet.

"Doesn't she look just like a turtle sundae? All we need is a giant scoop of ice cream for her to curl up to."

Violet giggled at her own creative observation, but Frankie thought otherwise.

"If you ask me, this kitty looks like she's been living on a steady diet of ice cream. She's kind of pudgy, Vi."

"Poor Sundae, looks like nobody cares that your food dish is empty. That's what happens with us old ladies. We're just forgotten." Tia seemed to have read Frankie's insulting thoughts.

While Carmen smirked in her aunt's direction, Frankie wanted to remedy the situation.

"Oh my goodness, Tia. I've been meaning to ask you about your niece's wedding. There's just been so much going on around here, I forgot. Did you have a good time?" Frankie watched Tia heap canned cat food into Sundae's dish. Thank goodness they were buying the high-end brand that was healthier. Sundae was developing a waddle in her walk.

Tia's face brightened. "Izzy was a gorgeous bride. Here, let me show you some pictures." She looked meaningfully at Carmen and cleared her throat. Since Tia didn't have a cell phone, she clearly meant that Carmen should get hers out and pass it around.

Everyone made sure to ooh and ah over the bride and Tia too, who wore a yellow and black flared dress resembling flowing butterfly wings, trimmed in turquoise spangles. A large Swallowtail butterfly brooch perched on her right shoulder in case there was any doubt about the dress's design.

When the conversation turned toward the shooting and Clay Cooper again, Aunt CeCe intervened.

"Listen girls, what we need is something relaxing to take our minds off this. I have an excellent idea." Frankie was thinking a peaceful pontoon ride around the lake sounded good, sipping wine while the sun went down. But, if Aunt CeCe had an idea, anything was possible.

"The Turner farm is offering Goat Yoga classes. Coral and I are hosting a group of artists on retreat this weekend, and yoga is definitely on the agenda. I wanted to try the goat version before I sign the artists up for it."

Nobody said a word for a minute, wondering if CeCe was serious. Like a gust of stormy air, they began talking all at once.

"What are you trying to do—kill me?" Tia Pepita's voice rang the loudest. "Do I look like I could do any kind of yoga, much less with a goat using me for a step ladder?"

"Did you say the Turner farm?" Carmen huffed. "Nope, no way will I go to the Turner farm. There's bad blood between the Turners and the O'Connors." She made it sound like an old-time feud, and Frankie was surprised Carmen had never mentioned it before.

Tess would be back in Madison by six o'clock. Jovie was working back and forth between the kitchen and wine lounge tonight. That only left Frankie, who studied Aunt CeCe's sorrowful expression. On the CeCe emotion meter, Frankie figured she was somewhere around an 8 for feeling hurt.

"What an exceptional idea, Aunt CeCe. I'd love to try it." Frankie hoped her acting skills were convincing. She had no intention of going on this escapade alone, and if she couldn't drag Carmen along, she planned to coerce her mother.

"Jovie, would you be able to finish my mother's shift tonight? I know she wouldn't want to miss out on this. She absolutely treasures her yoga time."

Carmen and Tess stood slack-jawed, staring at Frankie and her velvet-worded delivery. CeCe gave an excited hand clap. Jovie looked from Carmen, who shook her head, to Frankie, who nodded hers. Jovie decided to take the safe road.

"Tara and I can manage if Peggy wants to go," Jovie offered, emphasizing the words *if* and *wants.*

* * *

Just before six, the trio arrived at Happy Flocks Farm, home of sheep and goats, owned by Dewey Turner and sons.

Frankie insisted on stopping at the O'Connors' first to see if she could convince Carmen to join them.

Carmen met her friend's SUV in the driveway, standing with hands on both hips. CeCe and Peggy didn't bother to get out.

"I mean it, Frankie. I won't be seen at the Turners' after the way they've treated my family."

Offering a short version of the story, the problems began after Ryan purchased the farm from his uncle. Dewey Turner offered advice on sheep breeds and Ryan accepted half of it. They agreed on raising Rambouillet or French Merino, known in the Midwest for their quality wool and meat, but Turner insisted the Columbia breed was the second-best breed. Ryan decided on the Targhee instead.

At that point, Turner was just annoyed. The annoyance became outrage when both farmers were contacted to help a young Amish family set up a farm nearby. Unbeknownst to the two men, the couple wanted bids from both of them to purchase some starter ewes. Ryan remembered how little money he and Carmen had, along with substantial debt, when they started out. He underbid Turner by quite a lot and offered the services of his ram for free the first fall. Once Turner found out about it, he let Ryan know he was no longer welcome on his property.

Small skirmishes ensued ever since. Turner's son ran against Ryan for a position on the Lamb Council, and lost. Turner often undercut Ryan's sales at the lamb auctions and in March, Turner hired the shearing crew out from under Ryan, forcing Ryan to scramble to find another crew on short notice.

"Sorry to hear all that, Carmen. Would you like us to sabotage his farm? Steal a goat maybe? Or one of us could pretend to get hurt and sue their butts." Frankie's suggestions made Carmen smile.

Peggy couldn't contain her contempt for the notion of goat yoga, holding her nose at the farm smell as she carried her yoga mat into a fenced in grassy area.

A 30ish woman in loose knit pants and spandex tank top, greeted them warmly.

"I'm Hannah Turner and I'll be leading this therapeutic experience. Just choose a place to put down your mats and get comfortable. Maybe settle in and take some deep breaths."

"As if anyone would want to take a deep breath here," Peggy harrumphed quietly. She found a patch of grass in the back corner against the fence to squat. CeCe placed her mat in the same row, so Frankie wisely settled between the two women. Peggy hung her tote bag on the fence post, hoping it would stay clean.

There were nine participants for the class; even a couple of men had signed up. Hannah explained the rules of the experience. "Don't put your fingers near the goats' mouths. They may be kids, but their lower teeth can draw blood. Otherwise, feel free to pet them if you're in a position to do so comfortably."

"Comfortable yoga position? Ha, that's a good one." Peggy was on a roll. She shot darts at Frankie from her icy blue eyes. Frankie had cajoled her mother with a sob story about CeCe being snubbed by everyone after her helpful idea to de-stress. The icing on the cake was Frankie's reminder that her aunt had been left out of the family barbeque the night before.

Hannah continued. "Don't be alarmed if one of the kids climbs on your back when you're in plank or on all fours. They are known for climbing. If it happens and you don't like it, just wave a hand in my direction and I'll get the goat down again." She smiled broadly at the participants and nodded for their agreement.

"Okay, well, let's get started." She looked at the farmhands who were leading very cute goat babies into the people pen. There were four goats in all, not enough for everyone to have their own personal kid, but maybe enough to attempt avoidance.

Frankie prayed her mother had selected a secure spot in the back corner. Hannah laughed when some of the misbehaving kids piddled on a few mats. "Don't worry. I have disinfecting wipes. I'll be playing goat butler along with giving instructions."

Somehow it didn't feel very relaxing at all to Frankie. Between trying to maneuver through poses and watching her mother's area for stray goats, she lost her balance most of the time. CeCe however, managed to look positively serene as if goats and yoga were made for each other.

Frankie couldn't have prevented the worst from happening any more than Hannah could. A rambunctious black and white kid frolicked over to Peggy and with no effort at all, sprang onto her backside during a cat-cow move. Frankie leapt to standing and tried to gently remove the goat. Hannah rushed to the back corner as well but lost her footing on a tiny mound of droppings and landed right in front of Peggy's mat like a runner sliding into home plate.

Like a silent movie scene, another attendee dashed over to help Hannah get up, just in time to see a rude bearded adult goat stick its head inside Peggy's tote bag from outside the fence. The farmhands rushed over, shouting and waving their arms.

"Saint, you grab Betty. I'll go in and get Natasha out of there." Frankie knew the voice and lifted her head in time to see Stubby (isn't that what Carmen had called the man who propositioned Frankie?) bolt over toward Peggy. Natasha promptly launched herself off of Peggy and a merry chase began through the pen, and thankfully, out the gate.

The hand called Saint tried to wrangle Betty, but she wasn't about to give up the treasure from Peggy's tote. A pair of earbuds dangled from the corners of the goat's mouth; the long blue cord holding them together snapped in two and was slurped up like spaghetti. Worse yet, Betty was wearing the tote around her neck like a chunky necklace. Peggy groaned and Frankie was certain an expletive tumbled out.

Both women glared at CeCe who was lovingly stroking a little ginger-coated kid that had curled up next to her on the mat, docile as a dove.

Hannah looked no worse for wear and laughed merrily as if this kind of thing happened every day. Who knows? Maybe it did. She dismissed the goats and played some quiet meditation music while participants curled into child's poses.

Afterwards, Hannah called the hands back to clean up the yoga corral. She offered an apology to Peggy and an invitation to come back for a free session.

Careful to avoid being recognized by Stubby/Shorty, Frankie walked over to Saint, hoping to retrieve her mother's tote, while Aunt CeCe complimented Hannah and signed up the artist retreat patrons for a special Sunday morning session.

An older man was talking to Saint, and Frankie noticed one of the herding dogs was tugging aggressively on the farmhand's boot laces.

"Doc, knock it off," the older man spoke with harsh authority, and lowered one hand as if he might strike the animal. When he saw Frankie, his bushy eyebrows shot up as if they might take flight. "Say, aren't you the baker?" The man sounded like a carnival barker.

Frankie held out her hand. "Francine Champagne. Do we know each other?"

"No, we don't. But I can see bad luck follows you around. You smell like the company you keep." He plunked his taupe ranch hat over his thinning gray hair and turned toward Saint. "Monty, after you and Shorty put the goats away, I want you to go up to the north pasture. A few ewes need their hoofs trimmed." He turned back toward Frankie to give her one last look of disgust. "And tell O'Connor he should do his own dirty work, instead of sending spies to my place." He stalked back toward the barn, Shorty following behind.

"Sorry about him, Miss." Frankie noticed an accent coming from Saint, but couldn't pin it down..

"Who is that?" Frankie guessed the brute's identity but wanted confirmation.

"Dewey Turner. He owns the farm." Saint handed Peggy's tote bag to Frankie.

"Thank you. I appreciate your help." She paused. "Is it Saint or Monty?"

"Same difference." The hand tipped his cap to Frankie and finished rounding up goats.

After dropping off Aunt CeCe at Lovely Lavender Farms, Frankie turned to Peggy.

"Well, that was something else, wasn't it?" She hoped she sounded sympathetic.

"It's nothing I'm ever doing again, Frankie, no matter how many free coupons Hannah Turner offers me." Peggy was still pulling grass out of her ponytail.

"At least Hannah seemed nice. I can't say the same for Dewey Turner. That man is beastly." Frankie filled in Peggy on Turner's insulting comments.

"Well, there're more Turners that didn't fall far from the tree. Dewey has four sons and they all own shares of the farm. They have mean reputations, just like Dewey."

"Poor Hannah, to be married into that family," Frankie took a swig from her water bottle.

"Hannah is lucky enough to be married to Nate, the

youngest of the four. He's decent, like his mother. After Jeanette died, anything kind that was living inside Dewey, packed up and moved out. She was the best part of the whole family."

"Well, I give Hannah credit for trying something new to bring people to the farm. With four families trying to make a living there, it must be hard." Sne knew enough about the expenses of running a farm from Carmen and other area farmers. There were a host of easier ways to make a living, that was certain.

"Sorry I forced you into going, Mother. But thank you for doing it. It seemed to make Aunt CeCe very happy."

"That woman is strange, Frankie. Goat yoga, of all things. Guess I'll be buying new ear buds tomorrow."

Frankie couldn't shake off Turner's remarks and she was bothered by the way the dog Doc reacted to Saint. Dogs are such a good judge of character. Frankie's musings led her back to the O'Connors' to take Sonny for a walk around the farm.

There was about an hour of daylight left when she knocked on Carmen's door. When Carmen ushered her inside, a pungent rush of air greeted her. Frankie spied Tia Pepita in the expansive great room, swaying around the furniture, waving a smoldering stick.

"Don't mind her. She's been smudging the house and around the barns ever since she came home. Says she's going to keep at it until the shooter is caught." Carmen continued stacking clean dishes in the cupboards.

"What kind of herbs is she using? I've heard a little about smudging, especially with sage, but sage can have such a harsh odor."

"That's just it. Tia lit sage the first day, but it sent the twins out the door gagging. So, she switched to mint, which you might think would be better, but let me tell you—it wasn't. Yesterday she got some lavender from Coral's place, but it still smelled skunky. Today, I think she's smudging with cedar. So far, so good." Carmen sighed with an exasperated snort.

"Want to walk around the farm with me and Sonny?" Frankie enjoyed Carmen's company and thought it would look less odd than Frankie walking the O'Connor dog alone on their property.

"Sure, I could use some fresh air. Besides, I want you to fill me in on goat yoga."

As Frankie recounted the tales of goat yoga and prickly Dewey Turner, Carmen busted out laughing at the scene, but her demeanor shifted when she heard about Dewey. "That man has no right. He better watch himself. One day he's going to cross me at the wrong time." Carmen was a warrior when the occasion called for it.

Sonny enjoyed trotting beside Frankie, and paused to sniff the early evening smells of a summer farm. Frankie gave him a gentle pat on the neck. She knew what it felt like to be an underdog and imagined it couldn't be easy for Sonny, who spent his life herding sheep only to become obsolete.

"How's this boy enjoying being a house dog?" Frankie asked.

"Between Sonny's poor eyesight and Tia's, I don't know who's worse off. The two have had to stumble around each other at times." Carmen snickered a little, despite the unfortunate circumstances. "At least I can give Sonny the backyard to ramble around in, which is more than I can say for Tia."

Frankie knew Carmen didn't mean anything by poking fun at Tia. The two were close or Carmen wouldn't have her staying with them. The experimental drug Tia was taking for her eyes had not produced the results her doctors hoped for, so she would be undergoing a new regimen in a few weeks. Tia always claimed she would return to Texas as soon as cold weather set in, but Carmen wondered if that would prove true.

Now that a few days had passed since the shooting, Frankie wanted to know how everyone was coping.

"It's messed up, Frankie. Ryan is so suspicious of all the workers. He doesn't say much and it's hard to get him to smile. The boys have mostly disappeared to their rooms except for chores and meals, and well, you saw Tia. Her superstitions are on overdrive." Carmen heaved a sigh.

Frankie paused to let Sonny sniff around a tree, turn circles, and select a prime pooping spot. She reached over and put an arm around her friend.

"And what about you, Carmie? How are you managing?" Wide green eyes searched her friend's amber ones.

"I want this to be over. I want things to go back to normal. I want my Ryan back." Carmen bit her lower lip but didn't allow herself to cry.

"We need to find the shooter, Carmen, or at the very least, let's eliminate your farmhands, one by one." Frankie strode forward, her mouth set in a determined line.

The trio walked along the right side of the property where the employee parking area loomed ahead. Suddenly, Sonny pulled at the leash and started yapping.

"Must be a squirrel or rabbit up there." Carmen was accustomed to dog behavior.

Sonny's barking intensified as they neared the parked vehicles, and Frankie let out a length of leash so he could explore. The sheltie sniffed around one of the trucks, then Clay's compact car, a third truck, and back to the first truck. He jumped at the tailgate, growled and barked with purpose.

"That's not normal Sonny behavior unless he spots a coyote near the sheep pasture," Carmen concluded.

"Okay, time for a peek in the bed of that truck." Frankie's muscles began to twitch a little.

The women climbed on the back end and looked inside. Except for dirt and wind-blown straw, the bed was empty. Sonny barked louder.

"Let's get our phones out and shine them around the bed, just in case."

Frankie did her best to shine her phone's flashlight around, too quickly at first but then slowly sweeping the interior. She saw something shiny and leaned her body further over the tailgate.

"Look over here, Carmen. Shine your light where mine is."

Carmen stood next to Frankie. "Looks like glass particles, maybe?"

Frankie nodded, adrenaline flowing through her veins. "I think so, too. Like maybe from a broken headlight?"

"Dios mío, do you think this truck was used to shoot the guy?" Carmen jumped down from the bed. "Come on. Let's walk over there so nobody sees us." She pointed to a wooded copse. "Call Alonzo."

"Good boy, Sonny. Such a good doggy." Frankie lavished praise upon the sheltie after hanging up with Lon. "He's on his way out. We're supposed to make sure that truck doesn't go anywhere."

"You stay here with Sonny. I'm going to talk to Ryan. He needs to handle this situation."

Frankie had been out to the parking area before, so she knew the shiny black Ram belonged to Jonesy. Jonesy, who had stayed overnight at the farm when the shooting happened. Jonesy, who wouldn't give Frankie a straight answer about hearing the gunfire.

Chapter 11

I am not afraid of an army of lions led by a sheep;
I am afraid of an army of sheep led by a lion.
- Alexander The Great

The Whitman county squads arrived minus lights and sirens, thankfully. They found Ryan in the feed barn, a .22 rifle trained on Jonesy, who sat on a folding chair, arms lying open-palmed on the nearby card table.

Ryan had confined Clay to the sheep shed, Goat to the equipment shed, and Reggie to an outside picnic table, all waiting to be questioned. Frankie, Carmen, and Sonny stood guard in the grass parking area, making sure nobody left or touched anything.

Alonzo introduced Detective Evans from Grant County, who was still in town after bringing the file on the fertilizer truck driver. Shirley and Officer Green emerged from the second squad.

Frankie wondered why she hadn't seen Donovan Pflug working the case, but figured that asking for his whereabouts would only jinx her lucky streak. She hadn't had a scrape with Pflug in months and hoped to keep it that way.

Shirley and Green donned gloves, opened an evidence kit, and began with a walk around the Ram truck.

Alonzo and Evans opened the barn door slowly, and saw Ryan holding the .22.

"Ryan, it's Alonzo. You can set the gun down now." Alonzo spoke gently. He'd been in too many situations where tension made people jumpy, and a jumpy person with a gun was never good.

Ryan cased the rifle and asked if he could return it to the house. He glared at Jonesy.

"Ryan, where are the twins?" Alonzo had both eyes trained on Jonesy.

"Ryan stopped mid-step, uncertain. "In the house with Tia. Why?" The words came out sharp, defensive.

"One of us should talk to them, Ryan. They may know something or heard something."

Ryan shook his head, a mirthless laugh tumbled out. "I doubt they know anything. You honestly think the shooter would confide in teenagers, my sons?"

Alonzo gestured with his head for Evans to follow Ryan to the house.

Within an hour, Alonzo accompanied Jonesy for a free ride in the sheriff's Jeep for further questioning. The other hands were dismissed to head home, and the evidence team packed up their bags. A tow truck was called to haul the Ram up to the county highway department, which served as an impound lot. The tally of vehicles impounded on this case was mounting, and so was the number of hands the O'Connors had to do without.

Ryan brought fresh bedding into the sheep barn, resigned to taking the night shift himself. Carlos and Kyle each commanded a pair of dogs to round up the sheep. By now the lambs were independent and night shifts were unnecessary, but since the shooting, Ryan insisted someone stay overnight until the case was solved.

Frankie and Carmen brought iced tea to the barn and a Yahtzee game. Ryan sat at the card table, staring off into space.

"Hey Ry, we brought refreshments and a diversion—time to let it go for now," Carmen rubbed her husband's neck and kissed his earlobe.

His sullen expression retreated slightly. "You should have brought something stronger." He grunted and raised his iced tea glass.

Frankie practiced utmost restraint during two games of Yahtzee, although she fidgeted at times and frequently chewed her upper lip. Thank goodness Sonny had tagged along to the barn, where he lay near Frankie's feet and raised his head to be petted at every jiggle of her leg.

After game two was scored, Frankie's voice rang out louder than necessary. "Can I ask you a few questions about the farmhands, Ryan?" When his sullen look returned, she added, "Please. I'm hoping to eliminate suspects . . . and that will help you know who you can trust." She hoped Ryan saw the value in her pursuit.

His sharp intake of breath was followed by a go-ahead hand wave.

"What do you know about Bucky? You said he hasn't worked here long."

A sharp exhale from Ryan. "Yes. What do you want to know?"

"Is he friends with anyone else here? Or in the area? Does he hang out anywhere, like The Oasis?"

"I guess he might hang at The Oasis since his girlfriend used to tend bar there. I mean, he had to meet her somewhere. He's pretty easy going. Gets along with all the guys."

"Are you going to keep him on here?" Frankie knew Ryan was the type of man to give people a second chance.

"I don't have much choice. He's already trained, and who knows if I'm going to be short-handed after Lon is finished with Jonesy."

Since the cat was out of the bag, Frankie broached the Jonesy topic. "Do you think Jonesy could be the shooter?"

Ryan gulped iced tea and ran a hand through his thick hair. "He's a gifted dog trainer with lots of experience. He's a quiet man, keeps to himself. I mean, he seems like he'd rather hang out with the animals than the other guys. But, there's something about him."

Frankie was clueless where Ryan was going, but she jotted down everything he said, wondering which revelation might lead to something important.

"Something about him, you were saying. Like what?"

"The guys respect Jonesy. Maybe because he's top dog around the sheep. Maybe because, I don't know. It sounds corny but there's an air of mystery about him. I don't know anything about his past, though."

"So are you saying he has a past?" Frankie held her pen above the notebook.

"Doesn't everyone?" Ryan's gaze fixed on Frankie's.

"What about Clay Cooper?" Frankie waited to ask about Clay until the end. Her question spoke volumes: Tell me every detail you know about him. She held her breath and noticed that Carmen was leaning into this bit of the conversation, too.

Ryan smiled broadly and his jaw relaxed for the first time as he surveyed the two women, looking like cats ready to pounce.

"You two. It's great you want to help investigate but do you really think you're going to find out anything the police don't know?"

Frankie flushed, partly embarrassed, partly miffed. It was true she'd only been involved in a couple of crime investigations, but she was gaining skills each time. Her self-confidence had risen dramatically, even though she still had a long way to go in proving herself to the outside world.

Even Carmen gave Ryan a deflated look. He raised his hands in surrender.

"Okay, let's talk about Clay. He's been on the shearing circuit for a couple of years now, and he's fast. He's also a quick learner, so when he said he might want to take the rest of the shearing season off and stay in one place, I hired him."

"Why would a shearer want to take the season off? Won't they lose out on good money?" Frankie was skeptical.

"Yes and no. Coop is serious about ranching. He wants to raise his own sheep, so there's no better way to learn the business than to work the whole farm."

That made sense. "What about the rest of the shearing crew? What happened to them?"

Ryan scowled, remembering how he happened to hire his crew. "I originally hired a different crew. One of the farmers at the sheep auction recommended them, but Dewey Turner hired them out from under me. I had to scramble and was lucky to find Clay's team."

Dewey Turner's name seemed to crop up quite often these days. Frankie wrote it down on a clean white page and circled it. "Why would Turner do that?"

"Part of the ongoing feud, I suppose. He must have gotten wind that I'd hired them. The team was willing to go to Turner's farm the next day, but Turner insisted he needed them the exact date I hired them for. He offered the crew double, maybe triple."

Carmen's lip curled into a sneer and she said something in Spanish. Frankie patted her hand, but smiled at her friend's chutzpah. She wouldn't want to cross Carmen Martinez O'Connor.

"Let's back up a step. How many were on Clay's team?"

Ryan held up two fingers. "I don't remember the other guy's name offhand. But, he wasn't interested in staying on for the season."

"What about Turner's crew? Did he keep anyone on?" Frankie was sure Saint, the goat handler, had an accent, but Ryan said he didn't know.

"I don't chit-chat with Turner or any of his family for that matter. I try to steer clear of them at the auctions."

Once the lambs were around 110 pounds, they were sold at weekly auctions, along with prize breeding stock. Ryan frequented auctions most of the summer and fall and even a few spring ones. So did the Turners. With four sons buying and selling along with Dewey, it was hard to avoid them all.

"I will admit that Nate, the youngest son, is tolerable. He's a lot like his mother. You know, Jeanette Turner and my Aunt Sally were close friends." Ryan was practically raised on his aunt and uncle's sheep farm, and since they had no children of their own, he'd bought the property on an affordable land contract. After his uncle passed away, the property transferred ownership free and clear to Ryan.

"What are you thinking, Frankie? I know that look. There's practically steam coming out of your ears." Carmen poked her gently.

"I'm thinking we need to take a closer look at the

Turners. That is, after I find out what went down with Jonesy. It's time I made some butterhorns." With that, Frankie bid the couple a good night. *Butterhorns were the surefire way to get the inside scoop from Shirley Lazzar.*

Chapter 12

Sometimes, the biggest secrets you can only tell a stranger.
– Michelle Hodkin

Frankie beamed at Garrett as he waved a Dirty Chai latte under her sleepy nose Friday morning at the bakery. Taking it gratefully and none too gracefully, she knocked her cardboard cup to his in a clumsy toast.

"Late night or just a lousy night?" Garrett carefully brushed back the bangs that had escaped her headband; his fingers lingered sweetly on her cheek.

She clasped her palm over the back of his hand, relishing his touch. "I'd say both." She held up a commercial tray of butterhorns she'd prepared the night before, let rise during the wee hours before dawn, then rolled, baked, and finished icing just after dawn.

He gave her an impish grin and reached for one of her signature pastries, half afraid he might get slapped. "Are these off limits or ..."

She giggled and passed him a napkin. "Nothing is off limits to you, Mr. G."

He cocked one eyebrow. "In that case ..." He pulled Frankie in close for a long embrace. The two sat in a corner of the wine lounge as the morning sun streamed through the windows, promising summertime warmth and comfort. She didn't have much time to chat before opening, but asked if Garrett had new information about the shooting.

"I wasn't part of last night's interview, if you're wondering. So I'm going to assume these butterhorns are a bribe for Shirley." He mocked sternness, but his face relaxed into a lopsided grin as he winked at her.

"After last night's discovery and talking to Ryan, I'd like to find out anything that might help. Besides, Clay Cooper is dating my daughter, so I need to know if he's innocent." Her voice rose and quavered a little.

Garrett pulled her in closer beside him on the low sofa. "I know, Frankie, and I can't blame you for wanting to find out the truth. But you really do need to be careful. Whoever shot the driver is not someone to monkey with."

She nodded agreement, but simultaneously stuck her chin out defiantly. "No matter what, I have a job to do as a reporter. Magda is after me for updates." At least that was the excuse she planned to use to get more information from the county. And, it was true. Magda wanted a daily progress report even if there was nothing new.

Worry lines formed on Frankie's brow, so Garrett changed the subject. "So, pig roast this weekend at the famous Oasis Bar, huh?"

Frankie stared blankly. "I have no idea what you're talking about."

"I thought Carmen would have told you this morning. I stopped out to see Ryan earlier, and he said somebody named Grizz invited the four of us to a Poker Run and pig roast at the bar. Sunday afternoon if you'd like to be my date, little lady." Frankie cracked up at Garrett's poor imitation of a biker cowboy.

"I wouldn't miss it for the world." She followed him to the front door and turned on the open sign. There were at least eight or so customers standing on the sidewalk waiting. Another sellout day seemed certain.

Tess and Aunt CeCe were in place to run front of house sales for the day, and would switch to wine tastings and sales for the afternoon. Frankie and Carmen would assume the Friday evening shift until closing, with Jovie's help.

Tara took the weekend off for a girls' getaway with Violet, Haley, and Paige. Surprisingly, they were off to Dubuque to kick up their heels on the Daisy Belle, a riverboat casino docked on the Mississippi. The girls booked a hotel just feet from the dock and planned to eat, gamble, and be dazzled by the nightly entertainment.

Frankie was puzzled by their plans, as she tried to deduce how her Disney World princess had changed to a partying woman-about-town. Gambling and other nightlife didn't jibe with the Violet she knew.

"However Francine, aren't you glad she's going out with the girls? She could be with Clay instead . . ." The Golden One interrupted her bewilderment; Pirate floated beside her, nodding.

What was with her fireflies, anyhow? Since when were they so closely aligned?

She shook the voices off and meandered back to the kitchen, her safe haven. Tia Pepita was working on her famous ChaChaCha quiche, or five of them, that is, which undoubtedly wouldn't last through the weekend.

Carmen, too, was busy preparing the vegetarian quiche offering for the week, a light summery offering the shop christened, Leeky Ceiling Pie. The rich aroma of thinly sliced leeks sauteed in butter with fresh herbs permeated the kitchen. After nestling the cooled mixture on the bottom of the crust, Swiss and Monterey Jack cheeses and lemon zest crowned the leeks before being bathed in whole milk, cream, and eggs. Carmen looked up at her partner, who was reading the agenda board.

"What do you think about adding Sad Tomato Pie to the mix? I thought I'd put a twist on it by adding bacon, since you're working on the meatless ones." Frankie was a firm believer that bacon made everything better.

Carmen nodded in approval. "I guess Garrett told you about Sunday at The Oasis?"

"He did, and I think it sounds fun. Maybe we'll see someone or something while we're there." She glanced sideways at Carmen, raising her eyebrows.

A sly glimmer shone in Carmen's eyes. She set down the sturdy whisk. "I actually hope we don't see anything there, I mean anything related to the shooting. You see, I asked Grizz to call Ryan and invite us out." She picked up the utensil and began whisking vigorously. "That man needs a break, Frankie, a stress reliever. So, let the case go on Sunday, okay." It wasn't a question.

Before Frankie could tell Carmen she was on her side, Tess swung through the kitchen doors, looking a little undone. "There's a woman here to see you." She jabbed a finger at Frankie, breathless.

"Says her name is Hannah Turner. Isn't she bad news?" Tess's head swiveled from Frankie to Carmen and back again. Clearly, Tess paid attention to all the shop talk, or she wouldn't have recognized the Turner name.

"Actually, Hannah seems nice. I'll go see what she wants." Frankie poured a mug of coffee from the back counter, grabbed her Dirty Chai, and slid two butterhorns onto a plate. Carmen made a sour face, her eyes suddenly lit with disgust.

Frankie's buttery reply, "Like bees to honey, Carmen," met with comprehension and a curt nod from her partner.

Hannah was seated at a table overlooking Granite Street, where the morning sun was muted. The table was the farthest one from the door and bakery traffic. A large box of assorted pastries sat on the back edge of the table near the window ledge.

Frankie said good morning, set down the coffee mug and plate in front of Hannah. "Do you take cream or sweetener in your coffee?"

"Both please. Thank you." She looked at her folded hands, which were sitting in her lap; a forlorn expression had settled on her face. Hannah sported the same messy ponytail she'd worn for goat yoga but her spandex workout duds were swapped for denim trousers, and a yellow Brad Paisley shirt announced, "I'm sunshine mixed with a little hurricane."

After seeing Hannah at goat yoga, Frankie saw no reason to doubt it. "What can I do for you, Hannah?"

Hannah raised her eyes demurely to meet Frankie's. "First, I want to apologize for yesterday. Not just what happened with your mother, Ms. Champagne, but for my father-in-law. One of the hands told me he was very rude to you."

Frankie sensed Hannah wasn't surprised about Dewey's demeanor. "Look, I don't even know your father-in-law, Hannah, but can I give you a little friendly business advice?" Hannah nodded solemnly. "Don't allow that man anywhere near your yoga clients. It's not just the way he talked to me, but even the way he shouted at the farm dog. His negative energy is detrimental for business."

"Yes, I couldn't agree with you more. To hear my husband Nate tell it, his father's belittled people his whole life, even his own children. I guess it's been worse since his wife passed away. I never knew Nate's mother, but I've heard good things about her."

"I didn't know her either, but I've heard she was kindhearted. Anyway, you can't apologize for Dewey, but you need to figure out how to keep him away when you're hosting yoga sessions. I think it could catch on, especially with vacationers, and let's face it—'tis the season to make money."

Hannah's face lit up with renewed hope, and her round cheeks pinked. ""Do you really think I can make a go of it, Ms. Champagne?" She leaned forward, anxious to hear more.

Suddenly, Frankie worried she'd sounded too optimistic about the venture. What did she know about goat yoga? "Well, I don't know for sure, but what I do know is that farm life is popular, small animals are popular, and yoga is popular, so what the heck? It's worth a shot."

Hannah sat back. Her shoulders slumped. "I have to try something. It's expensive to keep a farm running." She bent her head toward Frankie's and spoke just above a whisper. "I don't think the Turner farm was meant to support five families."

Frankie leaned in closer, her face mixed with empathy and interest. She pushed a butterhorn in front of Hannah, inviting her to open up about the family.

"These are simply amazing, and that brings me to the other reason I'm here. We're going to host Breakfast on the Farm in two weeks, before Dairy Month is over."

"June is Dairy Month" was an oft repeated Wisconsin slogan for decades and afforded many dairy-centered events in rural areas. But the Turner farm wasn't a dairy farm as far as Frankie knew.

"Are you diversifying to dairy, too? I mean, the goats

are a new addition, right?" Frankie recalled what she'd learned from Carmen on the Turners.

"Right. The goat herd is a business venture Nate and I started a couple of years ago. We're not milking yet but are considering it. I'm hoping goat yoga will bring in some extra income and I think the breakfast event would bring out more people, too." Her brows curved downward to match her mouth and she began massaging her temple with one hand.

"We've sunk all our money into an event barn—you know, for weddings, parties, and entertainment. It's just finished and we need to show it off, so people will want to rent it."

Frankie understood the risk involved. After her house burned down, she used the insurance money and took out a loan to buy the Bubble and Bake building and vineyard land. She'd gone all in, but it took time to start operating in the black.

"I'd love to see your event barn. That's something new for our area, and Deep Lakes is a destination spot in Wisconsin. Your barn could become a happening place. I hope you're consulting with someone for marketing advice." She took out her notepad from her apron pocket and wrote down two reputable consulting firms in town. "Here, give one or both of these a call. See what they have to offer."

Hannah thanked her and slipped the paper into her purse. "I want to order some things for the breakfast. I don't have time or manpower to make everything myself.

I was thinking quiches and pastries, definitely some of these things." She waved the last bite of butterhorn in the air. "We're taking reservations until the 20th. Can I let you know the count then?"

Since the breakfast wasn't until the 28th, she figured they could manage. She knew she could prepare quiches and butterhorn dough in advance anyway. There was never any problem selling those items during tourist season, no matter the quantity.

"Will you be offering Bloody Marys and Mimosas?" Frankie suggested. The beverages were staples at a fancy breakfast and would likely bring in more customers.

"I'm not sure we can. I've applied for a liquor license but it hasn't been issued yet." Hannah frowned.

"Don't worry. You can offer mock varieties instead, and I have a killer recipe for cake bites made with booze that you can offer?" Frankie added that to the order at Hannah's enthusiastic nod.

"Will all the Turners be helping with the breakfast?" Frankie hoped Dewey and the disagreeable sons would vacate the premises during the event.

Hannah sighed heavily and her shoulders slumped again. "Of course, there's Nate and me. It's our idea and our building, so we will have to run the show. My sister-in-law Ashley agreed to help us prep, set up, serve, and clean up. Thank God! But her husband Franklin wants nothing to do with it, so I hope Ashley doesn't back out." She lowered her voice once more and narrowed her eyes.

"Ashley's worried about money, too. I offered her a cut for helping with the breakfast. She had a great marketing job at a Madison firm, but Franklin made her quit. He said she was needed at home. I don't get it. Their kids are both in middle school." Hannah held a finger up to her lips, mostly to remind herself to stay quiet.

"What about your other sisters-in-law?" Frankie knew there were two other sons and assumed they had wives.

"Well Cheryl won't lift a finger around the farm anymore. She's married to Wayne, the oldest. Wayne gets the biggest cut from the farm profits, they have no children, and Cheryl's a diva. I have no idea why she became a farm wife in the first place." Hannah's disgust was obvious, and she was on a roll.

"Eileen is another story. She and Daniel diversified a long time ago. They bought neighboring property and planted soybeans and corn. All of their corn goes to the ethanol plant in Vandenberg. They're making bank."

Hadn't Frankie just been thinking she needed to find out dirt on the Turners? Here was Hannah, a gift horse unloading an info dump right in her shop. When Hannah left, Frankie retreated to the office alcove and frantically jotted down everything she recalled from the conversation.

Onward to see Shirley Lazaar. Butterhorns in tow, Frankie sped out of the back alley, up Whitman Avenue and over to Kilbourn to the gray concrete block building trimmed in brick. She didn't have time to appreciate the sights of summer: tourists strolling along with dripping ice cream cones, kids squealing in delight at the splash park, bicyclists happily pedaling in tandem down the shaded streets.

Evidence of the annual Flying Fish Festival for the upcoming Father's Day weekend was visible everywhere. Colorful flying fish windsocks flapped in the June breeze from the light posts, while large banners hung all over town, detailing event activities.

Frankie barely noticed the changing signs—every weekend from Memorial Day until Halloween boasted some sort of festival enticing vacationers to come on up or come on back again. Events were not limited to the three big holiday weekends, because someone long ago figured out that summer itself was one endless holiday that bled into autumn. If there was a way to lure Illinois money northwards, a festival was invented to bag it.

She snagged the bakery box from the back seat, catching an apron tie on the door handle. She shook her head at herself. Always in a hurry, Frankie had forgotten to remove her shop apron, which turned out to be one more happy accident for the day. Her set of cryptic notes were in the pocket, and might provide the possibility of bringing the Turners into the investigation.

Shirley was typing on an old IBM Selectric model when Frankie plopped into a chair across from her desk. Shirley sat straight as a tree trunk and had the best posture

Frankie had witnessed in an older person. She waited for the speedy clacking to cease before saying anything.

"What gives, Shirley?" Frankie indicated the typewriter.

"The dang internet has been down more than once today. So, I resurrected this baby from storage. Works like a dream." Shirley gave the beige hunk of metal a friendly pat. "I even found a supply of unopened ribbon cartridges." She laughed heartily as if it were a joke on the 21st century.

Shirley perked up when she saw the bakery box. "That for me?" When Frankie nodded, she held her hand palm up in the "halt traffic" position, scooted to the break room to retrieve coffee, and opened her desk drawer for a napkin, which she dutifully tucked in around her collar to cover her tan uniform shirt. Between her stiff posture and fastidious manner, Frankie thought Shirley might have been ex-military.

"Butterhorns—my favorite. I suppose you'd like a rundown on Jonesy in return." Shirley didn't mince words.

"Yep, and anything else you have on the case, too." Frankie had learned to be direct as well.

It turned out, Frankie's lavish bribe of butterhorns didn't bear much fruit. Shirley opened a gray file folder labeled "Orson Harold Jahnsrude" and produced one sheet of paper.

"With a name like that, no wonder he went by Jonesy," Frankie said.

"For someone with a long-winded name, he didn't have much to say," Shirley chuckled at her own joke.

A recap of Jonesy's statement indicated he didn't know how the glass got into his truck bed, when it got there, or what kind of glass it might be.

"Of course, we already know he doesn't have an alibi since he spent the night on the farm. Nobody but the sheep and the dogs could testify he was bunked up with them the whole night." She closed the folder and placed it on a stack.

"Is he free then, and what happens to the truck?"

"We couldn't hold him. The shards have been sent to the lab to match with the delivery truck headlights. That'll take a few days. Jonesy's truck is being scanned for fluids and searched once more. If we don't find any residues, he'll get it back soon."

"Like today?" Frankie didn't like vague information.

"I'm guessing we'll know soon. I know they were going over it for evidence about an hour ago."

"Anything relevant in Detective Evans' Grant County file?" Frankie hoped to score something on this trip.

Shirley shook her short white curls. "Here. You can read the complaint filed by the Iowa fertilizer company." She handed Frankie a manilla folder.

An assailant hijacked the fertilizer truck at a Kwik Trip in Lancaster. The keys were in the ignition. The driver saw the perpetrator drive away but didn't get a good look at him. The truck was found abandoned and empty on a dead-end road near Waukegan, Illinois on October 10th. The fertilizer company recovered the truck October 11th.

An addendum to the report read: Grant County farmer, Chet Henrichs, age 59, identified the O'Connor farm victim as the driver who picked up manure on October 9. Henrichs said the scars and misshapen nose helped him identify the man.

"Do you think our victim is the one who hijacked the fertilizer truck in Grant County and later abandoned it?"

"It seems plausible," Shirley said. "Unless there were other players involved. Someone put a bullet through the man's head, but we don't have a motive yet, so I can't say for sure our vic is a criminal."

It was normal for the police to express uncertainty until all the facts were gathered, although Frankie knew there was always room for speculation or why bother investigating?

She snapped a photo of the report pages with her cell phone. "Please tell me you have some juicy tidbit you've been saving for last, Shirley?"

"We're digging, Francine, but we're casting a wide net right now. We have a lot of suspects in the mix. Plus, I'm training a rookie intern how to investigate. It ain't easy." Shirley looked like she'd been logging a lot of extra hours.

Frankie passed Shirley her set of notes on the Turners as narrated by Hannah.

"And you think Dewey Turner should be investigated because . . ." she shot Frankie an accusatory look.

Frankie was indignant. "Dewey definitely has a grudge against the O'Connors. Maybe he's involved somehow. His farm property butts up against Ryan's. He had access . . ." her voice faded as she realized there was nothing concrete that warranted an investigation.

Shirley smiled reassuringly, chewing thoughtfully on her third butterhorn. "Maybe we can ask Mr. Turner if he saw or heard anything unusual on the day of the shooting."

Outside, the summer blue sky had given way to gray skies with thunderheads. Rain put the kibosh on outdoor activities and often brought more customers to the wine lounge. It could be busier than usual tonight.

Abe Arnold, editor of the *Whitman Watch*, was camped next to Frankie's SUV.

"Anything new on the shooting?" he asked Frankie, while methodically scrolling through his cell phone.

"Nope, afraid not." Frankie's answer was short, but truthful. Abe was a skilled reporter, sharp, quick-witted, and crafty with his questions. Frankie couldn't deny she admired the man, but she couldn't find it in her heart to share information with him.

Before Bubble and Bake opened, Frankie planned to use her communications degree to pursue a journalism career, but Abe wouldn't hire her. Frankie was certain it was because she was a woman. After all, she was good enough to write features about wines, grape cultivation, and culinary fare, just not the heavy stuff. She jumped at the opportunity to be a stringer for *Point Press*, a large regional paper, where she garnered some modest recognition for investigating and reporting on two Whitman County murders. Abe had swallowed his pride and suggested they team up, but Frankie found his ask too much to choke down.

Now Abe rolled up his car window with a small wave to Frankie and started the engine. Something gnawed in her brain. She trotted over and rapped on his window.

"Did you think of something?" Abe asked, a look of amusement playing on his face.

"Yes, I did. You're sitting next to my car. You know I just came from the sheriff's office, but you're not going there yourself. Why are you here, Abe?"

"I've already talked to the sheriff today, Francine. I know there's nothing new. I just wanted to see if you'd tell me the truth or not." He rolled up the window once more, shutting out Frankie's parting rebuke.

Chapter 13

Birds rising in flight is a sign that the enemy is lying in ambush; when the wild animals are startled and flee he is trying to take you unaware.
- Sun Tzu

Since Frankie didn't need to be back at the shop until just before four, she considered walking Sonny the sheltie as time well spent. The rain clouds had moved on, replaced by a light breeze and partial sunshine. She wanted a chance to talk to Jonesy, thinking it may be her last chance if the police found other evidence in his truck.

Sonny smiled with his whole body when Frankie brought out the walking leash and clipped it around his collar. She rubbed his ears and mane and was rewarded with a sheltie slurp on the hand.

It didn't take long to find Jonesy doing his normal routine, standing at the edge of the south pasture outside the fence, Fly and JoJo standing guard on the inside.

"What can I do for you?" Jonesy's smarmy tone was on full display, so Frankie figured she'd get straight to the point.

"I thought you might want a chance to tell your side of the story, so I'm here to offer that."

Jonesy held a stalk of long grass between his lips, removed it, examined it for who-knows-what, then planted it back in his mouth. He never took his eyes off the grazing flock.

"What makes you think I want to tell *you* my side? I'd rather just be left alone. Having my name in the newspaper don't mean a thing to me."

Not to be deterred, Frankie volleyed back, "It might be nice to get your story in the paper just in case you get arrested. Telling your story after the fact won't help you much." Frankie told him that spinning a positive story before the bad news comes out was known as "getting ahead of the story." "Good publicity is what you could use right now, I'm thinking."

Jonesy paused but his demeanor didn't budge. "They have my cell phone, too."

Frankie raised her eyebrows. "What will your cell records show for that day?"

Jonesy shrugged. "There's a couple calls to the Turner farm. I imagine they'll make a deal out of that."

"Should they?" Frankie felt the adrenaline pumping.

Jonesy shrugged a second time. "Tell you what. I'm not going to say anything, but it wouldn't hurt you to talk to Jenks at the Turner farm. He's one of the goat handlers." Then Jonesy opened the gate to enter the pasture, apparently dismissing Frankie.

"Come on, Sonny. I promised you a walk." Frankie turned down the farm lane that connected the O'Connor property to the Turners'. Sonny was on familiar land and bounded off in a flying run down the lane, his walking leash nearly out of slack, and Frankie charging along behind him, doing her best.

Naturally, Sonny stopped obediently at the property line to sit and wait for Frankie. It was clear the well-trained dog knew his boundaries. Frankie caught up, paused for a breather, and tossed Sonny a treat.

The two resumed a side-by-side walk onto the Turners' lane that led to the farm driveway. Frankie kept alert for signs of people, so she could give them a friendly wave, something that would keep her from looking like a trespasser. After walking up the drive, past the barn and the yoga arena, she finally spied the goat corral.

Grateful for the downward slope, she and Sonny picked up the pace to a trot while she waved a couple of times to two men in the corral. She prayed that one of them was Jenks, and prayed even harder that neither of them was Dewey Turner.

A tall, lean man in work jeans walked partway down the path to greet her.

"Hi there. I'm Nate Turner. Can I help you?" Nate's smile was warm as he held out a hand to shake hers firmly. Good looking with sun-streaked brown hair and honest eyes, he looked like a good fit for Hannah, as far as Frankie could judge from a first impression.

"Hi. I'm Frankie Champagne. It's nice to meet you."

Nate cut her off from saying more. "Oh, is this about catering the farm breakfast? Hannah's not here right now, but you can give me any information you have for her." It was nice that Nate was being welcoming, and Frankie hoped she wasn't treading dangerously by taking Jonesy's tip.

"No, Mr. Turner. I'm not here to see Hannah. I am hoping to have a few words with Jenks."

Nate's stunned expression left the opening for an afterthought.

"I do hope the farm breakfast will go well. I think it's a good way to showcase your new venue. I'm excited to be part of the event," Frankie believed it was good practice to acknowledge her customers and their endeavors.

"All right then. Well, Jenks is right there." Nate gestured with his thumb behind his right shoulder. "I'd be happy to show you the new building, but I think you'd appreciate taking a tour with Hannah. She's the one with the eye for design and details." Nate spoke with sincerity and admiration for his wife. She could imagine the two would get along famously with Ryan and Carmen, given half a chance.

Nate spoke briefly to Jenks, then took over feeding the goats so the hand could leave the corral.

Jenks was a sprightly young man with dark hair, freckles, and arms the size of tree trunks. He looked warily at Frankie and rocked back and forth on his boots. "Ma'am?"

Frankie introduced herself as a local reporter who was interested in any information about the shooting at the O'Connor farm or anything Jenks might know about the hired hands there. She kicked herself for not rehearsing what she would say as her inroad for asking questions. It turned out, this time it didn't matter.

"Let's go talk over here, Ma'am." He pointed to a small open space where a picnic table and benches stood, probably a lunch spot for the workers. Frankie sat down, but Jenks stayed on his feet, occasionally rocking on his heels.

"I honestly don't know anything about the shooting, but I know that Mr. Turner has it in for the O'Connors." His pace quickened and he looked over both shoulders before continuing. "You see, me and my shearing partner, Tinker, were supposed to be working the O'Connor farm, but all that changed when Dewey offered Tinker triple the money to shear here the same day."

Jenks took a breath, kicked up a dirt clod with his boot toe, then raised his eyes to Frankie's. She was surprised to see the emotion there, a look of righteous indignation. "That was bad enough, but then Dewey didn't keep Tinker. Instead, he hired that Monty guy and Tinker was SOL, if you know what I'm saying."

Frankie was trying to catch up. "Well, maybe Mr. Turner just hired the better worker?"

Jenks beamed and stood straighter. "I'm one of the best there is, Ma'am. But so is my buddy, Tinker. We're the best team." His face darkened again.

"So, what happened to Tinker?"

"Don't know for sure. He worked at the O'Connors' the next day, shearing with that Coop. He didn't stay on, so that is that. Tinker doesn't have a cell phone. Don't know if I'll ever see him again. Damn shame. He's a helluva lot better worker than Monty." Jenks's accent gave him away as Australian, so Frankie was curious to ask if he knew Clay.

"Not really, no. I've seen him around is all."

Dead end: Time for another trail. "I get the feeling you don't think much of Monty? Or you don't like him because he kept your friend from getting hired?"

"Ha. You're quick. Me, Tinker, and Monty worked together last fall right here in Wisconsin. Had a shearing job on the Henrichs' farm, south of here."

The Henrichs' farm. Why was that name ringing a bell? Oh, of course, Shirley had told her Henrichs was the farmer who identified the dead fertilizer driver as the same man who had picked up manure at his farm, also in a hijacked truck. She waited for Jenks to embellish.

"Let's just say that Monty's a schmooze. He's nothing but a bludger, but he's got a velvet tongue." Jenks spat on the ground, then apologized.

"A bludger? What's that?" Frankie wasn't up on her Aussie colloquialisms.

"Just straight-up lazy. The worst. Please excuse me. I need to get back to work. Mr. Nate is a good man, not like his dad."

"Thank you Jenks, for taking the time. Please let me know if you think of anything else that might help find the shooter."

Jenks spun around, his face bright red. He pulled off his hat and slammed it against his leg. "Bugger! I almost clean forgot what I wanted to tell you. Monty borrowed Jonesy's truck the day of the shooting. I saw him driving it."

"What?" Frankie couldn't contain her surprise. "What time did you see him?" The time could make or break Jonesy's involvement.

"It was the middle of the night, maybe three or four in the morning, Ma'am."

"Was the truck leaving the Turner farm or returning to the farm?"

"It was parked in the farm lane between the properties, but I didn't see it leave. That's all I know. I didn't see the truck after that."

"How can you be sure it was Jonesy's truck?" Frankie was skeptical; after all, she couldn't identify any specific features of the truck she saw leaving the O'Connor farm in the early hours herself.

"One of the prettiest farm trucks in the area. Engine hums like a song and he keeps it shiny. You can see that sheen in the darkest night. Besides, Jonesy is known for loaning out his baby. There's a lot of us don't have vehicles."

"One more thing, Jenks. Can you explain these nicknames you all have?"

"Sure, but why do you want to know?"

"Just curious." Frankie smiled brightly and shrugged.

"Well, my last name's Jenkins so nothing special there. Tinker, he could fix anything, no matter what it was."

"What about Monty? I heard someone call him Saint, too. Is there a connection?"

Jenks spat in the dirt and excused himself. "Sorry about that. The wind is kicking up a good amount of dust. Monty's a Canuck." Jenks spoke Monty's name as if it were a dirty word. "He's from Montreal, you see. But his last name is Saint something or other. When it comes to nicknames for hired hands, we keep it pretty simple."

The world had grown strangely quiet around them as they walked back toward the O'Connor farm. Frankie speculated about Jonesy loaning out his "baby." She imagined many of the guest workers didn't have money or reason to buy a vehicle. Most were used to carpooling any place they wanted to go. She found it interesting that Clay owned a car and wondered if he planned to stay in the U.S. Hadn't Violet said Clay had spent more than two years here already?

Frankie's mind was buzzing with the particulars Jenks shared. Things didn't add up, however. Why wouldn't Jonesy tell the police he loaned out the truck to Monty the night of the shooting? What possible reason could he have for protecting Monty?

She was slogging through the facts as she knew them when she heard a popping sound. More popping noises came from somewhere behind or above her; she wasn't sure. She and Sonny broke into a simultaneous run, but they were out in the open, almost to the property line. A few more pops erupted, while Sonny jumped into action and herded Frankie behind a brush pile on the Turners' line.

Frankie gasped for air, too shocked to cry or shout. Then Sonny dropped down on his haunches and fell over. His breathing wasn't slowing down, and Frankie could see a little blood on his chest. Shooter or no shooter, she hunched down behind the brush, pulled out her phone and called Ryan.

Ryan's old blue Dakota rattled down the lane in no time. The two of them carefully scooped up Sonny and laid him on the small backseat of the cab. Ryan whipped a U-turn in the lane, baja'd across the field and squealed onto County HH.

"What happened, and what were you doing down by Turners' anyway?" Ryan looked like a parent who had to pick up his drunk kid from a party, a mix of anger and concern on his face..

Frankie was crying resentful tears. How dare anyone shoot at an innocent dog. Of course, she had just enough time to imagine the gunfire was meant to warn her to stay away. But was she supposed to stay away from the Turner farm or from the O'Connor shooting, or both maybe?

Ryan asked Carmen to call Dr. Sadie, so the vet was ready to take Sonny. "Don't worry about the shop; Carmen said she'd call Cherry in to help.

It was easier getting the sheltie out of the truck with four people, as Sadie and her assistant manned the front end of the sheltie, and they settled him onto a doggie stretcher.

In less than an hour, Sadie pulled out one of the red plastic chairs in the waiting room and sat facing Ryan and Frankie. Inwardly, Frankie was feeling nauseous, and half expected Sadie to say she couldn't save Sonny.

"I think Sonny will be fine. He was grazed in the chest by some kind of projectile and took a few BBs to his front leg. I shaved the hair around his wounds, cleaned and bandaged them. I'll give you an antibiotic in case of infection and some pain reliever. Just watch for any changes in the wound areas or his behavior."

When a couple of tears escaped Frankie's eyes, a bewildered Sadie asked: "Are you okay, Frankie? What happened?"

Frankie would only say that she'd been walking Sonny on and off for a few days and somehow had been shot at. "I think we may have been mistaken for trespassers." A little tick developed in Ryan's jawline, but he didn't add to the story.

Once the trio was heading back to the farm, Ryan broke into Frankie's thoughts. "I'm going to report this to Alonzo if you don't, Frankie. The Turners are not getting away with shooting at either one of you."

* * *

Frankie accepted a bear hug from Carmen but declined a beverage and chat, wanting only for the day to be over. She felt bad about messing up Ryan's day, about getting their dutiful Sonny shot, about not being at work when she was supposed to run wine tastings that night. Carmen gave her friend a firm push toward the stairway.

"You need to call Alonzo and probably Garrett. Cherry and Jovie could run the shop tonight without my help, so don't sweat it."

Back in her apartment, Frankie called Alonzo, found him at home, and filled him in on the information she gleaned from Jenks. She knew an officer would have to take his statement anyway, but she tried to recount his words as accurately as possible, including a description of where she and Sonny were when the shots were fired.

Alonzo grudgingly told her that Jonesy had been arrested about an hour ago, after blood spatter was found in the bed of his truck, identified as human blood. Along with the circumstantial evidence of the broken glass that appeared to be from a headlight, it was enough to bring him in. "Of course, we'll see if the blood matches our victim."

"I think you need to stay away from Ryan's farm and as far away from this case as possible, Frankie. You might be the next one to get hurt. Whoever shot Sonny was sending you a message. I don't think it was an accident that they hit the dog instead of you."

Alonzo's words brought fresh tears. Frankie balled her hands into fists and jammed them in the air, whacking an imaginary target. She hated feeling vulnerable. She hated that she'd put Sonny in danger. She hated being told what to do.

"I'm going to bed, Alonzo. I promise to think about what you said." Frankie's full emotional restraint was on display.

She phoned Garrett and told him the whole sordid story. There, her slate was clean, wasn't it? But she slept fitfully, worried about Ryan and Carmen losing Jonesy, a valuable employee, but mostly worried about Sonny and the feeling that his suffering was all her fault.

Chapter 14

Give me wine to wash me clean of
the weather-stains of cares.
- Ralph Waldo Emerson

Yowling cat noises woke Frankie ahead of her Saturday alarm. Her open bedroom windows offered more than fresh air: A conclave of tomcats were hissing at each other in the backyard by the stream. But, that wasn't all. Sundae was serenading the toms and Frankie from inside Violet's room, sounding like a caged animal.

Frankie opened Violet's shut door and saw the dark outline of an arched back. The feline pawed at the window screen, advertising herself. The tortie wasn't happy to see Frankie, nor to be pried away from the window and her waiting suitors.

"I'm doubly unimpressed, Sundae. You should never have been shut up in here in the first place, and why haven't you been spayed? I'm calling Sadie later to find out." Sundae responded with a hiss and tried to claw Frankie's arm as she vaulted off of the window sill and streaked out the door. Frankie yelled at the toms, shut the apartment windows, and pushed start on the coffee maker before seeking the lost kitty.

Sundae was hunched at the bottom of the stairway that led to the Bubble and Bake kitchen, pawing and meowing at the door. "Out you go Sundae. See you later, kitty." Frankie slammed the door a little too loud before traipsing back up the steps.

The coffee was just the remedy she needed to organize her day and the early start was a blessing in disguise. She was hard at work making orange cinnamon rolls in the shop kitchen when Tess arrived.

"Look at you, already hard at it this morning," Tess smiled cheerfully with her whole face, and she was dressed like a summer picnic, red and white checkered cotton shirt and a paisley bandana that matched.

One long finger trailed down the agenda board as she hummed a tune. Tess often hummed or sang Ethiopian tunes she'd learned from her mother and aunts. Most days, Bubble and Bake's kitchen was filled with chatter or songs, and Frankie insisted the baked goods turned out better for it.

She skipped over and handed Tess a mug of her favorite tea, a black blend with cinnamon and cardamom that Frankie purchased in bulk after she discovered Tess's penchant for it. She would do anything she could to remind her star baker just how much she mattered.

Tess smiled her thanks, made a mark by the scone varieties she'd be preparing, and headed to a station.

"I want you to know that my brother James is coming by Monday to look at the upstairs space over Rachel's store. I've been considering remodeling it into a small apartment, and I think now might be the right time to get that going." Frankie hoped the news would brighten Tess's worry of being displaced in August.

"You mean it might be a place for me to live?" She perked up when Frankie nodded.

"I'll keep you posted, Tess."

After Tia Pepita and Carmen breezed in the back door, the kitchen took on an array of chit-chat and music. Carmen gave a report on Sonny's wounds, saying the medicated sheltie slept peacefully and was still slumbering when she left. Tia hunted down Sundae to spoil, which reminded Frankie to call Dr. Sadie after she shared her early morning escapade with the crew.

"Well?" Carmen paused in counting out an order of scones and cookies for a church fellowship when Frankie walked back into the kitchen.

"Sadie said Sundae isn't on tap to get spayed until she's six months old, so she was surprised to hear she was in heat. As soon as it's over, I'll take her in to get it done. Meanwhile, lucky us."

Carmen giggled. "Guess you'll have to keep your windows shut for a few days, sorry to say."

"I'm going to tell Violet the cat needs to stay downstairs until this is over. In the meantime, I've made a diaper for her. She looks kind of pathetic, but really, she's so annoying I can't feel sorry for her right now." Frankie scowled at the tortie.

Baking, counting, boxing, and checking items off the task board continued while Tess manned the front of the shop. Aunt CeCe would be busy all day at Lovely Lavender Farm leading painting classes, but Tia was getting the hang of making croissants in her absence.

"You're really something, Tia," Frankie praised, "to learn French baking skills when you've been making empanadas and pan dulces so long."

Tia made a clucking noise and shook her head. "I like all kinds of sweets, even that hoity-toity French stuff." She stuck her nose into the air and sniffed for emphasis, but then a cloud of worry crossed her face.

"Frankieee . . ." Tia exaggerated the last syllable whenever something was on her mind. "Are you getting anywhere on the shooting at the farm? I want that person caught, so I can sleep at night!"

Frankie and Carmen exchanged sympathetic glances; both crossed the room at the same time to enfold Tia in a tight squeeze, which made her laugh. Simultaneously they chimed in, "We're trying."

"After what happened yesterday with you and Sonny, you better be careful. I think one of those coldhearted Turners is responsible." Tia's eyes were on fire and the tender croissant dough took a pounding.

Apparently Carmen thought so, too, but Frankie was skeptical.

"Someone wanted to send a message yesterday, but was the message to butt out of the case or just get off the Turner property?"

Late morning ushered in a western breeze and lapping creek waters outside Bubble and Bake. Late risers took to the back deck with their coffees and baked treats. Tia and Tess finished cookies, pastries, and quiches, then headed out the back door as the noon shift clocked in to staff the wine lounge.

Cherry's black and white uniform was trimmed in yellow bows, and her hair was curled and pulled back into a long ponytail clipped with a yellow daisy barrette. She bounced around the lounge like a happy bumble bee flitting from flower to flower, setting up tables as needed with flameless candles, napkins, and other complements.

Jovie took out tasting bottles—some from boxes, some from the cooler—and opened two of each. Cherry's sister, Pomelo, was a regular fill-in at the wine lounge during summer while on vacation from her middle-school teaching duties. Jovie set up Pom on one end of the tasting bar, and laid out a pad of tasting lists, pencils, and palate-cleansing crackers.

Frankie checked on the front of house before taking off a couple hours to do accounting and run errands. The Parker sisters, though not twins, wore the same buoyant expressions and walked with a certain bounce on slender frames. Pom and Cherry were blessed with the golden blonde hair many craved or would dye for. Their youthful faces sported gleaming skin and they were fit; Frankie knew the women were avid volleyball and softball players, even now in their mid-thirties.

"It's good to see you all. How's everyone?" Frankie believed in using a soft touch in business.

"Just a reminder we have a bachelorette party on the back deck. They will be here around six and there are eleven in the party. Carmen and I will be back around four to take over tastings, which will leave all of you free to circulate the lounge and check on the chick party. We can help you as needed. Just give us a wave."

The crew knew the ropes and nodded agreement. Frankie went over wine inventory with Jovie and the two clambered down to the basement to retrieve a few more cases before Frankie's phone jangled.

Manny was calling from the vineyard.

"How's the grape whisperer today?" Frankie marveled that Manny had a way of coaxing extra grapes out of the vines.

His reply had an edge to it. "Do you have time to come out here today? There's something I need you to see."

"I was just going to run errands. I'll come out right away." Frankie wanted to know more, but didn't want to waste any time, and Manny didn't elaborate but disconnected.

Frankie pulled into the drive and parked next to an older model Toyota, perfect for a frugal college student. Nelson and Zane habitually carpooled together from

Stevens Point. Since Nelson graduated in May, Frankie would be woefully sending him off to a full-time professional gig at the end of harvest. She was lucky he agreed to stay that long; she was still paying him intern's wages, although he was worth a great deal more.

Zane had another year left before graduation, and she hoped he would supply a name or two for another intern to work at the winery.

She scampered past the front row of La Crescent vines, barely registering the forming clusters, and made a beeline for the fruit trees. Manny said they would meet in his office, which was at the bottom of the orchard hill next to the equipment building. The office was just a wooden shed that housed a small desk, two chairs, and a rectangular table set against one wall with shelves above it.

Manny was sitting at the computer, staring at the screen. Next to him on the desk were two of the vineyard trail cameras, one of which was plugged into the computer. "Come over here and take a look."

Oh, oh. Frankie wondered what new critter was munching on her grapevines now. They decided to invest in the cameras last year due to the increase in the deer population and other animal life, hoping to set up deterrents rather than having to do away with the wildlife.

She wasn't prepared to see a two-legged intruder prowling around the rows of grapevines. "What in the world?"

"I've gone through all the cameras and footage. This

is the only camera that picked up the prowler. And we've only got two photos. See, I put them up side-by-side."

Both were night photos, time-stamped from Tuesday at 11 p.m. and a few minutes after that. The figure might be male or female, hard to tell what with the dark baggy clothing and hoodie. No face was visible at all. The figure was carrying a sack and small implement, and was hunched over the ground in one photo, possibly digging.

"Did you show these to anyone else? Nelson or Zane or Violet?"

Manny shook his head. "I can tell you this person isn't either of our two field workers. Rico is much bigger than this and Gil is much shorter." Manny drew his face closer to the screen, squinting. "I'm mad at myself for not checking the cameras sooner this week. I pulled them on Wednesday and haven't looked at them since then." He kicked the desk leg.

"Hey, it's okay. We usually have intruders in the spring and fall. Nothing much happens during the summer months until there's fruit for the taking," Frankie reassured him.

"So, there's nothing before Tuesday that you can see?"

Manny assured Frankie he went through all the camera footage with a fine tooth comb. "I already hung the other cameras back up. But, there's more. Come with me."

Manny carried the cameras back up to the vineyard as they walked up the hill. He placed them back in their opposing trees and ushered her into the row of Frontenac vines across from one of the cameras. About a third of the way, he stopped and pointed to the ground.

"See how the mulched area around the vines looks different here?" He kept moving, rounded the end and entered the next row. "And here." About half-way down, he pointed at the soil again.

Frankie nodded. "But couldn't anything be rooting around in the mulch? A chipmunk or squirrel or even a stray cat?"

"Yes, I suppose so, but I checked the whole vineyard. Every row has mulch that's been stirred up by something. An animal can't be in every row. And the camera picked up the intruder in two different rows. So it seems like we have a prowler digging around every row."

"Are any of the vines damaged or dug up?"

Manny said they weren't. "What would somebody be digging around out here for?"

Frankie sighed heavily. Well, there was another question that needed answering. "I think we should call the sheriff. Maybe this is connected to the O'Connor shooting, maybe not. And maybe they can use their equipment to zoom in on our photos and come up with something we can't see."

Frankie made the call and asked Manny to relay the details he'd discovered that day to the responding officer. She had a business in town that needed her, and right now, wine tastings and customer chats would be a peaceful hiatus from being preyed upon by unknown enemies.

* * *

Fresh-faced from a shower she hoped would revive her desire to mingle with customers, Frankie changed into a white linen skirt with buttons down the front and a pink lace-trimmed top. She could see her mom's frown as she selected practical shoes, a pair of walking sandals in natural tones. She never learned to walk in heels and her clumsiness always got the best of her, so she rarely took the risk of donning dressy shoes.

Carmen was already in position, doing a tasting for six on one end of the polished walnut bar that was cut horizontally from a dead tree. Carmen had changed, too, from bakery rags into a casual floral dress on a bright lime background and black braided sandals. Her long hair was pulled into a neat chignon, held in place by barrettes covered in the same fabric. She offered Frankie an encouraging smile, but the fatigue showed on Carmen's knitted brow and drooping eyelids. Frankie had called her with the latest fracas at Bountiful, adding to Carmen's worries.

It was strange to see so many locals on a summer day at 5 p.m. At Frankie's prodding, Carmen checked in with the Farm Femmes, a group of area women involved in some form of agricultural pursuit.

The seven women were huddled into a corner alcove on the Meriwether side of the lounge, enjoying glasses of various wines and sharing flatbread pizzas. Hannah

Turner was taking notes on a tablet and smiled at Carmen when she interrupted their chatter to see if they needed anything.

"Carmen, it's nice to meet you at last," Hannah's voice was bright as she held out her hand to shake Carmen's. "It's about time we met since we're neighbors and all. You'd be welcome to join our group anytime."

"Here's our business card. I'm the organizer this year, so you can contact me if you want to join or come to a meeting as a guest." Marnie Grey, a local beekeeper and alpaca farmer shook Carmen's hand, too.

"What exactly does your group do?" Carmen clearly needed convincing to even consider the proposal.

"We meet to exchange ideas to promote our farms and products around the state. We're part of a Wisconsin cooperative where we sell some of our items. We also chat about fundraising events and ag-related issues. Sometimes we just sound off about our significant others." Marnie laughed and tilted back her wine glass. "By the way, I would love another glass of your Sweet Tia chardonnay."

Carmen pondered the idea. "I'll give it some thought. I don't have a lot of extra time with two teenagers, helping with our farm, and running this place. I need to be two people half the time." She laughed good-naturedly toward the women though, as she collected a few more wine orders.

"We hear you, Carmen. That's why we only meet every other month, so it's not such a huge commitment."

Hannah spoke lightly, scrutinizing Carmen's expression. She knew the history of the fallout between Dewey and Ryan.

While Carmen retrieved refills, she noticed Frankie was handling an unlikely group of locals for a tasting and wondered what brought them together. Only three were actually tasting while the other two imbibed on lemonades. Another two women sat down near the five for a tasting, so Carmen scuttled back to the Femmes to deliver wine, and hailed Cherry to let her know she'd taken care of refills, but was heading back to the bar.

About dead center, Carmen recognized Donna Stauffer and Lena Hagen, both of whom owned lake resorts for decades.

"What brings you two here on a Saturday? Shouldn't you be checking in campers and running around like madwomen about this time?"

Donna laughed heartily. "Not anymore. I finally talked Bruce into selling the place to our nephew, Jason. It took me three years, but he agreed. That man runs slower than molasses in the Arctic." Donna was known to speak her mind, sometimes in funny idioms. "The paperwork's signed, and after a season or two, we're out of here." Donna pointed her thumb like a hitchhiker toward a destination far away from Deep Lakes.

Just then another six sat down at Carmen's end of the bar. Carmen waved and nodded acknowledgement. "Why don't you two make your tasting picks on here, and

I'll get this other group going?" She pushed tasting lists and pencils in front of the two.

Frankie finished with the three/fifths tasters, a group that included the school administrator, the school board president, local librarian Sue Pringle and two outspoken pillars from different local churches. The two pillars were all business, so Frankie was quite happy to escort them from the tasting bar to a far table near the bookcases. She was surprised when the public officials purchased two bottles of wine for the three of them, piquing her curiosity further. But now they were Jovie's to handle for the duration.

Frankie waved a greeting at Donna and Lena, washed her hands and scooted their direction, wine glasses in tow.

"I haven't seen either of you in the summer since I don't know when. I didn't know you existed this time of year!" Frankie turned their checklists around to face her and did the first pour, bigger than what she normally offered customers.

"Do you want the spiel about each kind or . . ."

"Yes, ma'am. Treat us like you would any tourist with money to blow." Donna's bawdy sense of humor was well known. She looked like a wild woman with her long silver hair pulled severely back from her face, a rough face that made her look like she'd done time. She smiled with full lips that covered half her face and revealed unusually large stained teeth. She was the first in line to donate to every charity event in town, and her lineup of repeat campers was the envy of the lake region.

"I'm surprised to see you two here on a weekend, during the busy season no less?"

Lena jumped in before Donna could take over the entire conversation. "Bob and I retired two years ago. Sold the campground and bar to a Chicago area family."

The Hagens ran the Happy Campers resort and bar on Lake Joy for 30 odd years, and Frankie wondered about the renovations she observed going on last fall.

"Oh yes, it's now Stairway to the Clouds resort. The new owners tore down the bar and replaced it with a swanky restaurant sitting atop the outcropping on the property. No more camping either. They're putting the finishing touches on a lodge, parking lot, and small golf course." Lena made a face like someone had just laid a dead fish on her lap.

Frankie whistled. "Wow, that's a huge investment. I hope they get a lot of customers."

Lena nodded, smiled approvingly at the Two Pear Chardonnay, and marked a star by it on her sheet. "I think they have money to burn. Two families bought the property together. Both own some kind of investment firms in Chicago. They didn't bat an eye at our asking price."

This phenomenon was nothing new in Deep Lakes. Local realtor Bram Callahan had the market cornered on transforming the area from family campgrounds to posh condos, lodges, and resorts on the pristine lakes of Whitman County. Frankie couldn't argue that some of the old resorts needed a facelift from their 20th century offerings, but she often balked at change, especially when it messed with tradition.

"What about you, Donna? Is Mischief by the Lake going to be razed for condos or a millionaire's paradise?" Frankie loved the point on Lake Loki where Mischief perched, facing west into sunsets every tourist dreamed about for vacation photos. Distraction caused her to pour half glasses for their next taste.

Donna sniffed loudly, her words blaring. "Ha! No way. Jason wants to keep Mischief just the way it is. Hell, the bar makes bank every weekend until December, what with hunting season and all. It's only the winter that's a downer." She tossed back the Riesling without tasting it.

Frankie remembered a summer she spent plenty of time at the Up To No Good bar on the Mischief property. Between college semesters, she cleaned cabins six days a week, working for three neighboring lake resorts. Rick Davidson, the man she would marry, tended bar at the Up To No Good, and every female tourist swooned in his presence. Years later, she couldn't recall why she fell so hard for the man.

As if reading her mind, Donna broke in. "Do you ever hear from that no-good ex of yours?" Donna never minced words.

Frankie shook her head. "Not since the girls were small. Last I knew, he was in Wyoming, still driving long-haul. But, that's forever ago." Rick was like a ghost memory now, and she didn't want to conjure up bad memories.

"I've seen Violet out at the Mischief. She's so grown up and sure is a pretty girl." Donna's voice took an air of mystery mixed with possible revelation, so Frankie shot her a cursory glance to continue.

"She's been hanging with one of our renters." Donna's face took on a sour expression.

"Those old shacks on the lowland need to be torn down, but Jason wanted to make a quick buck this summer by renting them out cheap for the season, then demolishing them in the fall."

Frankie remembered the tiny shacks that were weekly rentals for fishermen or hunters, who weren't in town for the scenery or lake life. They didn't care if the places were run down, had faulty plumbing, and weren't insulated. The so-named lowland was just that: flat, marshy, and stinky in the summer, on the backside of the property, accessible by trail and dirt path. She wondered what condition the shacks were in now, some twenty years later. Her interest was piqued.

"So, Clay Cooper is renting there? By himself?"

Donna nodded, tossed back the third vintage and pointed one arthritic finger at the tasting sheet. "I think it's time for some reds. I don't care much for the whites. I need something more substantial, if you get my drift."

Frankie pulled the stopper from her favorite red

blend, Dark Deeds, and watched Donna's dreamy smile of approval as the stream of garnet red splashed into the glass. "Has Clay caused any problems?"

Donna tasted, savored the flavor, and shook her head. "None that I know of. I mean, he and his sheep shagger friends paid for the whole summer up front." Donna's profane name for the shearers didn't surprise Frankie.

"Friends? How many shearers are renting from you?"

"I think there's three. I'd have to check with Jason or Bruce to know for sure." The effects of the wine were beginning to show, and Frankie worried over her decision to make the samples too large. She looked over at Lena, who was attentively listening to their discussion, but still sipping on her third sample.

"Donna, can you let me know if there are any problems out there with those men, and can you get me their names, please?" The woman raised her brows. "A mother wants to know," came Frankie's reply.

Donna never had children of her own, but treated Jason as if he belonged to her. She understood and promised she'd find out.

Frankie set the two women up at a table by the window where there was plenty of activity to keep them alert, and brought them water while they waited on their food orders.

The night ramped up after the first shift of locals were replaced by tourists roaming around town after the dinner hour. Pom and Jovie took turns running interference for the bachelorette party and announced last call at 8:30 to nudge them off the property by 9.

Carmen and Frankie were alone to finish the closing details by 9:45, so Frankie discussed more details about the hooded figure caught on the vineyard camera, and Donna's information that Clay was slumming it on the marshy part of Lake Loki.

"Any news about either shooting? Do the police have any ideas about who shot at me and Sonny? Or the evidence in Jonesy's truck?"

Carmen's voice wavered, showing her distress at all that had happened. "We know so little. Almost everyone in Whitman County owns a BB gun, especially out in the country. We had to hire Bucky on full time, what with Jonesy in jail for now."

Frankie patted her friend's shoulder. Both women were weary from a week of too many misadventures. "How long can they keep Jonesy without more evidence?"

Carmen shrugged. "We were told the blood on the truck is being tested for a match with the victim's. Ryan's beside himself with worry. I mean, which workers are we supposed to trust?"

Stress crossed Frankie's face. One of those workers was Clay Cooper, her daughter's boyfriend. Could he be trusted? She had to find out.

* * *

Interlude:

Neill Starr ran both hands through his unkempt hair and swigged his spiked morning coffee. Looking out past his deck and formal gardens to the bay, he scanned the water for answers. What was keeping Sawyer? Why hadn't he heard from him yet? The rendezvous at the docks was supposed to happen yesterday. He swore and slammed his mug on the glass table, startling nearby songbirds into flight.

Starr's agitation was not unfounded. This third shipment would be the feather in his cap, the final feat in the wager against his big brother. He was so close now to getting the advantage he'd been waiting a decade to achieve. There couldn't be any glitches standing in the way, and yet, here he was, downing scotch at six in the morning, waiting for a phone call. A phone call he'd been anticipating for two days.

As if willing it, his burner phone rang. Starr blew out his breath, but he couldn't quiet the ire in his voice.

"What?"

"It's Pierce at the docks. We're still watching that container, but I've got nothing new to report, Sir. There's been no movement."

Starr swore a blue streak as he paced the deck.

"Give it another 24 hours. And keep me posted if so much as a rat shows up near that pier."

The fact was, Starr needed 24 hours to come up with

an alternative plan. What would he do if Sawyer didn't show? He needed some hired guns just in case his crew failed to deliver. Sawyer was seasoned and trustworthy. Surely he would show up. There had to be an explanation, and he thought he knew who to contact to find out. If only he could locate her.

Chapter 15

Chance encounters are often the routes through
which opportunities manifest themselves.
- Ashwin Sanghi

No matter the season, Sundays usually began quietly
in Deep Lakes. The morning sunlight danced on Sterling
Creek as the water played a tune of its own, easily heard
absent the typical weekday morning traffic. In summer,
Frankie's body clock was locked in daylight mode.
She rose with the promise of dawn's entrance and was
continuously surprised when twilight arrived. Without
Violet or Sundae to create the whisper of a noise, she
stretched leisurely to a sunrise yoga video, hoping it
would foretell a day without stress.

The first phone call interrupted her *namaste* ending.
Shirley Lazaar was calling before 5 a.m.

"I hope I didn't wake you, Frankie, but I wanted to
call before you head off to church this morning. Do you
have time for a quick coffee?"

She hated to break it to Shirley that church didn't
start for another three hours, so she just agreed to coffee

at six in the shop kitchen, which would give Frankie time for a shower.

Shower massages were the rule on most Sundays, since Frankie had time to enjoy the spray and pulsing water, maybe even warm up her voice for church choir. Today would not be a spa shower day, thanks to Shirley. In fact, the phone call kicked Frankie right back into a state of antsy anticipation, wondering what the news was. She pulled on a church outfit, and donned an apron over it to avoid wearing her morning brew.

Shirley was at the back door a little before six when Frankie waved her inside as she put the finishing touches on two lattes and a plate of Saturday's leftover bakery. Shirley carried herself differently out of uniform; she almost looked relaxed in denim capris, an "Up North" tee, and raffia sun hat. If she hadn't been wearing her gun holster, Frankie would have mistaken her for a tourist.

She slapped the hat on the counter and pulled out a sheaf of papers from a denim tote. She inhaled the latte before taking a sip and scrutinized the baked offerings before choosing a cherry tart and mocha muffin. Frankie wondered at the woman's metabolism after witnessing her eating habits and felt a twinge of envy at the elder officer's lean frame.

Guilt stabbed Frankie, so she retrieved an orange from the cooler and began peeling it into sections. After all, she was going out later to the Oasis Poker Run, where healthy food choices would be non-existent.

Ready with pen and notepad, she nodded at Shirley to offer up her news.

Shirley's eyes gleamed like a hound bearing down on prey. "We've got an ID on the victim. Came in late last night."

"I'm all ears."

"His name is Gerald Sawyer, age 37, from Kingston, Ontario." Shirley paused, took a large bite, and waited for Frankie to write.

"Wait, Ontario? As in Canada?"

Shirley nodded and washed down the bite. "Yes indeed. He works for a shipping company there called Envee Express. Kingston is a major port, so it looks like he works on the docks. We're still gathering information."

"Who identified him?"

"Well, there's a story. Turns out Officer Evans from Grant County has a buddy in Chicago who works at the Port Authority. Evans's friend was in town to pick up some evidence and the two were shooting the breeze about unsolved cases. One story led to another, and the port authority guy recognized Sawyer as a person of interest detained in Chicago a few months back."

"So, you have or have not validated the port authority information?" Frankie wanted factual reporting in her news story.

"We're working on it. But, it's Sunday, so it'll be tomorrow before we get confirmation from Envee Express. Meanwhile, Sawyer's face matches the victim's.

We've sent the vic's fingerprints down to Chicago for a crosscheck. If those come back a match, we won't be contacting Envee at all."

"You think the shipping company might be involved somehow?"

"It's a gopher hole worth poking into, Frankie. We don't want to tip the company off that we're looking into their business." Shirley tossed back the coffee.

"Any news on Jonesy? Did the blood spatter match Sawyer's? Any other evidence inside the truck?" Frankie poised her pen, ready to write again.

"DNA confirmed the blood on the truck matched Sawyer's. One way or another, that truck was involved in the shooting. I'd bet your last butterhorn that the glass particles in the truck bed match the shot-out headlight."

Frankie paused mid-sentence, looked thoughtfully at Shirley, her lips pursed. "Something's bothering me. Jonesy's truck is his baby. He keeps it immaculate, so how did he miss the glass particles in the bed? And, wouldn't he have cleaned the blood spatter if he had shot Sawyer?"

"Good thinking. I agree with you. I don't think Jonesy's our man, especially since we found four sets of prints on the steering wheel. The problem is, one set of prints are Jonesy's but the others prints are not on file." Shirley picked up the three leftover tarts and asked for a to-go bag.

"Yeah, about those fingerprints . . . has anybody checked out Monty as a potential suspect? You know, from what Jenks said about seeing him driving Jonesy's truck?" Frankie wanted to get the most bang for her buck with her bakery bribe.

"We're looking into it. Gotta run now. Tony and I are going on a nature hike out by Devil's Lake."

Frankie thanked Shirley, amazed that she could switch gears from discussing a murder to climbing along the Baraboo bluffs to take in the scenery.

"I wish I could flip a switch like that."

At least she planned to try. It was still more than an hour before she needed to be at Mass. She took a second coffee out to the shop deck, hoping to log some new birds on her life list, but she hadn't made a single checkmark before her phone rang.

Manny Vega was breathless on the other end of the call, anxious to fill in Frankie on his early morning discovery.

"I found an ash pile, boss. It looks like some kids were partying on the property near the east edge of the woods beyond the orchard."

"That area's pretty remote. How do you think they even knew how to get there?"

"There are a lot of trails through that woods. It crosses over into James's land, but it also intersects with the marsh preservation, and that's public land. Area kids would know it." Manny felt certain the vineyard intruder was probably just a partier. "He may have come up to the vineyard on a dare or just wandered in the dark after drinking too much."

"Hmm," Frankie didn't feel as certain as her vineyard manager did. "I hope you're right, Manny. That would make both of us feel better. It doesn't seem right to me though. Why is a partier poking around in the grapevine rows?"

"Just to make us both feel better, I bagged some of the ashes to give to the police, but I can't imagine there's anything to identify. There were charred beer cans laying around, too. I tried not to disturb the area in case the cops want to look for footprints and such." Manny could be counted on to be thorough when it came to vineyard property matters.

"Thanks for letting me know. Maybe we need to discuss putting up a fence. You know how much I hate barbed wire, though. Anyway, I'll be out early tonight to do some work. I need to make some grape notes and get my hands dirty."

Manny laughed. He and Frankie were similar souls; both were intoxicated by the smell of fresh earth and became giddy around nature's plants and critters.

*   *   *

Later that afternoon, Frankie muttered to herself as she poked through her closet, shoving aside one hanger after another in search of something appropriate for the Poker Run so she could blend in. She almost called Carmen several times to borrow the outfit she'd worn on their last excursion to The Oasis, but her mind flipped on her and she continued to browse her wardrobe instead. Posing as a biker chick was out of her comfort zone no matter how much Garrett teased her about it.

Finally settling on a denim sundress she pulled out of a plastic tub from the back of the closet, Frankie giggled. "I think I hear the 1980's calling from a cordless phone and it wants that dress back." She spoke out loud, picturing her first cordless phone, beige with antenna and push buttons, heavy enough to use as a weapon.

She pulled on a light blue tee then pulled the sundress over her head, adjusted the thin straps in place over the tee, and pulled the skirt down over her hips. Thrilled about the loose design that forgave a couple extra pounds, she turned circles in front of the mirror and decided it would do for an outdoor casual summer event. She'd saved the dress years back, telling herself that denim comes back in style frequently and besides, the length was perfect, hanging just below mid-knee.

She shoved her feet into a navy blue pair of Keds and grabbed her sun hat, then thought again. She wasn't going out for a day of sailing or to a church picnic; she'd need a more suitable hat for The Oasis. A bandana wouldn't work well with her getup, so she rummaged through her hat drawer and pulled out a denim ball cap embroidered with tiny flowers. "Good enough."

She raced downstairs to the wine lounge where Garrett was chatting with Peggy at the bar while a group of tasters were finishing a bottle of wine on the other end. Several customers were making final selections before the shop closed. Then she spied Lori Hansen waving her over to the unoccupied register on the bakery side of the business.

"Sorry to bug you, Frankie. Mike and I tried our hand at making dandelion wine and were hoping we might borrow one of your floor corkers for bottling." Lori perched a case of wine on the checkout counter. The Hansens ran the Hotel Divine, a restored historic hotel, now a B and B furnished with Victorian era antiques . They were frequent wine customers, offering guests bottles bearing the Bountiful label.

"Sure, we recently replaced our manual models with high-powered corkers, but I still have the manual corkers at the vineyard, and you're welcome to use one of those. When do you need it?"

"Wednesday would be great and thank you. I'll comp you a bottle or two." Lori winked.

"Better yet, please pass along that chocolate rhubarb cake recipe I've heard rave reviews about." Rhubarb was abundant this time of year and any new recipes were always welcomed. Lori promised she'd have the recipe ready to exchange for the floor corker and left.

Peggy and Garrett turned their attention to Frankie. She gritted her teeth waiting for her mother to make a comment on Frankie's wardrobe choice that was sure to set her hair on fire.

"Well Frankie, don't you look dressed for fun. I hope you two enjoy the Poker Run, but watch your back. I'd leave my purse in the car, if you know what I'm saying," Peggy stage-whispered, eyes wide and brows pointed.

Frankie smiled appreciatively at Peggy. Her mother would never change, and she couldn't imagine any scenario where Peggy would find herself at The Oasis. "I'll be on high alert, Mom," Frankie promised. She was grateful her mother hadn't insulted her outfit.

Garrett looked Frankie over ardently, put both arms around her waist, and smiled warmly. "Why Miss Francine, you look positively delectable," he drawled like a southern gentleman, which made Frankie laugh.

"Seriously though, you look relaxed and carefree, which is a nice change from the past several days." Garrett took her hand and they waved to Peggy on their way out the door.

The Oasis was a happening place and the small country road was lined with vehicles on both grassy shoulders. The parking lot was chock full of motorcycles except for the side lot where a pavilion stood next to a barbecue pit that sent out mouthwatering billows of smoked meat on the breeze.

Carmen and Ryan waved at Frankie and Garrett from a picnic table under the pavilion where they were talking with Grizz and a couple Frankie didn't recognize. Carmen had donned the same outfit from their last visit. Ryan, too, was dressed in biker wear, looking exactly not like a sheep farmer. Frankie couldn't help but notice how comfortable her friends looked. The change of scenery and clothing seemed to transport them back to their youth.

Grizz shook Garrett's hand and looked at Frankie momentarily without recognition. Then he let loose a round of deep chuckles as he patted her shoulder.

"Now this look suits you much better, if I may say so, Frankie." Grizz was obviously having a great afternoon that included a number of drinks, but his comment to Frankie was harmless.

Frankie laughed too. "Where can we get some drinks? Looks like we've got some catching up to do, Garrett."

Circling his thumb and forefinger between his lips, Grizz whistled loud enough to scare away the local wildlife. Customers in the vicinity paused their conversations and the horseshoe throwers stopped their game. Once they noticed it was just Grizz, all activity resumed. He'd gotten the attention of Katie, one of his servers, who trotted over to take their orders.

Carmen gestured toward the couple at the table and introductions commenced. "These are friends of ours from our younger days—Jake and Rosie." Jake looked suspiciously at Garrett after finding out he was the county coroner, but Rosie was cheerful.

"Hope you won't be needed at the Poker Run today, Garrett," she winked meaningfully. "I mean, Grizz's parties have been known to get out of hand."

To Frankie she said, "I've heard a lot about you, and

your business sounds like a winner. Seems like you and Carmen are having a blast. I'll stop by someday with the girls for a wine tasting." She clinked her Corona bottle with Frankie's.

For the next couple of hours, the six of them drank and told stories while Grizz ran back and forth with plates of pulled pork, and mounds of slaw and potato salad for them. Finally Frankie announced she had to use the bathroom and Rosie decided to accompany her.

The buxom woman linked one rose-tattooed arm through Frankie's, laughing as they tried to match each other's strides up the steps and into the dimly lit bar. Rosie led the way, taking Frankie's hand to guide her through the loud crowded interior and down a narrow hallway that ended in two restrooms and a back door to the deck on the riverside.

Just their luck, the bathroom door opened right on top of a raven-haired woman swaying at the sink as she tried to reapply eyeliner and smokey eyeshadow. Frankie couldn't understand why anyone would want to look like a raccoon on purpose, but to each their own. The woman scowled at them as the bump from the door created a long black streak across her face.

"Both stalls are occupied so you should wait in the hall," she offered. Since there was no getting into the cramped room anyway, they closed the door and broke into a fit of giggles, which only made their need to use the facilities a whole lot worse.

Soon the door opened and one of the servers emerged, took a deep breath and steadied herself to jump back into the fray of bodies wanting more drinks and pulling cards for their poker hands, before they headed out to the next bar on the Run.

Rosie graciously offered Frankie first dibs on the bathroom, which she accepted gratefully. When she exited the stall, the woman at the sink had gone, leaving Frankie room to wash and squeeze out the door again to wait for Rosie in the hallway.

Frankie looked out the back door, noticed a number of boats docked along The Oasis pier, and wondered how many people over the capacity limit were here. The back deck was occupied by smokers or friends of smokers chatting away, most with drinks in hand. Beyond the deck were permanent patio tables, some with umbrellas, and a few more picnic tables that descended toward the river. Every square foot of the property was occupied.

Then she saw him. Clay Cooper was standing next to a beautiful blonde woman on the pier. They appeared to be having a heated conversation and their familiarity with one another couldn't be mistaken. The blonde shook her head many times at Clay, placed her hands on his arms and shoulders to soothe him, then squared her own shoulders, raised her chin determinedly and seemed to be lecturing him.

Frankie ducked out the back door for a closer look and wormed her way to the deck railing, but tried to stay out of sight. Clay was mostly turned away from her as he faced the river and the blonde. Frankie fumbled with her phone to find the camera and snapped as many rapid-fire shots of the pair as she could. She couldn't hear any of the conversation and didn't dare go any closer, but she did see the woman hand something to Clay. It could have been anything: a note, a key, a trinket. She didn't know but hoped her phone would capture something useful.

Abruptly, the conversation ended and the blonde climbed into a vintage Chris-Craft Runabout, ripped the engine, and pulled away from the pier before heading north up the river. Clay turned toward the deck, making Frankie's heart pulse hard along her jawline. But Clay was too occupied by his own thoughts, and he trotted doggedly toward his car, which was parked on the edge of the property where no parking existed.

Frankie turned to go back inside but collided into the ample chest of Rosie, who had spotted her on the deck and wondered if all was well. Rosie was a head or so taller than Frankie, and in a scoop-neck tank, Frankie found herself face to face with the sprawling rose garden inked across the woman's chest.

Thankfully Rosie laughed at the situation. "Is everything okay, Frankie? I saw you out here watching those people and taking pictures . . ." she trailed off.

"Let's go back to our table. I'll explain there." She quickly added, "Sorry for running into you. Nice tats though."

To Frankie's surprise, Rosie smacked her bottom. "Thank you. You're not the first woman to admire them," she laughed heartily.

Garrett caught Frankie's glower from several yards away. "Oh oh, I think there's been a change in the weather." His head darted toward the fuming figure of Frankie as she stomped their way.

A chorus of concerned questions greeted her. Frankie pulled out her phone, loaded the camera roll and centered it on the table as she scrolled.

"Clay Cooper and another woman," she seethed.

Garrett put his arm on hers to calm her fuming. "There's no telling what's going on here. Maybe nothing. Probably nothing?"

"Right, Garrett, and if your daughter were dating Clay . . ."

Garrett nodded. He would have confronted Clay; that was certain.

Carmen picked up the phone. "Let's get Grizz over here and see if he knows the woman."

Grizz looked over the photos carefully. "I've not seen either of them before. But the fact that the blonde showed up here in a boat—a very expensive boat mind you . . . Well, she's probably from the city and owns one of the high end cottages or summer houses at the far northern end of the river where it empties into the lake."

Frankie confirmed that the speed boat went that direction. "But how in the world would Clay, a sheep shearer, someone who's only been in the area a couple of months, know this woman? Where would their paths have crossed?"

Frankie explained that Clay was staying in a rattrap shack in the swamplands near Lake Loki. "He's rented the place for the summer from the Stauffers at Mischief Resort. There are three hired hands renting out there."

Grizz assumed a knowing look as he stroked his chin and looked out toward the river. "I've seen a lot of dirty business coming here from the city. A lot of rich folks look for someone who wants to make a quick buck and doesn't mind getting their hands dirty to do it. Maybe that's what this is all about."

Garrett interjected that they couldn't know for sure. "And it's probably not worth digging into, Frankie."

Grizz agreed. "If I were you Frankie, I'd stay as far away from this as possible. Nothing good can come from poking around in it."

Frankie raised blazing green eyes to Grizz and Garrett. "But this involves my daughter. Don't ask me not to look into it."

Chapter 16

Stones of small worth may lie unseen by day,
But night itself does the rich gem betray.
- Abraham Cowley

The party mood had soured and Frankie's temporary tipsy bliss had been replaced by a smack from reality. It was time to work out her frustrations in the vineyard while there was still daylight.

She and Garrett basked in the calm quiet beauty at Bountiful in contrast to the noisy raucous atmosphere at The Oasis. They both breathed in the fresh air, gazed at the even rows of green grapevines, and admired the rolling hills that wound out to the orchard.

Garrett took Frankie into his arms and stroked her hair. "Now this property would be an ideal place for you to build a house, Miss Francine. Who wouldn't want to wake up here every morning?"

"Maybe someday, Garrett, maybe someday." Frankie allowed herself a few moments to daydream, then turned her attention toward the orchard.

"Well, guess we better get to it. Manny left some of

the mulch mix for me to spread in the herb garden. It's piled behind the equipment shed."

The pair stopped enroute to pick up rakes, shovels, and a wheelbarrow, then sauntered behind the shed adjacent to Manny's office. They donned work gloves and Frankie handed Garrett a face mask to keep out the dry mulch particles.

Garrett grinned at the proffered mask. "Nothing worse than dried doo-doo up your nose!"

Frankie made a face beneath her mask but her eyes smiled playfully. They started shoveling mulch into the wheelbarrow, and in no time, they had a heaped up load which Garrett maneuvered between the orchard and top side of the vineyard to the framed herb patch.

Frankie couldn't help but smile at the newest addition to the Bountiful farm that she and Garrett had crafted together last month. Using a design from a New England cottage garden, the herbs were laid out in a lovely mosaic with a fieldstone pathway winding around the framed beds. The whole garden was bordered with zinnias, delphiniums, bee balm, lantana, and licorice plants to provide feasts for honeybees, butterflies, and hummingbirds. An old step ladder sat in one corner for nasturtiums to climb around, and garden gnomes squatted here and there to tend the plants or take naps among the flora.

Garrett dumped half the load at one end, then headed to the opposite end so the two could meet in the middle.

Frankie used a trowel to carefully dig the mixture into the soil around the plants. This was a perfect evening or early morning activity when the summer temps had moderated. Unfortunately, the mosquitos were looking for a free meal so the two were thankful they remembered to wear long sleeves and tuck their pants into their socks. They applied mosquito repellent to their faces, especially around their ears where the pesky fliers congregated. It had been more than a week since the last good rain, which made for the best time to spread the dry compost with minimal mosquitos.

Frankie swatted at one annoying bug when she was blinded by a brilliant particle in the soil that had caught the sun's rays. Forgetting the mosquito, she nudged a pebble from the outskirts of the oregano and blew off manure particles. It looked like a small clear rock, quartz maybe. She settled it into an empty pocket of her garden apron to look at later and resumed her work.

Minutes later, Garrett called out from the parsley patch down the way. "Frankie, can you come here for a second? I want to show you something."

She stood, cursed her leg muscles that had spasmed from squatting, and made her way to the parsley. Garrett stood too, briefly rubbed his lower back, and held out his gloved hand to Frankie.

"I found two interesting stones in the mulch just now. What do you think?" The stones looked similar in size and clarity to the one she'd just found in the oregano.

Curiosity took precedence over spreading mulch, and the two walked over to one of the soaker hoses by the border and washed the rocks for a closer examination.

The three stones were somewhat round and had a greenish hue. Frankie and Garrett shrugged, looked at the stones again, and spoke at the same time.

"Let's keep looking. There might be more."

"Oh my God, is this why someone was prowling around my vineyard?"

Garrett notified Alonzo and the two continued digging carefully through the mulch.

"This is nuts, Garrett. We need a strainer to make this go faster. I have some in the wine lab." Frankie scampered that direction, her mind on fire with ideas. *Could these rocks be diamonds or some other precious gem? What were they doing in her mulch pile?*

She quickly returned with three strainers used for fruit mash in the winery and handed one to Garrett. "If these are diamonds, I think I know why there was a shooting at the O'Connor farm. Manny got the manure from there. This has to be connected."

Garrett agreed. "Let's keep at it. There's a lot of mulch here to sift through."

They worked quietly and industriously, occasionally shouting out the discovery of another clear stone.

By the time Alonzo arrived, out of uniform in old jeans and a long sleeved denim shirt, they had a small collection to show him.

The sheriff let out a long low whistle. "We need to get these to a lab pronto to see what exactly we have here, but I think you're right. This might be connected to the murder and could be the motive."

He picked up a strainer and started sifting through the remaining mulch in the wheelbarrow. "How much more of this is there, Frankie?" They were losing daylight quickly now.

"Bad news, Lon. There's still a large pile behind the shed over there." She gestured past the orchard. "The worst part is that a lot of it has been spread in the vineyard and around the new fruit trees in the orchard already."

"I'm going to send out a couple officers tomorrow morning to do some raking and sifting. That okay with you?" Lon knew she was protective of her property and the fruits were her babies as well as her livelihood.

Frankie nodded. "I guess so, but I'd like to be here to supervise. I want to show them how to work around the vines so they don't hurt them. Besides, I can help, too."

Garrett laughed. "That's what a good investigator would say."

Lon smirked and elbowed Garrett, but he knew Frankie would not be deterred.

"Okay, how about I get my people out here early? Say seven a.m.?"

Frankie agreed, knowing full well that she, Manny, and his workers would already be hard at it long before the officers showed up.

Alonzo left with a small pail full of stones.

"What time should I be here in the morning to help, Miss Francine?" Garrett's honeyed eyes gleamed.

Frankie, hands on hips, pretended to be offended, then broke out into giggles. "I guess you know me pretty well, G. I plan to be out here at first light. And, I'm going to let Manny know, too. We'll have a lot of the vineyard sifting done by the time Lon's guys arrive."

Garrett kissed her firmly as they walked back to his truck, hand in hand. On the ride back to town, Frankie reached into her apron pocket and pulled out a wayward stone.

"Oops, guess Alonzo missed one."

Garrett pretended surprise. "I bet I know your plans for the rest of the night. Computer searching?" He reached over and patted her leg. "How about an extra investigator? I'll grab my personal laptop and head over."

To say Frankie was excited would be a gross understatement. The prospect of looking up gems and missing gem shipments produced a wave of questions and adrenaline coursing through her body. The fact that Garrett was a willing accomplice made it that much more enticing.

She stopped in the dark Bubble and Bake kitchen, scooped up a leftover charcuterie, cheese, and veggie platter; snatched a box of crackers from the pantry and a bottle of Two Pear Chardonnay, Garrett's favorite, and vaulted up the stairs. Violet was still on her girls' getaway, but could be arriving home anytime. Of course, she hadn't been in touch, so Frankie sent a text casually asking if she was having fun and what time she could be expected home.

Twenty minutes later, Garrett was bounding up the apartment stairs, thrilled to see the platter of snacks and two glasses of wine on the breakfast bar. He plunked down his laptop across from hers and grabbed a seat.

Frankie's phone pinged. It was Violet saying not to wait up for her. She figured it would be past midnight before she got home. "It's Violet, saying she'll be home late. At least she messaged me, I guess." Frankie frowned, worried about her youngest daughter. The sooner she got to the bottom of this crime, the better, and nothing helped Frankie more than research.

The pair nibbled on snacks, sipped wine, occasionally jotted a note, and exchanged worthwhile bits and pieces. It was possible the stones they found were green diamonds but they could also be sapphire, peridot, or just quartz.

Garrett told Frankie he was shifting his search to jewel thefts on a notion that maybe it was the common denominator in the two fertilizer truck hijackings.

Minutes later the two looked up at each other in exclamation. "I found something," they said at the same time. "You go first," they echoed.

Garrett turned his screen to face Frankie. "Look at this. Green diamonds were found in a mud bog last fall in Arkansas." Frankie looked at the photos taken of the raw gems.

"They certainly look like this one, don't you think?"

He agreed. "There's more. The locals hired to excavate the diamonds finished in May, after a winter hiatus. They were transporting them to Chicago when they got into an accident on a rural road, rolled down an embankment, tipped over, and were seriously injured. Someone who witnessed the accident called 911, but when the police arrived, the witness was gone, and so were the diamonds!"

Frankie jumped off the stool. "Come here; I want to show you something." She pulled Garrett by the hand and led him into her bedroom.

"Wow, Miss Francine, if I had known investigating would get you this excited, I would have come over weeks ago," he teased.

She gave him a look, opened her closet, and pulled out a cork board easel with pictures, notes, and strings crossing every which way.

"You made a crime board?" He couldn't have been more dumbfounded.

"I've never done this before, but this case is so complicated. I mean there's so many suspects, and I was watching a detective show one night, and thought—that's what I need. All the good detectives use them."

Garrett laughed and almost couldn't stop, but saw Frankie's hurt expression and gently pulled her in for a warm hug. "Sorry. This is great Frankie. It's just that you never cease to surprise me." He asked her to go over the details with him.

"Here's the O'Connor hired hands. We know Goat had an alibi since he was in a bar fight that night, and he's right-handed, so he couldn't have shot the handgun used to kill Sawyer. I don't think Bucky and Reggie should be suspects, even though Bucky ran from the cops, but that's because he'd been driving without a license. That leaves Jonesy and Clay."

"But Clay has an alibi," Garrett interjected. "Provided by your daughter."

Frankie sighed. "Right. So that leaves Jonesy. Neither Shirley nor I think he's the killer. There are three other sets of fingerprints in his truck. But why won't he tell the police what he knows? He must be protecting someone."

"Could be. But you can't clear Bucky and Reggie without more information." Garrett read through more of the notes on the board. "Okay. So you have a connection going to the Turner farm with a lot of question marks. Tell me about this."

"Well, the Turner family is a hot mess. Dewey seems to have it out for Ryan. This guy, Jenks, said Dewey hired his shearing team out from under Ryan. Jenks also told me that this hand, who goes by Monty or Saint, borrowed Jonesy's truck the night of the shooting."

"Did you tell Alonzo that?"

Frankie nodded. "I did. That was the same day that Sonny and I got shot at with the BB gun on the Turner property."

"Why did you include these details?" Garrett pointed at the photos of Clay, Monty, and Jenks.

"Well, Jenks and Clay are both Australian. Monty is Canadian, according to Jenks. I think it's an odd connection, especially now, after my last search." She motioned him back out to the kitchen counter.

While Garrett discovered the Arkansas green diamond theft, Frankie had been poking around for information on Envee Express, the shipping company Sawyer worked for.

"Envee Express is an American company, but it's a subsidiary of Five Starr Woolens, which is an Australian corporation." The more Frankie spoke, the more authoritative she sounded. Garrett admired her adeptness at gathering and combining facts.

Frankie added a card to the board for Envee Express and Five Starr. She pinned a new card for the Arkansas diamond accident and theft.

Underneath Clay's photo was a picture of the blonde he'd met with at The Oasis with more question marks.

"You should show your board to Shirley. I mean, the department may already have most of this information, but they may not have made the same connections as you."

He pointed at a dark, fuzzy photo off to one side by itself. "What's this?"

"That's the surveillance photo from my vineyard. We still don't know who that is, but I'm pretty sure I know what they were looking for."

"Okay. It seems like we've got motive for murder. We know the weapon is a .480 Ruger, and we haven't found it.

Jonesy, like most of the guys around here, owns a shotgun, but he could own a handgun, too. It was likely ditched somewhere, though."

Frankie picked up the discussion. "A lot of people had opportunity, including Jonesy and the Turner hands. Heck, maybe even the Turner men for that matter. But, we have to tie them to Sawyer and the stolen diamonds."

Garrett jabbed a finger at the vineyard security cam photo. "If only we could identify this person."

They were both spent for the night. Garrett kissed Frankie a long leisurely goodnight, told her to be careful, and said he'd see her bright and early at Bountiful.

Frankie checked the kitchen clock. Eleven p.m. She figured her mind would just somersault the case details around her brain in a continuous swirl, so she might as well wait for Violet to come home.

A tired and tipsy Violet quietly came through the living room an hour later, trying to tiptoe past Frankie who was dozing under a lightweight throw on the couch. Frankie's mother's intuition kicked in, however.

"Hi Violet," she whispered. "Come sit by me. Did you have a good weekend?"

Violet nodded, but sat on the recliner across from the couch. "We had a great time, Mom. But, I have to get up early, so I'm heading to bed. Can we catch up tomorrow?"

Frankie sat up straight and set aside the throw, then scrutinized her daughter. Violet looked flushed, and Frankie suspected the girls must have been hanging out at a bar somewhere before calling it a night. Worry overtook her and she leaned toward Violet and took both of her hands in her own.

"You know, I only ever want what's best for you. I want you to be happy—happy and safe. I hope you know that."

Violet looked down at their hands, her head bowed. Frankie noticed she was wearing a necklace that looked new. She clasped the pendant in her fingers and examined it. It was a four-leaf clover, perhaps made from jade. She couldn't tell in the low light.

Violet stammered, her eyes fixed on her mother's hand. "Clay gave this to me. He said I was his good luck charm."

Now was not the time for an interrogation, so Frankie logged the information and wished Violet a good night.

"I'll be up early in the morning. I have some work to catch up on at the vineyard, so maybe I'll see you at the lab." Frankie did her best to sound nonchalant. Now was not the time to talk about the gems in the manure pile.

* * *

Interlude:

That evening, Neill Starr found himself once more sitting at his office desk staring out into the harbor. Another 24 hours had passed and he'd heard from nobody, not Sawyer, not Melanie. He tossed back a second scotch, drummed his fingers on the desk, and looked out where dark sky met darker water. What could possibly be delaying things? Especially when he was so close to getting exactly what he wanted.

He swore, jerked open his desk drawer, moved a latch at the back, and opened a hidden drawer where he grabbed one of three burner phones. He hadn't spoken to her since things ended badly between them last month, but now he had no choice. Sawyer was incommunicado and Neill had to talk to someone.

He swore louder and punched in her number.

"What is it?" The voice on the other end was silky and icy at the same time.

"Where the hell have you been, anyway? I need to know what's going on. Nobody's been to the docks." Starr knew his voice was harried from panic and slurred from scotch.

It didn't help matters in the least that she laughed curtly in his ear. "Poor cell service on this end. We're not dealing with a finished product, so it's going to take longer. I thought you'd figure that out . . ." she trailed off but her voice remained calm, cool, passive.

It only made Starr more agitated. "How the hell was I supposed to know?"

She didn't dare use Sawyer's name, even on a burner phone. But the obvious hung in the dead air. Shouldn't Sawyer have told Starr about the delay?

"When, then?" He sounded like a beggar.

"Two or three more days." She hung up.

Starr cussed a stream of curses at the empty office, all aimed at her and Sawyer. He felt wildly out of control, and he loathed the feeling almost as much as he loathed the man standing in his doorway.

"Anything wrong, little brother?" Sam Starr, debonair and gallant in his Armani suit and leather wingtips, strode across the office to stand beside Neill where he was pouring a third scotch.

"Drink?" Neill asked and handed the tumbler to a nodding Sam.

"What's the word on your shipment?" Sam gave him a sideways glance, a look of amusement in his eyes.

Neill swore again. "It's going to take a little longer, but it's going to happen. You mark my words."

Sam toasted his little brother, but the gesture was empty and mocking. "To endings and beginnings," Sam smiled and held out a manicured hand to shake Neill's, a reminder of the deal they'd made.

Neill hated him. He hated that Sam was given everything by virtue of being born first. That while Neill worked his way up in the company from the bottom rung, everything came easily to his older brother.

Neill clasped Sam's hand, making sure to scrape his own calloused hand against the silky smooth one, a reminder of the physical strength Neill possessed in contrast to his brother's charisma and intellect.

Sam narrowed his eyes as he dropped his brother's hand. He stood nearly a head taller than Neill and believed himself superior in every way. Even now, Neill's disheveled appearance couldn't be offset by his expensive suit, nor could the calloused hands become elegant, adorned by the emerald ring he wore. Neill would never be better than a dock worker in Sam's opinion.

Sam set the empty glass cooly on the desk, and looked down sharply at his brother. His voice conveyed something akin to amusement. "I expect you'll keep me posted, Mate."

Chapter 17

A gem cannot be polished without friction,
nor a man perfected without trials.
- Lucius Annaeus Seneca

Garrett was already waiting in the driveway when Frankie's SUV slid in to park beside his truck. Despite the early hour, Nelson and Zane were already at work. She'd managed to make coffee for her and Garrett before leaving, but at the last minute decided to stop at the drive-thru for fast food breakfast sandwiches—something she deemed distasteful when one owns a bakery.

Garrett laughed and made a face when she held up the drive-thru bag. He encircled his arms around her and drew her in close. "Did Violet get home okay?"

It was Frankie's turn to grimace. She told Garrett about the clover necklace from Clay, that she suspected Violet had been drinking, but that she didn't hash over anything with her.

"Good for you. I know that couldn't have been easy, but it's for the best until you have a clearer head."

Turning toward the wine lab, she said, "I'll meet you

in the vineyard rows in a few minutes. I want to talk to Nelson and Zane first."

Garrett said he'd grab the tools they used yesterday and see her in a bit.

Nelson and Zane, energy drinks in hand, looked chipper as usual. They were morning people for the most part—Nelson more than Zane, but since they carpooled, Nelson usually set their working hours.

"Good morning, Ms. Champagne. What brings you out here so early?" Nelson's business formality was the norm.

Frankie confidentially filled them in on the underhanded happenings at Bountiful. Both gasped in surprise.

"Is there anything we can do to help?" Nelson asked.

"Yes, there is." She hesitated. "I hate to ask you this, but please don't say anything to Violet. She's been gone all weekend and I haven't had a chance to talk to her. She needs to hear this from me."

They nodded earnestly, and Frankie had one more clandestine request to make. She pulled out her cell and presented the photos of Clay and the blonde before her two scientists. "I want to find out who this woman is with Clay Cooper. And, I want to find out more about Clay, too." She gazed sternly into each one's eyes. "You don't have to do this, but if you do, I want it to stay among us, and only us."

Nelson appeared startled. "You should know by now,

Ms. Champagne, we are willing to serve." He bowed in deference, making Frankie chuckle.

Zane added, "If there's anything to be found on Clay, we'll find it. We have our ways." He produced a foreign accent, rapidly raising and lowering his eyebrows simultaneously.

She placed a hand on each one of them. "You two are the best. Now, I need to get out to the vineyard and get going on gem hunting before the police arrive. I'll text you the photos." Hesitating a moment at the door, she turned back and pressed her lips together. "Don't do anything illegal though."

In the vineyard, Manny, Gil, and Rico were already hard at work, sifting mulch mixture in the strainers. She wished them good morning and thanked them for coming in early to do the "dirty work" before seven.

Manny stood up and followed Frankie to the next row where Garrett was trawling through manure. "So I guess we know what the prowler was after." Manny was on edge. He'd been in situations before where he and people who looked like him were blamed for things they hadn't had any part in.

Frankie put her hand on his forearm. "It's going to be okay, Manny. But, I do have a question for you—which hands at the O'Connors' saw you loading manure?"

Manny stared off into the distance, thinking. "Let's see. The shooting was Saturday. I came by on Thursday to pick up manure. It was Reggie who showed me where the driest stuff was that would be best for the vineyard. I drove down to the lean-to and shoveled the stuff right into the bed of my truck.

He scratched his head a minute, thinking. "I mean, there were a lot of people around. I saw Ryan standing in the pasture with Jonesy. We waved at each other but didn't talk. I think Goat was working in the pasture."

"What about Clay or Bucky?" Frankie sucked in her breath.

Manny shook his head. "Maybe, but I don't know either one of them or even what they look like."

"Did you notice a pallet with a big pile of manure stacked on it for pick up?"

Manny couldn't remember and huffed at himself for not being more helpful.

"It's okay. I'm going to ask Ryan, too. We haven't told him yet what's going on, but we should fill him in." She looked from Manny to Garrett for agreement and they both nodded.

By the time Alonzo and two officers descended the hill toward the orchard, Frankie and her crew had finished combing the vineyard and were straining the last of the composted mulch around the young fruit trees.

Alonzo stood with his hands on his hips. "Looks like most of our work is done, huh?"

Frankie cocked her head toward the equipment shed. "The last of the compost is behind the shed in a pile. We wanted to get a head start on the vineyard and orchard, you know, to keep the roots from getting damaged." She was matter-of-fact, coming from the perspective of a farmer, and Alonzo couldn't find fault with her actions.

The sheriff sent Officer Green and the summer recruit to get started on the shed pile, Manny trailing behind them.

Frankie pulled a few rocks from her work apron and handed them to Lon. "We didn't find anything in the vineyard, so the prowler probably got away with those. But here's a few from around the new trees."

He looked at her and Garrett. "Have either of you filled in Ryan?"

They shook their heads, wondering if they should tell Lon what they discovered on the internet last night. Garrett waited for Frankie to make the call.

"We think we should talk to Ryan, don't you Lon? Garrett and I did some internet snooping last night and found this." She pulled out a printed copy of the article on the missing Arkansas green diamonds, even amazing Garrett with her candor.

"Huh," Alonzo shook his head and pocketed the article. He waggled a finger in Garrett's face. "It doesn't surprise me in the least that Frankie is playing amateur detective, but you? I'll say it again: If you really care about her, you won't encourage this kind of malarkey."

Frankie stood between the two men, pushed them apart, and looked directly into their chests. She almost laughed at the situation but then raised her chin defiantly. "Look Lon, you may not like it, but I'm just trying to help. Ryan and Carmen are my dearest friends. Someone's been trespassing in my vineyard, and I got shot at!"

"Which is why you should butt out and let us do our job." He looked again at Garrett. "And you should know better." Lon retreated to his jeep and left the officers behind to comb the mulch.

Frankie beat it to the jeep on Lon's tail. "Any updates you can share?" She hesitated. "Anything at all about Clay Cooper?"

Lon placed one huge hand on her shoulder, covering it entirely. His voice was gentle and kind. "Look Frankie, I know how worried you are about Violet, and I promise I'll let you know if she's in danger in any way from Cooper, but we've found nothing on him. He's not on social media and has trekked all over the U.S. the past two years—hasn't left a trail. We showed his photo to the Grant County farmer, and he didn't know Clay."

Frankie was about to protest but Lon squelched it. "That doesn't mean we're not still looking. I'll let you know when there's something to know." He climbed into the jeep and shut the door.

Less than an hour later, the officers summoned Frankie and Garrett from the orchard where they were sitting with their cold breakfast sandwiches. Since Manny was working with the officers, they must have decided a report was expected.

Green held out his hand, revealing several marble-sized stones and three that were larger than a golf ball. "We're going back to the department now to get these logged as evidence. We'll keep you posted, Ms. Champagne."

Green had been schooled once by Frankie at a crime scene a few months back, and he hadn't underestimated her ever since. If only Alonzo had the same respect for her skills of observation, she thought. Their encounter made her sullen. She didn't want Garrett under fire professionally; she just wanted Lon to be the friend he'd always been to her in the old days. Was that too much to ask?

Frankie excused herself to the restroom and returned to find Garrett ending a phone call.

"That was Alonzo. He said he's going to talk to Ryan this morning and asked if we'd wait until he had a chance to do so."

"G, I'm sorry to put you in the middle of my squabble with Lon." She took his hand in hers, but he pulled back and gave her a little punch in the shoulder.

"Good grief, Miss Francine, I can handle the sheriff. Don't worry about my job. You know he's always going to be protective of you. He doesn't see you the way I do. To him, you might always be the damsel in distress that needs to be saved." Garrett kissed her cheek.

"Well then, I guess we both better get to work. I've got pastries to make today. The July 4th celebration is just around the corner and I'm going to need every butterhorn

I can muster for it. And, Hannah Turner ordered some for the farm breakfast, too." She gave him a smooch on the lips and they walked arm-in-arm to their vehicles. The weather promised to turn up the heat, and Frankie's day was about to rise to a fever pitch.

Chapter 18

Before you can see the light, you have to deal with the darkness.
— Dan Millman

The Bubble and Bake women were in a natural baking rhythm when Carmen and Frankie received phone messages at the same time. It was Ryan and he wanted to talk with them as soon as they could take a break.

The two partners looked at each other. "I'm almost done with these donut holes for tomorrow, but I still have dough to make before Tia arrives this afternoon to make tarts." Carmen looked at her list. "And it would be nice if I got going on Wednesday's order for the July 4th committee meeting." She blew a tendril of damp hair off her face.

The temperature was warm and humid, and the weather looked like it would stagnate for the week. Summer made for uncomfortable work in the Bubble and Bake kitchen. It was next to impossible to keep the place cool, no matter how many fans whirled around the ceiling. The AC was only meant to keep customers happy in the retail area, so, like it or not, the partners decided to block off the front from the kitchen with a pocket door during the summer. It was simply too expensive and a waste of energy to run AC into the baking area.

Frankie looked at her recipe card, sticky with brown sugar and butter. She was making butterhorns like an automaton. "I'm going to be awhile with these butterhorns. I really can't leave them. I guess we'll have to talk to Ryan later?" She wanted her friend to make the decision; Ryan was Carmen's husband after all, and she would know the best course to follow. Still, the call must mean that Alonzo had filled Ryan in. Frankie was chomping at the bit for an update.

"I'll call him right now and see if we can talk this afternoon." Carmen was back in the kitchen a few minutes later, ready to burst.

"Ryan remembered that he had a trail cam at the edge of our property, down by the Turner farm. About a year ago, we had a few sheep go missing, so he wanted to keep an eye out in case the Turners were involved somehow. But, we haven't lost any more sheep, so he forgot about the camera."

Frankie picked up on cue. "You mean Ryan might have footage from the night of the shooting? Or maybe even something showing who shot at me and Sonny?"

"Bingo. I told him we'd meet him at home after we're done with all this." She spread her arms wide at the array of preparation happening in the kitchen.

Tess piped up. "If you want to go, I can make the dough for the tarts, and I can finish these butterhorns. I'm here all day, and we're basically set for tomorrow."

As much as the two wanted to jump ship, their responsible business-owner side won the moment. Frankie scampered over to Tess for a hug. "You're such a dear to help us, but we're going to finish what we're working on here, and then you can take over. Meanwhile, take a break Tess. It's only going to get hotter in here, and you've got a long day ahead." For a moment, Frankie registered that Tess was arriving earlier to the shop lately and made a mental note to find out her reasons.

After stopping at Tyke's Deli on Whitman Avenue around 1 p.m., the women drove in tandem out to the farm, pulling up next to the house where Ryan was ready to devour lunch and fill them in. Sonny was sleeping peacefully on the screened-in porch and raised his head heartily when he felt Frankie lovingly stroke his fur. She was pleased that Sonny wasn't afraid of her and didn't seem to associate her with being injured.

Ryan offered Carmen a hasty kiss and small, tight squeeze, then the three hurried to the table and ate, talking between bites. When Ryan jabbered about the gems discovered in the sheep manure, Carmen jerked her hand in the air to cut off the discussion.

"What are you talking about, and how come you know about this and I don't?" Carmen pointed a finger at Frankie.

Frankie gulped air, almost choked on her salad, but Ryan saved the day. "Sorry, honey. Frankie found the gems but was told she couldn't talk about it, not even to me, until Alonzo notified me."

Carmen wasn't letting that slide, and she spoke louder and faster. "Since when do you do what you're supposed to do, Frankie? And you . . ." she shot a glare at her husband, "why didn't you tell me this when I called you from the shop, huh?"

Ryan grinned and held his wife's hand. "There was so much to tell you, and I thought it would keep until we could sit down and sort it all out."

She made a face, but sat back down. "Ok. Let's sort it out."

Neither Ryan nor Carmen could offer any theories as to how green diamonds, if that's what they were, had found their way into the O'Connor sheep manure. While Carmen suspected the Turners were somehow involved, Ryan determined the most logical explanation was that one of the hired hands was a rat.

"A criminal rat, Ryan. But which one?" Frankie weighed in, then changed the subject. "The videos from your property line?"

Ryan confessed that it had been nearly a year since he looked at the trail camera footage, but since it was date and time stamped, they could probably skip to the week of Sawyer's shooting through the day Frankie and Sonny were attacked.

Nothing showed up during daylight on June 7th, but a dark truck rolled into view on the dirt lane between the two farms at 11:30 p.m.

"Could this be Jonesy's truck?" Frankie wondered.

"I remember what Jenks said about it. That it's so shiny, you can tell it's Jonesy's truck, even in the dark."

Ryan nodded. "Looks like it could be. But, it could also belong to one of the Turners. Black trucks are a dime a dozen. Hell, it could even be my truck, Frankie." Ryan frowned.

The footage continued to roll without any action, so Ryan forwarded it for several minutes at a time, stopping when it picked up movement. He backed up the film. Someone had exited the passenger side of the truck. In the low light, they could see the figure was a woman with long hair held back from her forehead by a headband. She was slender, wore jeans, a light-colored blouse, and flip flops. She gazed up at the night sky, smiling, speaking now and then. But to whom?

The driver exited the truck, but stood in shadow the whole time. From the camera angle, he appeared to be a little shorter than the woman, but wore a hoodie and cowboy boots.

"Does this guy look like your vineyard intruder?" Carmen wondered.

Frankie shrugged. "We'd have to compare footage. Even then, we might not be able to tell. These cameras don't take the best video. Do either of you recognize the woman? Is she one of the Turners?"

Ryan and Carmen shook their heads and shrugged. They continued to roll through the video, pausing from time to time, but seeing nothing helpful until 3:30 a.m.

flashed on the screen. The truck was on the move! Did that mean this was the truck used to murder Sawyer?

Ryan backed up several minutes and rolled it at half-speed while they watched for anything revealing. A flash of light appeared in the frame at 3:27. A second vehicle arrived in the lane. It was coming in hot, almost rear-ended the truck, then reversed course and parked so only its front bumper and a partial hood were in view, enough to tell it was a car rather than a truck.

A hooded figure flashed past the camera, stopped near the driver of the truck, and shoved him into the front door. The driver shoved back. The two people were about the same height and build. Go figure. But, that ruled out the tall, lanky Jonesy anyway.

The person doing the shoving approached the female, pointed to the car, and she quickly went toward it. Then, the shover presumably got into the truck with the driver and left. The car disappeared from the camera's view just after the truck left. They couldn't tell if the woman was driving or if a fourth figure was at the scene. Nothing else of interest showed up that day.

In fact, nothing else of interest other than white-tailed deer, some cats, a few bats, and a possible coyote on the hunt showed up on camera through the day of the BB gun incident. The camera did pick up Frankie and Sonny walking, then dashing for cover behind the brush pile, but the shooter remained out of sight.

Well, at least the footage might be helpful to the police.

Again, Frankie hoped their sophisticated equipment might uncover more details.

"Before you turn that over to the police, Ryan, could you make a copy of it? I think I'd like to watch it again with Garrett. He might see something we're missing."

She paused a moment, pondering the latest information, wondering how to assemble all the pieces. "Hey, Ryan? What happened to the manure the fertilizer guy was supposed to pick up?"

Ryan looked confused, then comprehension dawned. "The police examined it since it was part of a crime scene, but they never said anything about it. It's still sitting on the pallet for the next pick up."

"Well, I bet they comb through it on their next visit when they pick up the video footage. Let me know if they find anything."

Frankie said her goodbyes, happy to be back in Carmen's good graces. She told her about her late-night encounter with Violet and the lucky clover necklace, rolling her eyes when she repeated Violet's words that she was Clay's "good luck charm."

Carmen gasped. "So, Clay was with Violet at least part of the weekend, but he must have left early to meet Blondie at The Oasis yesterday. I wonder what it all means."

"I've got Nelson and Zane snooping around the internet to see if anything turns up on Clay or the blonde. I sent them the photos. Keep you posted." Frankie needed to get back to Bubble and Bake to run payroll. She'd lost track of the calendar, but received a text from Tara asking when she could stop by for her check. "Better get back to the shop. I'll bring Tia home after I run checks; I'd like to take Sonny out for a leisurely stroll anyway."

*   *   *

Tara was sitting at the Bubble and Bake kitchen counter talking animatedly to Tess when Frankie ambled in the back door. She gave Tia an attentive hug, followed by a compliment on the pan dulces: traditional Mexican pastries that were works of art she'd concocted. Slowly but surely, the bakery had expanded its cultural offerings, thanks to Tess, Tia, and Aunt CeCe.

"I'm going to run payroll right away, Tara. I got way behind today. Sorry."

Tara barely acknowledged her boss but continued her stream of conversation with Tess, something about an African studies class she'd taken that year. Apparently, Tara was sharing what she learned while Tess was confirming or revising the information based on her real-life experiences.

Frankie retreated to the office alcove where Sundae was snuggled next to the computer on the desktop, soaking in the warmth. *Leave it to a cat to locate the hottest spot for a nap, even on a warm summer day!* At least Sundae had become less agitated the last two days, so maybe her time was about over. She did look awfully cute in the little dish towel diaper she was wearing.

A bouncy phone tune sounded before Frankie even opened the payroll program. It was an unknown number and she almost let it go to voicemail but for the tingle she felt on the back of her neck.

"Hello." She used the annoyed voice to answer numbers she didn't recognize.

"Frankie Champagne?" A gruff yet familiar voice questioned.

"Yes?"

"It's Grizz from The Oasis."

The prickly sensation elevated a notch. "Yes, hello Grizz. What can I do for you?"

"I kept thinking about that blonde woman and your daughter's situation, so I asked around, quiet-like, you know. Anyway, people have seen her on the lake and river the past week or so. Nobody knows her name but they say she's Aussie. Supposed to be here for a business conference."

"A business conference in Deep Lakes?" The only conferences Frankie knew of in town were associated with fishing, hunting, and boating. Of course, if hotels were booked up in the area, the woman might have been forced to stay further from the city.

"Thanks for the information, Grizz. I appreciate it, and it might help." Frankie was sincere.

"Hey, Frankie. I understand. I have a daughter, too. If someone was doing her wrong, they'd have a lot to answer for, and it wouldn't be pretty. Let me know if you need anything."

Frankie wouldn't want to be on Grizz's bad side. He was the picture of intimidation, and he had a whole posse of the same kinds of friends at his disposal.

Brow furrowed, she sent herself a text logging the information about the blonde. It wasn't much to go on, but the Aussies were multiplying like face cards in a poker hand. If she were a gambler, she'd bet the house the Aussies were up to their Outbacks involving the crime at the farm.

She wanted to call Shirley to see if they could swap information, especially since Garrett suggested she show the detective her crime board, but she didn't want to put off Tara for too long or subject Tess to her endless questions on Africa.

In less than half an hour, a handful of envelopes in tow, Frankie heard chatter coming from the wine lounge and walked that way. She set paychecks in front of Tia and Tess, who were taking a break from the heat, sipping on iced tea. "Okay, you two, where's Tara? Did you chase her away?" Frankie snorted.

Tess pointed to the restroom just as Tara exited, pouting. Frankie figured it was time to relieve the other women of the Tara drama hour. She rose and met the young beauty halfway, nudged her back into the shop kitchen, and pulled a pitcher of tea and lemonade from the cooler.

"How come you look so down? When I left you, it looked like you and Tess were having a marvelous discussion." Frankie sounded more like a teacher than a mother.

Tara moped. "They asked me about my weekend and it brought up bad memories."

"You didn't have fun on your girls' getaway?" Frankie mixed lemonade and tea together in two tall glasses and slid one across the counter to Tara as she sat down.

Tara frowned deeply. "If you could call it that. The girls part, I mean. It was supposed to be just the four of us." She looked at Frankie expectantly, clearly meaning she wouldn't say more without prompting.

Frankie pretended she didn't know that Clay had intruded on their fun. "I haven't had time to chat with Violet. So, who else was on your getaway?" She was going to make certain her questions were specific.

"Clay and his friend showed up on Saturday. All our plans went out the window because the guys wanted to gamble on the riverboat all day." Tara was gifted at storytelling, elongating the words for emphasis and huffing at the end for effect.

Frankie tried to look empathetic, but wanted more information. "Clay's friend? Who might that be?"

Tara groaned and palmed her cheek as if she had a toothache. "His name is Boots. He's not from Deep Lakes."

This was taking far too long for Frankie. "Is he a sheep shearer? Where does he live? How does he know Clay? Did he hang around any one of you in particular?"

"O-M-G, Ms. Champagne, that's a lot of questions. No, he's a mechanic, I think, or something like that. I don't know where he lives. He latched onto Haley or she latched onto him, more like it."

A mechanic—that struck a chord. "Do you know his full name?"

Tara looked pained but something pinged in her brain. "Yes, Janus something. I remember because it was an odd name. Those Australians."

It came as no surprise to Frankie that Boots was another Aussie. "Did you take any pictures of the couples?"

Tara's eyes flung open wider, baffled by the question. "Really? I didn't think you liked Clay. Now you want a photo?"

Frankie waited, her green eyes flickered fiercely as she stared directly into Tara's bewildered ones.

"Actually, I do have a photo." She pulled out her phone and began to scroll as she talked. "Haley asked me to take it after the guys gave them lucky charm necklaces. She made a big deal out of it. Her phone battery was dying, so I took the photo. Here."

Frankie studied the face of Boots. She didn't know him. "Could you send that to me please, Tara?" Tara complied, grumbling the whole time.

Frankie's empathy returned. "I'm sorry these guys ruined your girls' trip, Tara. How long did they hang around?"

Tara looked away, unwilling to say more. No way

was she going to spill the beans that the guys booked a hotel room, that she saw neither Violet nor Haley until breakfast the next morning. Instead, she stuffed her paycheck into her bag and left.

Frankie decided she had just enough time to check in with Shirley before taking Tia home. After four rings, Frankie was certain she'd be talking to voicemail, but the phone made a loud clunk followed by an exclamation on the fifth ring.

"Officer Shirley Lazaar, could you hold on a minute?" she sounded ruffled. Frankie could hear water running, whirring, and finally, footsteps.

"Sorry about that. What can I do for you?"

Frankie chuckled. "This is Frankie. Is everything okay, Shirley? Sounds like I took you away from something."

"Crazy Monday under the hot summer sun, Frankie. The phone hasn't quit all day, so I finally just had to take it with me to the john. So, what's up?"

Immediately, Frankie regretted bugging the officer. "Oh, if you're busy, this can wait. I mean I don't want to …"

Shirley cut her off. "Nonsense. Yours is probably the best call I'm going to get today, so let's get on with it. You got questions or answers for me?" The woman had a knack for knowing.

"Did Garrett talk to you? Never mind. I have questions and maybe a few answers, too. What I don't have is time, and it looks like you don't either, so can you talk now, on the phone?"

"Keep it short, and don't be surprised or take it personally if I hang up. Just means I got other business to tend to. Okay, Ace. Your move."

Frankie conveyed the short version of her search on Envee Express, Grizz's information on the blonde, and saving the best for last, the footage from Ryan's camera on the night of the shooting. She suspected there hadn't been time for the police to review it yet.

Shirley whistled. "Not bad for a newbie. What do you want from me?"

"Can I get the real names of the hired hands you interviewed? Might seem silly to you, but it's hard to find information on them when all I have are nicknames."

"Done. I'll send them by email as soon as we finish here."

"One more thing. Did you corroborate Clay Cooper's alibi during the shooting?"

"I thought you knew that we did, Frankie. Violet's a pretty reliable individual."

"But, did you check in with the mechanic?" Frankie hated to think her daughter would cover up the truth for this man, but love is blind, after all.

"We talked to the mechanic and to the waitress at the diner where they had breakfast. Both verified Clay's story . . . I already told you this the day we took Violet's statement."

"Right. I wasn't exactly firing on all cylinders that day. Could I get the names of the mechanic and the waitress, please?"

"Sure. What tree are you barking up now, Frankie?" But Shirley didn't wait for a response. She said a fast goodbye and the line went dead.

Chapter 19

*As the shadow in early morning, is friendship
with the wicked; it dwindles hour by hour. But
friendship with the good increases, like the
evening shadows, till the sun of life sets.*
– Johann Gottfried Herder

Tia Pepita stuck her head inside the alcove where
Frankie was reading Shirley's email and jotting down
the names in her phone notes app, underneath the
names she'd received from Donna Stauffer. She planned
to compare the names with the hands renting from the
Mischief resort to look for potential connections.

Tia tapped one rubber-toed shoe as noisily as she
could on the wooden floor. "Come on, Frankie. Time
to go home. I'm baking in here." She fanned herself
dramatically with a pot holder, making Frankie giggle at
Tia's inadvertent play on words.

"I know, I know. I just need to finish this email and we'll
go. Promise." She reached into her apron pocket. "Here,
take my keys and start the SUV. Get the AC running."

Tia shook her head and muttered something in
Spanish, but snatched the keys and left.

Email notes completed, Frankie stopped in the kitchen to wish Tess a good evening. "Isn't it about time you left, Tess? You've already put in a full day."

Tess smiled wearily. "I'm just getting a head start on some yeast dough for the week. Then I'll be leaving. See you tomorrow."

Tia was leaning up against the SUV chatting with Violet, who had just pulled in from the vineyard. She appeared to be in a good mood, so Frankie asked if she'd like to come out to Carmen's to walk Sonny with her.

"Okay. Let me just change clothes. I'll be quick."

Violet dashed through the back door, and Tia climbed into the much-cooler SUV to wait. Frankie checked the bird feeders that dotted the backyard and creek area, added some sunflower and safflower seeds to a couple, then checked the birdhouse that had a number of twigs sticking out of the entry hole.

"Silly wrens." Frankie scolded the absent wrens for filling the house with twigs so no other bird could nest in it. She emptied the house, shut the door and latched it, hoping some bluebirds or maybe a swallow would build a nest there.

Violet was wearing workout clothes and had hopped in the back seat. Frankie could see Tia impatiently drumming the window, but when she climbed in the driver's seat, Tia was merely tapping a rhythm to the song on the radio.

* * *

Frankie happily walked Sonny in the back farm field, far away from the property line. Thankfully, Sonny was healing quickly and loped along like his old self, soaking up the fresh air and love strokes from Frankie and Violet.

Violet asked her mother to identify the wildflowers currently in bloom, and together they spied a pair of bluebirds and some baby robins scratching around the tall grass.

"We've had quite a week or so, haven't we?" Frankie began, wondering if she was trying to mend fences with her daughter or punch new holes into the already broken one.

Violet made a tsk sound, tongue against teeth. "I guess it hasn't been easy for either one of us."

Frankie used the opening to voice her fears. "I just don't want anything to happen to you; I think we both need to be careful until the shooter is caught." She didn't want Violet to know about the gems, the blonde with Clay, or any other case details for fear she might spill the beans to Clay and mess up the investigation.

Normally, Violet would subscribe to her mother's opinions; she'd always been a cautious child and teen. Frankie noticed a sea change in Violet, who was finding her way into adulthood and seemed to have lost her mooring.

"Look Mom, I know you don't trust Clay, but I do. And you're just going to have to trust me." The chin, tilted upward in defiance, reminded Frankie of her own stubborn nature. Like it or not, she had raised a headstrong daughter and would have to decide how to properly navigate the new waters they were drifting into.

Frankie reached for Violet's hand, about to offer her soothing words, but Violet snatched her hand back and glared at Frankie. Her tone made Sonny search each woman's face to get a read on the situation.

"Don't treat me like a child!" was all Violet could muster from her quaking insides before she stormed back toward the house, leaving Frankie with a barking Sonny, who seemed to call her back to resume their happy walk.

Frankie soothed the upset sheltie and whispered, "I keep screwing things up." A tear slid down her cheek. She gazed around the field of grasses and wildflowers, feeling at sea. Staring up at the sky, she foolishly called: "Fireflies, where are you?" Her inner voices hadn't weighed in on her actions in a while, and she wondered why.

Sonny perked up, curiously cocked his head toward Frankie, then pulled on the leash for them to get moving. She nuzzled the pooch, thankful for his concern, and walked onward, finally circling back to the farmhouse after what she hoped was enough time for Violet to cool off.

Carmen met them outside. "I don't know what happened, but Vi is down there, talking to Clay." She nodded toward the pasture, where the two were leaning against the fence, happily chatting.

Frankie mumbled a cuss word, mostly meant for herself. She hadn't known if Clay would be working at the farm or not, but the squabble with Violet sent her right into his orbit. Shoot.

"There's something I want to tell you quickly before Violet comes back. I asked her to show me the clover necklace, so I could get a closer look. I think it's jade. It reminds me of the necklace my niece Izzy wore at her wedding." Carmen's voice was agitated, and Frankie was confused.

"Never mind. It's just something that's bothering me. Let me think about it some more." Carmen offered her partner a half-hearted smile.

Perplexed, Frankie decided it was time to collect Violet and go, when her phone rang, and Garrett's face popped into the corner.

"Hi Garrett," Frankie sounded glum.

"I got your message about looking at some camera footage. What's the matter, Frankie?" Good old Garrett, always intuitive.

"I'm okay. I just finished taking a walk with Sonny and Violet. Let's just say I overstepped my boundaries with her and we're at odds again."

"Sorry to hear that. Maybe you both need time apart to sort things out for yourselves. So, why don't you come over here tonight with your laptop, and we'll review the video. I'll even order pizza, like a real date." Garrett's attempt at joviality wasn't lost on Frankie, who agreed to be there in about an hour.

She looked at Carmen. "Should I walk down there or

send her a text that I'm ready to go? Honestly Carmen, I don't know my place right now. I'm second guessing every little move."

Carmen shrugged. "You're asking me? I have two teenage boys that seem to change every day. I think you should text Violet so she doesn't think you're checking up on them. Right?"

Frankie nodded and had just started her message when a Whitman County squad pulled into the O'Connors' and stopped outside the barn. Carmen could see Ryan speaking to Officer Green, then they disappeared into the barn. Green emerged with Reggie and helped him into the back of the squad. The episode was not missed by Clay or Violet—an agitated Clay kicked dirt with his boots while Violet stroked his arm quietly.

Ryan drove up to the house in the old blue field truck and jumped out, eyes alight with news. "They found messages to Reggie from Jonesy on his phone from the night of the shooting. They must be incriminating because they took Reg in for questioning."

Carmen was wide-eyed while Frankie was shocked. "Reggie? I don't believe it. Something isn't right."

"Yeah and there's more. Jonesy is being released tomorrow morning. He used his truck to post bond. I don't believe the police would let him out if they had evidence against him."

"What about our camera footage from the property line that shows the truck and the people?" Carmen folded her arms across her chest, troubled by the entire situation.

Ryan nodded. "I asked Green about that, but he said they're still reviewing the footage. So, why would they let Jonesy out? Things are not adding up." Ryan swore under his breath. He hadn't signed up for this kind of problem on the farm and just wanted things to return to normal.

Frankie finished her text to Violet, keeping it short and sweet. "I'm ready to go. Should I pick you up by the fence?"

Her phone quickly blooped back. "You go ahead without me, Mom. I'm going to stay with Clay. He'll bring me home later."

"Great, just peachy." Frankie read the text to Carmen and Ryan, scowling.

"Clay's shift is over, so I'll encourage them to be off," Ryan said.

Carmen's eyes lit up with an idea. "Uh-uh. Let's invite them for supper. I was thinking we could order pizza." She hoped this would give Frankie time to see Garrett without worrying about Violet and Clay.

Frankie gave her friend a squeeze. "Thank you. I hope that's okay with you, Ryan?" Ryan looked confused but figured Carmen would explain.

Carmen wondered if the two young lovebirds would even take the pizza bait. Moreover, how long could she keep them there before they decided to go their merry way? They were adults, after all, and didn't owe any explanations to the O'Connors.

* * *

Munching on pepperoni, sausage, mushroom, and black-olive pizza; Garrett and Frankie grew bleary-eyed looking at the same footage, willing their eyes to see something new in the fuzzy darkness.

Garrett yawned loudly. "This is like watching the *Ghost Hunters* show. I see these little flashes now and then, some strangely glowing circles, but nothing identifiable."

"Time for a break. Let's go outside and sit on the porch swing." Frankie loved Garrett's old Victorian farmhouse on County WH, even though one room or another was in a constant state of remodeling. Garrett was a gifted carpenter, but he only had so much time to work on the house.

Freya, his Norwegian elkhound, trotted along beside them, excited to go outside for business and sniffing around. Freya was responsible for the two of them meeting, since she had wandered into the shop's backyard after chasing a squirrel down to Sterling Creek. Frankie returned the hound to Garrett a couple of days later, but Freya and Frankie shared a lasting bond.

The couple sat silently in the porch swing, barely moving, each lost in their own thoughts. Frankie tried to push aside the ongoing conflict with Violet to focus on all the loose ends in the investigation, pieces that didn't fit together but seemed to multiply.

It was a dark evening with only a sliver of moonlight. Frankie imagined the night of the shooting again, remembered there was a much bigger moon, but that the haze created from the humid weather hampered her visibility. No wonder they were having so much trouble seeing details from the footage. She supposed the police were having no better luck. She sighed heavily.

"I feel like we're losing daylight on this case, like we're running out of time, Garrett. Whoever shot Sawyer is still here, waiting to make the next move. I just know it."

Garrett pulled her in closer and draped his arm around her shoulder. They both jerked their nodding heads up at the same time when Freya growled at a shadow. The elkhound was comical to watch, pouncing over the dark shadow of a large maple tree again and again.

"See, even Freya can't see clearly in the dark, can you, Girl?" Garrett laughed as Freya barked at Garrett's dark truck and pawed at the Whitman County emblem imprinted on the door. "Come here, Freya. We're not going for a ride tonight."

"Maybe we should switch gears, Frankie. What else is on your crime task list?" He was serious with just a hint of humor in his voice.

"Let's start again tomorrow, G. I'm spent, and I'm hoping to talk to Violet before turning in for the night." She stood on tiptoe for a kiss, snuggling into his chest as he held her tightly.

"No telling what tomorrow has in store for us, but let's connect and plan our next move. I think you're right: This case is on the move, and everyone involved needs to be ready. Whether Alonzo likes it or not, he's stuck with all of us."

"How about lunch tomorrow? I can make sure I'm not in the middle of dough if I have a stopping time. See you at noon?"

Sadly, Frankie came home to an empty, dark apartment. She checked her phone, but there was no message from Violet. She considered calling Carmen but decided that if Carmen knew anything, she would already have contacted Frankie.

Tonight she wasn't going to wait up for her daughter. She set an early alarm and turned on music to sleep by. She awoke sporadically all night long from a recurring dream of being chased by a car. The car had two occupants, but they were faceless; the car darted forward then backward over and over and she could see her reflection flashing along and something else too, just outside her grasp.

Chapter 20

The pearl is the queen of gems and the gem of queens.
– Grace Kelly

Long before her alarm chimed, Frankie was awakened by her phone's jingle. Maybe Garrett had found something in the video. Maybe Violet was in trouble. Maybe . . . oh, it was Carmen.

"Hi Frankie. I wanted to make sure you were coming in early today. We need to talk." Carmen sounded like she'd been up for hours. Frankie said she'd see her in the kitchen in fifteen minutes.

Downstairs, the partners were first on the scene, which wasn't always the case. Especially in the summer, Tess and Jovie liked to bake before the heat of the day made them feel like steamed vegetables.

Carmen handed Frankie two pieces of paper and an iced sugar-free caramel latte. "Don't read it now because I want to tell you the high points." She sat at the counter as far from the ovens as possible, even though they weren't even on yet. "By the way, where is Tess? Her car's out front."

Frankie walked through the swinging doors that led

to the shop and looked out the picture window facing Granite Street. Tess's car was parked in its usual spot down the block in order to save good spaces for paying customers. The car looked empty. She shrugged.

"I don't know. We'll check in a few if she doesn't turn up. Before we talk about this," she said, holding up the papers, "what happened with Violet last night?"

Carmen's smile flatlined. "They stayed to eat pizza with us, and we made small talk. She and Clay mostly chatted with the boys about music and sports. They left around eight. I'm guessing they didn't come back here?"

Frankie shook her head. "When I got home from G's house, the place was dark and empty. I didn't wait up. I checked to make sure her car was in the alley this morning though."

Carmen took a long sip of her iced cinnamon latte. "New subject. I told you Vi's necklace had me wondering, so I did some internet searches about Imperial jade to see if any had been stolen recently."

Frankie was about to interject that she couldn't imagine the small clover necklaces were anything of great value. Tara said the guys had purchased them at the casino gift shop. But, Carmen held up a hand and made an exaggerated slicing motion to cut her off.

"Let me finish before you start asking questions. Dios mío!"

Frankie promptly swallowed her comments and sat on her hands, but as Carmen talked, Frankie grabbed a pen and began writing notes on the back of the pages she'd given her.

"Imperial jade is very expensive. I know this because we have a family necklace, an heirloom, that has passed through six generations in my family. Last night I emailed you this photo of Izzy wearing it at her wedding."

Frankie gasped at the fine emerald green color of carved jade beads on a long strand that ended in the head of a jaguar with diamond eyes, trimmed in brilliant gold.

"I know. Stunning, right? There's an amazing story that goes with it. My great-grandfather grew up in a little village in the Yucatan. When he was a boy, he had a crush on a little rich girl, and watched her through the iron gate as she played in the garden. Suddenly, for many days, when he came to the gate the little girl wasn't there.

So, he bravely went to her window and threw small stones at it until one of the servants came out to chase him away. But, the servant recognized my great-grandfather as the grandson of a famous local Mayan medicine woman. So, the girl's father chased my papi down the street, told him the girl was very ill with fever, and the doctor had no hope for her. Would his grandmother come?

She did, bringing a bag of remedies with her. She used them to save the girl's life. The doctor called it a miracle from God, but the girl's family believed in the medicine woman. To show their gratitude, the girl's mama gave away her prized necklace of Imperial jade. She told the medicine woman the necklace held a secret curse, which she believed could only be broken by a powerful Mayan woman."

Frankie was mesmerized by the tale. "How much is it worth, Carmen?"

Carmen said her family had received many calls over the years from curators who wanted the necklace, auction houses, jewelers, and historians, but it was not for sale. The necklace was kept in a safe at her parents' house, because Carmen's mama was the next in line to keep it.

"The necklace only passes to the women in the family, starting with my third great-grandmother, the medicine woman. Every woman in my family wears it on her wedding day for good luck, good health, and prosperity. The last appraiser valued it at $75,000."

Frankie choked on her latte and almost fell off the stool. "Wow!" After she recovered, she asked about the printout Carmen gave her.

"A valuable collection of Imperial jade pieces was stolen about two years ago from the National History Museum in Guatemala City. The details are in the article, but the thieves were never caught. There was a small fire in one of the offices on the night of the heist, and a window was left open. The security guards never told the same story twice, making the police suspect that at least one of them was in on the heist."

Frankie skimmed the article, her eyes popping out as she read the value of the stolen gems. "The museum lost over $4 million in jewels! But, none of the items have surfaced, so they were either cut into other pieces or are sitting in someone's very private collection."

"Check out the second article. I noticed the green pearl in the center of Violet's necklace, so I started poking around for pearls, just in case."

"Did you get any sleep at all last night?" Frankie's shocked expression made Carmen giggle.

"No, thanks to you. I think you're rubbing off on me." Carmen was only half-serious. For the sake of her family, she wanted the case solved ASAP.

The article focused on a set of crown jewels stolen last October somewhere between the Maldives and Sydney, Australia. As Frankie scanned the article, she sniffed sharply from time to time while jotting stars in the margins where something seemed pertinent to their case.

The crown jewels included several items crafted from rare green South Sea pearls: a layered bib necklace, a choker, an eight-strand bracelet, and a Venus crown. The largest piece was a baroque pearl pendant, known as the Green Envy, weighing in at 52 carats.

Most intriguing of all, the shipment was tracked from Sydney to Chicago, then simply vanished into thin air. The estimated value of the collection was listed at $30 million. Frankie sucked in her breath.

"Do you really think it's possible these two heists are connected to the green stones we found on *my* property in *your* manure?"

Carmen shrugged. "Who knows for sure? It does seem far-fetched, but they're all green stones, and they're all unsolved thefts. And there does seem to be an Australian connection in two of the cases."

"Australia's huge. There has to be more than a few criminals there. What are the odds they'd be here in Deep Lakes?" Frankie wasn't sure if she was just playing devil's advocate in her cross-examination or trying to convince herself that Clay was innocent of any wrongdoing.

Carmen looked a bit miffed. "Just trying to play along. Besides, I'd like our lives to get back to normal." She glanced at the kitchen clock. Daylight was streaming in the windows, and Jovie and Aunt CeCe would be walking in the door any moment.

"Hey, we still haven't seen any sign of Tess. Let's go look in her car."

They saw the top of Tess's head pop up from the back of her little gray car as they were about to knock on the window. Tess looked sheepishly from Frankie to Carmen as she escaped from underneath a cotton throw.

Wide-eyed, the business partners looked at Tess in yesterday's clothes, wiping sleep from her eyes.

Tess rolled down the window to speak. "I'm so sorry I'm late. Let me grab my stuff and I'll get changed in the bathroom. Okay?"

"Did you sleep here last night?" Frankie, hands on hips, stamped one foot on the pavement.

"Um, well, yes. I did."

Both women believed the reason had to do with Tess's uncertain living conditions. They gave her the stink eye, arms folded across their chests, waiting to hear more.

"I didn't want to go back to my apartment. The college allowed someone else to move in, since I was supposed to be moving out. I have an extra room, but I don't know this person, and I don't want to stay there."

Frankie and Carmen had never seen Tess distraught. Each one wrapped an arm around her and held her close.

"You should have told us. You could have slept in the shop lounge last night or at my apartment, for Pete's sake, Tess. Don't ever sleep in your car again—understand?"

Tess sobbed harder. The three walked arm-in-arm down the street, Carmen carrying Tess's tote bag. Frankie took Tess upstairs for a shower, since it wasn't likely Violet would be up for another couple of hours.

Not much later, a refreshed Tess ambled down the stairs into the kitchen, and immediately took her spot at a station. While Tess was upstairs, both Jovie and Aunt CeCe arrived and Frankie told them Tess was using her shower due to a plumbing problem in her apartment.

The women noticed Tess wasn't herself, however. She wasn't singing, humming or smiling. Their looks of concern were directed at Frankie and Carmen, who said nothing. It was time to lighten the mood. Carmen turned on a favorite oldies music station and soon the baking tempo picked up. When The Isley Brothers "Shout" played just before opening, Aunt CeCe grabbed Jovie and the two whirled around the kitchen, waving their hands in the air as they altered their volume from a whisper to a shout on the chorus with the Brothers. Tess burst out laughing and Sundae headed for the hills with a grumbling meow. The dark cloud had passed for the time being, but Frankie reminded herself to help Tess find a new place sooner than later.

Frankie used the break in the action to call Garrett. "Hey, Mr. G. How's my favorite coroner?"

"Same as my favorite baker, maybe. I didn't sleep much last night. How about you?"

Frankie relayed the dream that played on repeat the night before. "If you're not too busy . . ." she began. No response on the other end gave her the signal to keep going. "Two things: Carmen gave me articles about two unsolved jewel heists. I'd love you to look them over, see what you think."

"Uh huh. Can do. What's the second thing?"

"How would you like to ride up to Waupaca to Forks and Spoons Diner for lunch?" she tried to sound perky, like they were off to indulge in a culinary delight.

Garrett's voice deepened on the other end. "And just why would we want to go there, Miss Francine?"

"Shirley gave me the names of the two people who corroborated Clay's alibi. I want to check them out myself."

"So, you have a hunch of your own, I suspect?" Garrett knew she wouldn't second-guess the police unless she had something valid to go on.

"Let's just say we're following up based on new details."

Garrett chuckled. "Okay, let's say that. What time shall I pick you up?"

"Nope. I'll pick you up at eleven-thirty. I don't want anyone to see your marked truck."

Chapter 21

There is always a pleasure in unravelling a mystery, in catching at the gossamer clue which will guide to certainty.
– Elizabeth Gaskell

Frankie and Garrett clocked the time from his county office to Badger Street in Waupaca at 43 minutes. Granted it was daylight with clear weather, but the two decided Clay might be able to make it back to the O'Connor farm by 3:30 a.m. if he left Waupaca at 2:30, right after Violet left. *Might* was the key word.

Forks and Spoons Diner looked like it had been shoved between two large brick buildings as an afterthought. Its wooden exterior might be held together by several coats of thick paint, but the front window was clean and a large red flower box sported well-tended geraniums and marigolds. Several bejeweled forks and spoons perched among the flowers, adding a whimsical touch.

Since it was a Tuesday, there were a few empty tables sprinkled among the booths occupied by the regulars. The red stools at the formica counter held several single diners who appeared to know each other, indicated by the loud back-and-forth among them and the servers.

A buxom woman in her 50s with brown and silver streaked hair pulled a pen from her updo and waved it around the room. "Sit anywhere you like. Someone will be right with you."

Frankie directed Garrett to a small side table near the kitchen door, as far away from others as feasible. The nearby booth housed three women in business attire, discussing a client, probably on lunch break from the courthouse or a downtown law office.

A young skinny gal with layered dark hair approached the small table with two waters. Her hair was streaked with a lovely shade of peacock blue and she had a tiny jewel stud in her nose. She handed them menus and pointed to the specials.

"Thank you, Jordan." Frankie considered exchanging pleasantries a must.

The waitress looked at her quizzically. "Do I know you?"

Frankie pointed to her nametag. The girl blushed.

"Oh, duh . . . Should I come back in a bit or do you know what you want?"

Frankie pulled her photos up on her phone. "Can I ask you a question? We're looking for a waitress here named Sheila. Sheila Kelly."

Jordan shook her head. "I've only been here a week, so I'm not the person to talk to, but I'll send Bobbi over. She's been here forever." Jordan elongated the last word.

It turned out Bobbi was the buxom woman who

greeted them at the door. Her appearance suggested sturdiness and a tough life, but she offered them a helpful smile.

"Jordan says you're asking about Sheila. She only worked here for maybe a week."

"Would you recognize her if you saw a photo?" Frankie wondered.

Bobbi nodded and kept her voice low. "Is she in some kinda trouble? The cops were here on her second day of work asking questions, and now you two."

Frankie clicked on the photo of Clay and the blonde. "Is this Sheila?"

Bobbi snorted. "That's her, sure as can be. I knew she wasn't waitress material the day she started. Fussing over her perfect nails and all. I knew she wasn't going to last."

"Any idea what happened to her? Oh, and did she have a foreign accent?" Not that it mattered, but any detail might reveal something worthwhile.

"Ha! No show, no call. She never asked for her pay either. I don't think she was a foreigner. She spoke kind of nasally." Bobbi pinched her nostrils when she spoke for effect.

Frankie laughed. "Oh, you mean she sounded like a Wisconsinite."

Bobbi looked annoyed. "*We* don't have accents."

"One more quick question: Do you know this man? Goes by Boots." Frankie showed her the photo Tara had taken.

"Well, your timing's good on that one. He's sitting up front there, in the booth, with three other guys. They come most every day from Al's Auto Shop. He's got a funny sounding name, Joonas or something. Did you want me to send Jordan back for your order?"

Garrett answered. "Yes, but please don't tell *Joonas* we asked about him." He handed Bobbi a twenty. She hesitated, but pocketed it just the same, nodding.

Frankie picked up the menu again and browsed the specials, and whispered over the top of it. "Isn't it interesting that Sheila started working the day of the shooting. How convenient." Garrett gave her a quirky half smile.

"So, we're actually going to eat here, then?"

"Don't be a snob G. I'm starving. A BLT and side salad couldn't hurt." Frankie closed the menu, Jordan's signal to return. She took their orders, and the food arrived in no time.

"The sign of a good line cook, speed and accuracy."

"It almost sounds like you did that job once, G."

"In another life. It helped put me through college." Garrett chowed down his cheeseburger appreciatively.

Frankie spoke quietly and leaned closer to him; she needed to process the new information out loud. "I'm certain Clay, Sheila, and Boots are thick as thieves in this. Maybe even jewel thieves."

She frowned. "I can't figure out how Jonesy's truck got tangled up in this. And Reggie. I can't see him being involved at all." Frankie paused as Garrett held up one hand.

"Reggie's not involved. He was questioned and released. Turns out the messages to Reggie were actually to Jonesy's sister, Regina."

"Garrett! How could you forget to tell me this?"

"Easy, Miss Francine. There are a lot of actors on this stage right now. Seems like we're changing scenes every few minutes. I just heard about it before you picked me up." Garrett slid his plate of french fries in her direction, a peace offering.

"You don't think Regina could be the blonde? Wait, that doesn't make sense. Grizz said Blondie is Australian, but Bobbi said Sheila didn't have an accent."

Garrett sipped thoughtfully. "An Australian accent would draw attention around here, so I'm sure Sheila/Blondie was trying to blend in."

"Right, but how is Jonesy's sister involved in all this?" She nibbled thoughtfully on a couple of fries. Still so many missing pieces to the puzzle.

She offered Garrett a lopsided grin. "Anything else you forgot to tell me?"

He returned a pained smile. "I don't think so; how about you? Turnabout's fair play, after all."

The two stayed long enough to allow Boots and company to exit first. Frankie insisted she pay for lunch since this lark was her idea and left Jordan a substantial tip.

She dropped Garrett off in the county parking lot, gave him a cursory peck on the cheek, and reminded him to read the articles about the jewel heists. She was anxious to update her crime board, and she hoped she would hear from her scientists at Bountiful with information about Clay and Blondie.

She noticed Violet's car parked behind Bubble and Bake, so she hurried up the back steps. Violet sat in the kitchen with a cup of tea, listless and moping. Aunt CeCe was diligently at work filling brightly colored macarons with lemon, strawberry or vanilla cream. She shot Frankie a warning look then smiled knowingly, humming a little song. Message delivered: Frankie would tread carefully.

She pulled a stool from the other side of the counter to sit next to Violet, who stared into her tea as if answers might emerge from its green interior.

"What's going on, honey?" Frankie's voice was the comforting mother's without edge or ulterior motive.

"I don't know, Mom. I didn't sleep well last night, and I couldn't concentrate at work. My head and stomach ached, so I came home. Aunt CeCe made me some chamomile tea with honey."

"I was just going upstairs. Why don't you come up with me and take a nap?"

Violet nodded and picked up her tea. Aunt CeCe presented a subtle thumbs-up to Frankie before they swung through the kitchen doors to the hallway that connected to the apartment.

As Violet rested, Frankie updated the crime board in her bedroom, wondering if her daughter was under the weather or simply emotionally drained. For better or worse, maybe she and Clay had a falling out. Whatever was wrong, the truth was bound to come out, and Frankie intended to be the safety net for Violet.

Frankie's phone rang, and when she saw it was Nelson calling, she stepped outside onto the deck, out of Violet's earshot in case she was awake.

"Nelson, good to hear from you. What's the news?"

"Good afternoon, Ms. Champagne. Two things here."

"Why are you whispering, Nelson?"

"I thought Violet might be nearby. She left early as she wasn't feeling well."

Frankie laughed silently. Nelson was brainy and typically logical to a fault, so the fact he thought he should whisper on his end was quite amusing to her.

"I think it's fine for you to speak normally on your end. Violet isn't going to hear you. Anyway, on my end, I'm on the back deck and she's resting in her room."

"Oh, very good then. I'll proceed. First, we need to ascertain a date for bottling. The process seems to be accelerating, so I'm afraid it's urgent for us to bottle within five days."

Frankie flushed, embarrassed she'd forgotten to check on her batches, knowing every day mattered during final fermentation. She'd been too preoccupied with the shooting and had shirked her crucial role as head vintner.

"I promise to get it scheduled this afternoon. I'll call to see who's available to help. Maybe we can even bottle tomorrow night." Wednesday was potentially the most practical day, with the wine lounge closed at 5 p.m. more people would be available. If not Wednesday, Frankie knew she'd have to wait until Sunday as the next feasible day.

"And the second thing, Nelson?"

"Zane and I have ascertained some information per your request. Do you think you could come out here this afternoon?"

Frankie agreed and signed off. Should she leave a note for Violet? Text her daughter? Get someone to watch over her in case she needed anything? Was leaving her alone the responsible thing to do? Once again, Frankie's priorities were entangled in a maze of duties pulling her every which way. Where were the fireflies to weigh in, to help her navigate these troubled waters?

Frankie managed to keep her curiosity reduced to a smolder, although she was itching to drop everything and head to the vineyard. Her first obligation was to call her regular bottling helpers for availability. She told herself she was being a good mother at the same time, hanging around while Violet rested.

Many phone calls later, she'd rounded up the usual crew minus Alonzo, who said the case was becoming a hot potato and needed his full attention. Even her brother Nick was available, which surprised her since Nick's social calendar always seemed to be bursting at the seams. Good old Nick, he might be a ladies' man, but he always made time to help his sister. She wondered if he was still seeing her employee, Cherry. That romance ran hot and cold as the need arose. Frankie would know tomorrow night when both Cherry and Nick were in the bottling room.

She tiptoed to Violet's bedroom door and peeked inside. Based on her quiet breathing, she was asleep. Frankie decided to leave her a note on the breakfast bar along with a chamomile tea bag. The note simply stated she was needed at Bountiful, that a bottling party was on tap for tomorrow night at eight, and that there was egg drop soup in the fridge from the Orient Express food truck she could have. Food trucks were a bonus of good weather; parked in the downtown lot near Lake Joy, they offered quick bites and a pretty place to eat in the fresh air.

Frankie loaded the rest of the takeout in the SUV and was off. The least she could do was bring a food offering for her informants. Her arms filled with takeout and her usual tote containing phone, tablet, and notebook, Frankie kicked at the vineyard door, hoping someone would open it.

Three kicks later, Nelson pushed open the door and took the jumbo takeout bag from her with relish. He inhaled the aroma of garlic and soy sauce and turned left into the break room. "Ah, Asian food. My favorite. I suppose you think you owe Zane and me for your research, but we do enjoy a bit of espionage, Ms. Champagne."

Frankie wanted to hug her chief scientist, who still looked like a twelve-year-old, despite 1950's black framed glasses and Hush Puppy loafers. His ways always brightened her day and his scientific methods were impeccable. How she would replace him left her insides churning.

Zane caught a whiff of the takeout and scampered to the break room to join them, laptop in hand.

If Frankie had known in advance what a trove of information they'd unearthed, she would have brought them something better than takeout.

Nelson delivered his report first, clicking through open tabs in a presentation of show and tell. "Clay Cooper—his real name, by the way—has a business and marketing degree from the University of Queensland. He graduated three years ago and began working for Five Starr Woolens in Sydney, in the marketing department."

"Wait a minute. Clay was in marketing and then went to shearing sheep? That doesn't add up." Frankie scribbled in her notebook.

A sharp intake of breath from Nelson indicated more was forthcoming. "About two years ago, he simply disappeared off the grid. No social media. Nothing. He was no longer listed as a Five Starr employee."

One of Nelson's screen tabs revealed Clay's old social media page and posts. The scientist scrolled to a shot of Clay dressed in business attire. Apparently there were many more similar types of photos. "I must say, he does clean up well, if nothing else."

Nelson scrolled back toward the top of the page and was just about to click to another tab when something caught Frankie's eye.

"Just a minute, Nelson. Scroll back down, slowly. There's a photo I want to check out . . . right there. Stop."

Staring happily outward from the screen were Clay and Boots, both proudly sporting spiffy crocodile boots. The post was captioned "dressed to kill."

"Well, well, well, the police are going to be very interested to see this. Nicely done, Nelson."

It was Zane's turn to present his findings. The other scientist in the lab was a study in contrast to Nelson's personality. Laidback, often appearing as if he'd just rolled out of bed, Zane spoke instinctively, the opposite end of the conversation spectrum from Nelson. But, when it came to microbiology, Zane was just as savvy.

"And now the moment you've been waiting for . . ." Seeing Frankie on the edge of her seat, he spoke like a game show host, on purpose. "I give you The Blonde!" He turned the laptop which showed a close-up of the woman, wearing a lab coat, no less.

"Frankie, meet Melanie Barnes, gemologist at the Gemmological Association of Australia in Sydney." He paused as Frankie's mouth hung open while she wrote.

Zane continued but dropped the act. "Here's the good part. Melanie is Clay's half-sister. They share the same mother, Marcia Cooper, who is employed by Envee Express shipping."

Momentarily, Frankie's hands flew to cover her mouth, but she recovered quickly and wrote the information down in a makeshift chart, showing the connections.

"Sawyer worked for Envee Express. All the major players are Australian, if they are the major players, that is," Frankie interjected.

Nelson took up the conversation again. He opened up another set of tabs on an incognito screen. "Envee Express is a subsidiary of Five Starr Woolens. The parent corporation is run by Samuel Starr. Envee is run by his younger brother, Neill. We found evidence on the web to suggest there's sibling rivalry afoot."

Zane raised a finger in the air. "We located one photo showing Melanie with Neill Starr at some kind of public gala about two years ago. Otherwise, they appear to keep a low profile."

"I need to call Alonzo immediately. Could you two forward all these links to his office email?"

Eager to be helpful, they started the process while Frankie disappeared to the lab office and punched in Lon's private number.

"Frankie, what's going on?" Lon knew she'd only use the private line if it was urgent.

She relayed the bare bones of the lab workers' discoveries and said all the details were coming in an email.

"The email's here." A loud whistle from Lon's end suggested he was reading it right there and then. "The question is, what do we do next?" He was thinking out loud. "You need to take a breath and step away now, Frankie. We have to tread carefully or we could blow the whole case. Timing is everything. Let me talk to Shirley and Green. I promise to keep you in the loop."

"Lon, Garrett has information for you, too. We went to lunch today at the diner in Waupaca . . ."

Lon cut her off. "He and I spoke. I got the 411. I need to run, Frankie. Meanwhile, don't let Violet out of your sight."

Frankie thanked her scientists, praising their talents and willingness to support her sleuthing.

"Finish up this food. You've more than earned a break. And, we have a long day tomorrow with bottling on the docket."

Nelson looked more serious than usual. "You know Ms. Champagne, I, I mean we have grown fond of Violet. We want to make sure she's safe from harm, too."

Frankie's look of bemusement wasn't lost on Zane. Well, what do you know? It was quite possible Nelson Raye had feelings for her daughter. She didn't say anything but simply patted his hand in gratitude.

Knowing the outdoors would help her think, she walked around the vineyard. She immediately called Vi's number, which went straight to voicemail, so she phoned the bakery only to find out Violet's car was gone. She hadn't come through the shop on her way out, so nobody knew when she'd left. Frankie's heart sank.

At least the countryside, with its shade and breezes, would help calm her nerves. And the beauty of the property was unmatched. Still, she found herself pacing at times, walking in circles at other times.

She checked the time periodically. It was after 4 p.m. Another day was slipping away; time was becoming elusive and the collection of case details in Frankie's head felt oily, shifting one way, then another. She was still adrift on a boat, tossed from the O'Connors to Violet, to Bubble and Bake, then violently plunged into the criminal underworld. It was hard to stay afloat.

When her phone rang, she jolted out of the nightmare, and noticed only ten minutes had passed since the last time she'd checked. She hoped to see Violet's icon on the screen.

Alonzo, Shirley, and Garrett were on separate lines, and Frankie was being conferenced in. Lon led the conversation. "We've made a plan, and for better or worse, we want your help, Frankie."

She found it difficult to believe how quickly the tide was turning now. The plan would be executed that evening at seven. Less than three hours to organize it, to make it foolproof. She wondered if it could succeed, and if she could steel herself enough to participate. Could she maintain a poker face? She had to, for Violet's sake.

Frankie spoke to Nelson and Zane, informed them they must be off the premises no later than 5 p.m., and explained the long and short of the plan. Then she called

Peggy Champagne, trying to quell her rapid heartbeat and disguise her quavering voice.

"Mom, I need a favor."

Peggy's womanly radar engaged.

"Could you get in touch with Violet and make up a reason you need to see her? Have her come to your house and stay there until I call you."

"Out with it, Frankie. What's going on? I'm not going to do anything unless you tell me."

As Frankie had no time to argue, she explained the gist of the seven o'clock operation. "And, Violet's not answering my calls. I don't know where she is." She hadn't expected her mother to go rogue.

"I'm coming out to the vineyard. You're not doing this without me right by your side. I'll call CeCe. She can occupy Violet. She's a better actress than I am." Peggy disconnected before Frankie could reply.

A new wrinkle showed up a few minutes later when Violet and Clay pulled up to the winery together. Frankie swore under her breath. Now, she'd have to enact Plan B.

She met the two at the door and willed herself to sound normal. "Violet, are you feeling better?"

"Yes, Mom, much better. I'm hungry, so Clay and I are going to grab a bite in town with friends." She was more forthcoming than usual. "I left my phone out here on my desk, so we came by to get it."

"Great," Frankie said. "Your timing is perfect. Can we take a few minutes to look at the setup for bottling while you're here? I'm going to be running around a lot tomorrow and will need you to help Nelson and Zane prepare." Her take charge voice kicked in.

While the two women, along with Nelson, dispatched themselves to the lab and bottling area, Zane occupied Clay, chatting away, talking casually about office dirt.

"This place needs a security upgrade." He pointed to the computer. "The tech security is outdated, and don't get me started on the property. I mean the vineyard should have security cameras, right? Those grapes mean everything to this business . . ."

Seeing Clay rapt with attention, Zane leaned in closer, his voice hushed. "You know, after Ms. C found a couple gems in the orchard, it seems like security cameras should be at the top of the list."

A fire burned in Clay's eyes. "Gems? You're kidding, right?" He tried to sound genuinely amazed, but his voice wavered suspiciously.

Zane looked uncertain, hemmed and hawed, but finally conceded more information. "They were turned over to the cops. They're really interested in digging through the rest of the orchard though. It's happening tonight."

Zane shared a few more details for Clay's benefit, doing everything to set the hook. Time would tell if the team would catch a fish.

Chapter 22

A woman is like a tea bag—you never know
how strong she is until she gets in hot water.
– Eleanor Roosevelt

With Violet and Clay gone for the time being, Frankie drove back into town, talking to herself the entire way, reiterating the plan and her role in it.

Somehow, her memory clicked a reminder she was supposed to unearth a floor corker for the Hansens to use to bottle their dandelion wine the next day. Although Frankie didn't need one more task to do, a promise was a promise.

She phoned her mom, said she would pick her up at 5:30, and explained she would be arriving early to get a floor corker out of storage for the Hansens. "We need to get out to Bountiful before Clay and his gang arrive. They know the cops will be there at seven, so they have to beat them to the digging."

She tapped the horn quickly as Peggy's house came into view and was shocked when Peggy scooted out the door, Aunt CeCe trailing right behind her.

"Aunt CeCe! I thought you were going to keep Violet occupied tonight. What are you doing here?"

CeCe's gray hair hung over her shoulder and down her front in a long braid intertwined with purple ribbon wrapped in dried lavender, matching her purple printed gauzy dress. She looked dressed for a summer party. "Aren't we bottling wine tonight? Won't Violet be coming?"

Frankie looked around her aunt, directly at Peggy with a smirk. "What's going on?"

"Peggy, I told you I'm not good at pretending. Frankie dear, I tried to call Violet but she didn't answer. I'm very sorry, sweety."

"Get in the car. We're on a schedule," Frankie commanded them, wondering how her daughter was going to be entangled in this mess now. She'd bet the vineyard that Clay would show up before seven that night, but where would that leave Violet?

Aunt CeCe broke into Frankie's thoughts. "Can you fill us in on more of the details. I didn't know you dug up diamonds at Bountiful. I had to hear it from your mother," she pouted.

"Nobody was supposed to know. And, I don't have time to fill you in. This case is overwhelming. Even I can't keep track of all the details." She grew less annoyed as she spoke and more weary. "Really, I just want to keep Violet safe."

Peggy squeezed her hand hard. "That's why we're here with you. We all want to protect her."

Frankie pulled behind a copse of trees just past the

driveway and headed down the fire lane; all three were alert to any other people or vehicles. The fire lane ended just south of a wooded trail where Frankie would walk to her storage shed to retrieve the obsolete floor corker.

"You two: Stay put and watch for anyone or anything weird. Got it?"

Surprisingly, both silently nodded. The two passed a pair of binoculars back and forth, trained on the vineyard and orchard. Minutes later, Peggy gasped as she spotted Clay and another man in the orchard. What she saw next made her tremble. Clay was roughly pulling a woman beside him, who had both hands behind her back and a gag around her mouth. Violet! The other man held the arm of another woman, forcing her around the orchard rows. She too, appeared to be tied up and gagged.

Peggy handed the binoculars to CeCe and they both sank down into the SUV, although it was concealed from the orchard vantage point. Aunt and grandmother put their heads together to devise a makeshift plan.

Meanwhile, Frankie pulled open the heavy door to the storage shed that was seldom used. Flashlight in hand, she navigated around a couple rows of metal shelves where empty wine bottles lived with cast off lab equipment and God knew what else. She vowed the shed would get a thorough cleaning before winter as she rounded the corner. If memory served her correctly, the floor corker would be standing right there with a cover over it.

Before she reached the corker, she tripped over something on the floor. She tilted the beam downward, revealing a large canvas backpack. Working quickly, she opened the pack and waved the beam inside.

She pulled out something heavy wrapped in a cloth, a wallet, and a cell phone. The light shone on a driver's license with the face of Gerald Sawyer. She bet the phone was Sawyer's too. She unwrapped the cloth, jumping out of her skin when the business end of a handgun peeked out. She rewrapped it and tried to shove it back inside the pack with the phone and wallet.

There was something folded in the bottom half of the pack. She pulled out a rolled sheep fleece. It felt knotty in spots, so she held the light over it, exposing facets of dancing lights. The green diamonds, cut and polished, were perfectly hidden in the wool on Bountiful property.

Fully cognizant of losing time, she stuffed the rolled wool carefully back into the pack, then the other items, gingerly handling the wrapped firearm.

Something flew out of the wallet sleeve and fluttered to the floor—a small piece of cloth. It was a label from Five Starr Woolens, the label missing from Sawyer's shirt, she bet. Without thinking, she jammed it in her pants pocket.

Frankie left the corker behind, hoisted the backpack over her shoulder, and surveyed the shed for anything she might use as a weapon that she could carry. She looked at the shovel with longing, but decided the wrench was a better choice. Hadn't Colonel Mustard used a wrench in *Clue,* after all?

As she pushed open the door, she paused to look around cautiously. Everything around her was quiet, so she worked her way back down the trail on high alert. When she got to the SUV, she saw it was empty, which started a thud in her chest.

She retraced her steps up the trail where it branched off toward the orchard. A silent scream filled her body when she saw Clay and Boots raking through orchard fertilizer, each one holding onto a fettered woman: Violet and Haley.

Frankie crept along the perimeter of the woods that ran parallel to the orchard. Eventually she would run out of cover, and she'd have to make a decision. She prayed the others were in place behind the equipment shed, waiting for the punks who expected to find manure there.

A slight movement near the vineyard distracted Frankie. Looking to her right, she saw her mother and aunt trying to conceal themselves behind the corner fence post not far from the orchard diggers. Frankie held her breath. Should she signal them to go back to the SUV? She couldn't risk it.

She pushed back another yelp and moved closer to the orchard, closer to danger. Just as she reached the open area beyond the woods, Peggy shouted.

"Let those girls go, now! You're surrounded!" This from a woman who said she couldn't act. Instead of hysteria, she spoke with contempt and authority, and she had the element of surprise on her side.

Startled, Clay and Boots dropped their rakes and looked around for the location of the intruder. Peggy was still out of sight, but Frankie couldn't see any weapons other than the rakes.

What transpired next happened at warp speed traveling through jello.

Peggy stepped into the sunlight with her compact mirror, waving it back and forth to blind and confuse the two crooks.

Seeing her chance, CeCe lobbed a rock at a wasp nest in the tree next to the orchard, yelling at the girls to run at the same time.

Violet loped crookedly to Frankie, who was running like a warrior at Clay, wielding the wrench. Clay laid on the ground, wasps stinging him in various places. Frankie untied Violet and hugged her close, then grabbed a nearby bucket sitting by a young apple tree and doused Clay's head with water, making the wasps retreat. She stood above him, the wrench in position. Then she dropped it in the dirt, figuring Clay was incapacitated enough.

Boots tried to run from the wasps and hoped to escape behind the equipment shed. Instead, he ran into the welcoming arms of the sheriff, who cuffed him on the spot.

Haley ran toward Peggy to safety. She and Aunt CeCe untied her and held the sobbing girl in their arms.

Peggy strutted over to the orchard where Clay lay crumpled in pain. She intended on giving him a piece of her mind while Shirley cuffed him, but Shirley shooed her away. "Not now, Peggy. We still have work to do, so back off. That goes for all of you."

Frankie escorted Violet and Peggy back toward the vineyard to wait with Aunt CeCe and Haley. Frankie unlocked the winery and they sat inside drinking water Peggy fetched from the fridge.

Haley spoke first. "How did you all know to come out here?"

It was Frankie's duty to confess what she knew about the plan. She carefully watched a shocked Violet as she relayed some of the information.

"Once I knew the identity of the victim, Sawyer, I looked into his business. He had a number of connections to Australia, and it seemed like the hired hands were connected, too. But, when I saw Clay with a woman at The Oasis, I knew I had to keep digging."

She informed them about Clay's sister, Melanie, her profession as a gemcutter and his degree in marketing. "It didn't add up for Clay to be shearing for a living. When Manny showed me surveillance of someone digging around the dirt in the vineyard, I had to figure out why."

Violet jutted her chin out. "I don't understand why you couldn't just tell me these things. I'm not stupid. I would have made up a reason not to see Clay." Her voice choked on a sob when she said his name.

Frankie wasn't too sure her daughter would have stopped seeing Clay. It was hard to believe bad things about someone you cared for; she knew that full well. Rather than respond, she added a few more details.

"When Ryan found surveillance video from the Turner property line on the night of the shooting, we knew more people were likely involved." She shared her dream of being chased by the blurry car in the video and how it flashed something from the side each time it passed her.

"Officer Green said sometimes things show up in dreams because our minds see them without us recognizing them. He convinced Lon to dissect the video, which is how they discovered the car was a loaner. And, that connected right back to Clay who was supposed to be having his car repaired."

"At that point, I knew Clay's alibi didn't hold up, and I suspected his mechanic friend was in on the crime."

Frankie wanted to say more, wanted to tell them the clover necklaces from the two guys were likely made from stolen gems, wanted to tell them it was their necklaces that made Carmen search online for other heists. But, she'd said enough for now, so they waited, silently hoping for the ordeal to end.

* * *

Outside the winery, a squad was parked behind the equipment shed where Lon stood and radioed Officer

Green, who was scoping the area for a getaway vehicle. Minutes later, Green called for backup and relayed that he sighted a vehicle with at least two occupants at the south end of the fire lane next to the vineyard driveway.

Alonzo and Shirley responded in pursuit while a deputized Garrett watched the two handcuffed criminals. The three officers did their best to surround the SUV, but they had their work cut out for them since it was equipped with tinted windows. They could see two people standing near the rear end, and Green pointed inside with a shrug, indicating he didn't know if there were more. The officers hoped they were only dealing with two.

They recognized Melanie Barnes from her photo and online information. The man she was talking to was a hired hand from the Turner farm, Sean "Monty" St. George. They weren't expecting a third individual, but had to be ready for anything.

Green, the youngest and most agile of the officers, volunteered to crawl around the SUV and pounce on Monty from behind, since he had his back turned. Green reached for Monty's ankles to pull him off balance, and he fell forward, knocking Melanie off her feet as well.

Shirley and Green dashed in to secure the two, but Melanie pulled a pistol from inside her waistband and pointed it at Green, who was cuffing Monty. Quick-thinking Shirley deftly kicked Melanie's hand, causing her to swear and the pistol to sail away.

Meanwhile, Lon used his bullhorn directed at the SUV. "Come out, hands in the air. You are surrounded."

The officers flinched when the passenger door slowly opened and Franklin Turner walked out blubbering, hands raised.

Chapter 23

Envy shoots at others and wounds itself.
- English Proverb

The next evening, Alonzo arrived at Bountiful for the bottling party after all, citing his need for a break from the paperwork that followed the major arrests he and his officers had made the night before. He looked exhausted but happily accepted the wine glass Frankie handed him.

"Any updates you can share, Lon?" Frankie grinned slyly.

Garrett pulled her away, reminding her, "We're not talking shop, remember Miss Francine? Unless by shop, we mean wine, that is." He gave her a playful pat.

Frankie was not to be deterred. Since Violet was at home resting, with Aunt CeCe at her beck and call, she knew tonight was her best chance to discuss the case without upsetting her daughter. Besides, she owed Violet more information, and she needed a way to regain her daughter's trust, too.

Alonzo was too tired to scold her. "Most of it is now in the hands of the feds and INTERPOL. We're small potatoes here. I just have a mountain of statements to organize and reports to complete, and they have to be perfect. Don't suppose you'd like to do your share of the paperwork, eh Frankie?" He teased, good-naturedly.

All teasing aside, Lon was impressed that the quickly-hatched plan had succeeded. Granted, they hadn't accounted for Peggy's mirror tricks or Aunt CeCe's crackerjack throw at the wasp nest.

Another unexpected surprise was the backpack of evidence Clay had stashed at Bountiful. Although Clay may have been genuinely attracted to Violet, he had used her for leverage and the vineyard as a safe hiding place.

"It's been a three-ring circus at the department. We've used every room we have to interview witnesses. Thank God we were able to pull in officers from other counties last night and today, especially with Pflug on assignment . . ."

Well, that answered Frankie's question about Pflug's whereabouts anyway.

Alonzo tossed the rest of glass number one and asked for a refill. "You'll all be surprised to know the murder weapon was registered to Franklin Turner. Piecing together all the data we have so far, it appears Turner's the shooter."

When he paused to let the news sink in, everyone was surprised at the sheriff's flair for storytelling or that he was disclosing the information at all.

"Are you supposed to be telling us this?" Frankie stood over the seated sheriff in astonishment. She'd never known him to be so forthcoming.

He smiled slyly. "It's all going to be in the press conference we're holding tomorrow morning. Well, almost all of it. I trust you all can keep it under wraps until then."

With the bottling finished, the only ones remaining at Bountiful were Frankie, Garrett, Carmen, Ryan, and Peggy. Lon was more likely worried about Frankie than Peggy, who was the picture of discretion.

"If Turner's the shooter, then what was Clay's part in this? He had the gun, Sawyer's ID, and phone. He even had the shirt label." Oops, Frankie pulled the label from her pocket and sheepishly handed it to Lon.

Lon picked it up, made a grim face and pocketed it. "This was in the pack, too, I assume?" She explained it had fallen out of the wallet and she put it in her pocket without thinking. She knew she would be giving a long statement to the feds within a day or two. Her file soon might be as thick as any criminal's.

Alonzo sipped wine, savoring the second glass at a slower pace. "Clay was part of the heist and original plan for Sawyer to pick up the gems hidden in the sheep manure. He and Turner were supposed to help load the manure, making sure it came from the right pile where the diamonds were stashed."

Frankie interrupted. "So, Clay must have checked the manure on the pallet to discover the gems were gone after Sawyer was shot."

Ryan interjected, "How did the gems get on my property in the first place?"

Shaking his head, Lon continued. "They were never supposed to. The gems were meant to be on the Turner farm. After the mechanic stole them from the Arkansas truck, he was supposed to take them to the sheep market in Milwaukee and stash them in Turner's truck trailer."

Garrett took up the story. "And we all know how many look-alike trucks there are around here. You and Franklin have the same truck, Ryan, and they were parked side-by-side at the auction. It was a mix up."

Ryan stood up and started walking around the room like an agitated lawyer. "So, the shearing team? That was all part of the plan. The team I was supposed to get—they were in on the operation?"

"Yes and no. Jenks wasn't part of the scheme, but his original partner, Boots aka Tinker, certainly was. Monty, er Sean St. George, was hired to keep his eye on Turner. Turner was a new hire for this heist only. You see, that farmer from Grant County? His son was a small player in the Green Envy robbery last fall. He recommended Turner, knowing he needed capital and would do almost anything to get it." Even as Alonzo gave the details, he wondered if Turner was a hired gun and able to glean more money than he would have from just loading manure.

Frankie was scratching her head. "So, why wasn't Clay at the Turner farm then, if he was in on all three jewel thefts?"

Ryan stopped pacing and answered. "Because our

properties butted up next to each other. Clay could keep a low profile if he was working nearby."

Alonzo nodded and held up both hands for attention. "There're still pieces to assemble here and that's where the feds come in. We can speculate, but we don't have the evidence attached to the other two heists to make an exact connection. So, we're impatiently waiting, just like you."

"Where are the suspects being held?" Frankie wanted to know, hoping Clay was under lock and key far, far away.

"Boots the mechanic, whose name is Janus Clary, Clay, Franklin Turner, Melanie Barnes, and Sean St. George were transported separately to Chicago this evening, in custody of INTERPOL. We know they are key players, but we're sure there's a kingpin out there in charge of the whole operation."

Frankie imagined they were looking into Envee Express Shipping and Five Starr Woolens this very minute. A question burned away in her mind: *If Turner was a two-bit player in the operation, why did he shoot Sawyer, and who ordered him to do it? Or was he acting alone?*

It seemed like Alonzo had read her thoughts. "When there are so many players in the game, one of them is bound to spill their guts. And the feds have the power to make deals. I think Turner got in way over his head. He's no hard core thug. If anyone will sing, it'll be him."

Chapter 24

It is never wise to seek or wish for another's misfortune.
If malice or envy were tangible and had a shape,
it would be the shape of a boomerang.
– Charley Reese

The afternoon was waning in Sydney where Neill Starr stood scanning the harbor, expecting a shipment from Envee Express, a shipment of green diamonds, expertly cut by the talented Melanie Barnes. She had texted his burner phone to expect the shipment today.

He salivated over his dream of owning the controlling shares of Five Starr Woolens, which his brother claimed was foolishly out of reach. Sam should never have agreed to the wager. He should have known how ambitious Neill was, how ruthless he could be when he wanted something.

Sam did know.

Neill's office door opened without a knock or announcement from his secretary, which must mean Sam was barging in, interrupting his reverie.

Neill continued gazing out the window, never turning to look at his brother until he realized there were several people in the office with him.

Men in black, wearing dark glasses, emptied his desk drawers, bagged burner phones, and confiscated his laptop. Neill's stomach knotted as his wall safe clicked open, revealing his cherished keepsakes: the Green Envy pearl pendant and Imperial jade Jaguar pendant. These tokens, accompanied by a mammoth Asscher cut green diamond, were meant to be his trophy collection.

Outraged, Neill leaped at one of the agents who was emptying the safe contents into a cloth bag. Starr was met with a gut punch from a powerful fist attached to a strapping body.

Neill laid on the floor and didn't get up; his mind was swimming in murky thoughts. Who turned on him? Was it Sawyer or Melanie? One of his two most trusted operators must have betrayed him. Why hadn't he seen it coming?

He sat up, despite the pain, just in time to see Sam standing in the doorway, an agent on either side of him. He wasn't cuffed, but was shepherded by escorts on either side.

Neill's heart ached momentarily for the older brother who played with him as a child, who taught him how to maneuver a soccer ball, who gave Neill his first surfboard. He smiled weakly.

"Oh, Sam ... I just don't know ..."

Sam's sneer and steely laugh stopped Neill from finishing. His stomach knotted into a ball of concrete. His own brother, of course.

"So, you thought we made an honest wager?" Sam kept his voice level and chiseled.

Puzzled, Neill glared at Sam. "You always thought you were better than me. I wanted to prove I could be just as good. All I've ever wanted is your approval, Big Brother." Too late, Neill realized he wanted a partnership with Sam more than he wanted a takeover. But that thinking wouldn't do now.

Sam arched one eyebrow. He hadn't expected this from Neill. He shrugged. "At one time, I thought we might become partners. But, your wager proved that could never happen. That's who you are, Neill. Always wanting more than your share. You're a leech."

The agents pulled on Sam's arms. Time to get going. Sam whispered something to one agent, who nodded.

"You shouldn't have dumped Melanie until after the job was finished, Brother." Sam drew his brows together in a flinty stare.

Chapter 25

Nature does have manure and she does have roots
as well as blossoms, and you can't hate the manure
and blame the roots for not being blossoms.
– Buckminster Fuller

Days passed, and Frankie filed her initial story with *Point Press,* drawing kudos from Magda, who implored her to stay with it until the case was closed. Frankie agreed, but her heart wanted to enjoy the rest of summer with Violet and the business of baking and cultivating grapes.

People were surprised when Bubble and Bake catered the farm breakfast a couple of days later at the Turners' posh barn.

Hannah called Frankie the day after her brother-in-law's arrest. The baker convinced her to go through with the breakfast the following weekend.

"You mean you're still willing to cater it—after everything?" Hannah was dumbfounded.

"Of course," Frankie said brightly. "Hannah, you didn't do anything wrong and neither did Nate. There's no reason not to move forward—for your family's sake."

"What about Carmen?" Hannah found it impossible to believe she would be quick to forgive the Turners, but Frankie reassured her that Carmen was a professional.

Carmen, on the other hand, was aligned with Hannah's thoughts. "Yes, the shop should still cater the breakfast, Frankie, but there's no way I'm setting foot on the Turner property, so you better line up someone else to deliver the food," she snapped, arms crossed tightly over her chest.

Frankie had anticipated Carmen's reaction and couldn't blame her for it, so she already planned on Peggy and Jovie to help.

Naturally, the small town buzzed with talk and gossip centered around the shooting and jewel heists. Deep Lakes hadn't been the locus of a federal crime like this before, and people there would never forget it.

Frankie imagined the story would become part of history and the facts would blur into a juicy tale. She worried about Violet's reputation and wondered if the town would treat her fairly. Mostly, she feared her daughter would not recover, that the incident would scar her and keep her from trusting anyone romantically again.

She thought counseling was the right avenue for Violet, so she asked advice from two people with divergent approaches: Officer Shirley and Dr. Sadie. It was no surprise they recommended counselors with wildly different methods; one who was direct and tough, the other who was empathetic and gentle.

She gave both recommendations to Violet and was amazed when her daughter chose the no-nonsense therapist.

Fortunately, many townspeople were kind and sympathetic toward Violet. They blamed the outsiders, as is often the case in small communities. They even blamed them for Franklin Turner's undoing, even though the Turners had a mean reputation. But, so it goes.

Franklin's greed caught up to him. He ended up being a gun for hire to make substantially more money.

Frankie had a lot of repair work to do to rebuild Violet's trust, so she kept her in the loop with each update that came her way on the case. Both eagerly awaited closure, hoping the feds would keep their end of the bargain and let Alonzo know when more arrests were made.

A week later, with July 4th looming on the calendar, Frankie anticipated a large picnic and barbecue at Bountiful with friends, family, and employees. A celebration of summer was just what everyone needed, in her opinion, to feel normal again.

The new summer vintages were selling like hotcakes, but it was too late to batch more for the summer season. Instead, Bountiful turned to autumn flavors to prepare for September, and that included Violet's experimental caramel apple mead. Mother and daughter planned a small launch party for a September weekend, wagering the mead would be a success.

Violet took the lead in planning the launch as she kept her eye on the progress of the vintage, pulling out samples that tasted promising.

"The name Green Envy crossed my mind, but I decided Golden Desire was more suitable," she confided in Nelson and Zane one morning. "I think Green Envy would just conjure up bad memories for no good purpose." Nelson and Zane applauded her selection. They both had been watchful over Violet since the incident, but Nelson didn't pursue his interest in her.

Violet coped by keeping busy. Although she still spent time with Tara, she wasn't socializing at the same places or with Haley and Paige. Instead, she immersed herself in the winery and mead venture, and spent Friday nights and Sunday afternoons working at Bubble and Bake, learning the language of wine and acquiring the finesse needed for tastings. Working with her mom and grandmother seemed to revive her spirits.

Late Friday afternoon, following the successful farm breakfast, Frankie and Violet were checking wine inventory for the weekend rush.

"We're going to need more Garden Patch and Enchanted Elderberry, Mom. They're currently outselling all your other summer varieties," Violet claimed.

The two offerings were new to the line-up: The Enchanted was the first time Bountiful crafted elderberry wine, while the Garden Patch featured a strawberry-rhubarb blend made with three red grape varieties.

"I'm so glad people like the Garden Patch. Strawberry wine is tricky to get the taste right. I didn't want to make cough syrup!" Frankie made a sour face.

As they continued restocking, she received a call from Alonzo.

"Hey Frankie," he sounded miffed. "Check your email. Looks like the Chicago Tribune got the scoop on the Green Envy case. Hope this doesn't get you in hot water with Magda."

Frankie promised the *Point Press* editor she'd stick with the story, but she certainly couldn't dog federal agents. It came as no surprise to her that the giant Chicago paper would have inside connections to the information.

"Magda will have to deal with it. Besides, I can add my local flavor to the updated article."

Lon laughed. "There's a new side to you. I've never known you to take things as they come."

Frankie snorted. "Even I can learn how to adapt. Things happen for a reason. Maybe this incident was supposed to include a lesson with my name on it."

"At any rate, check the email. I put in a call to my contact at the feds. Whatever I can tell you, I will."

Frankie asked Tess to help Violet finish stocking and trucked to her office to read the email. Lon included a link to the article with the headline:

Envee Express Mogul Arrested For International Jewel Heists. The subheading read: *Hunt for Missing Green Gems Continues.*

Frankie absorbed as many high points from the first reading as possible, knowing she would comb through the details later, taking copious notes for her own files.

Australian Neill Starr owned Envee Express and had an interest in the parent company, Five Starr Woolens. Neill's brother, Sam, the CFO of Five Starr, was also being questioned about his part in the heists, after agents raided their offices in Sydney. Among the items hauled away were computers, burner phones, and large gems from a wall safe.

Allegedly, Neill wanted a bigger piece of the Five Starr corporate pie and bet his brother that he could come up with the cash to buy controlling shares within three years.

Neill studied famous gem heists, then looked for museums where expensive jewels were touring. Since Neill owned a shipping company, he schemed ways to transport the gems, once his gang stole them.

Neill's plan to transport the purloined baubles in sheep manure was original indeed. The deals took longer because of their rural locations, but they could operate under the radar since most small towns lacked good surveillance and their cover gave almost no cause for concern.

It wasn't difficult for Neill to find hired helpers greedy for a cut. He assembled his team which included Sawyer, a loyal employee, and Starr's girlfriend, Melanie Barnes. She recruited Clay and Boots, who went undercover as shearers.

The first heist in Guatemala was easy because it was unexpected. The museum had poor security, and the Imperial jade collection was already crated, ready to be transported by ship from the Gulf of Mexico to New Orleans for display there.

Allegedly, a couple of security guards were paid off to let the intruders take the crates. From there, the crates went by Envee Express to New Orleans, where Sawyer picked them up at the docks in a stolen truck, then stashed them at a sheep farm in Arkansas where the shearers had a job.

Melanie dismantled the gems, recut the larger ones, while the centerpiece stones were claimed by Neill. The recut gems were ready for redistribution to buyers who didn't ask questions.

Clay, Boots, and Melanie skimmed off the top of the treasure trove, unbeknownst to Sawyer or Starr, mostly claiming average sized jewels that would be easy to market.

Things got sticky after the Green Envy and crown jewels pearl theft. For one thing, the feds were on the lookout for thieves after the Imperial jade heist and museums were on high alert.

The pearls were hijacked at the Sydney docks, transferred to an Envee freighter, and made their way to the U.S. where Neill's band of culprits awaited them. Since Envee had large operations in Canada, the Great Lakes made for optimum transport to Kingston, Ontario where an interested buyer waited. But, Sawyer was detained in Chicago at the docks, as were employees of other shipping lines, so the gang had to scramble to find a farm to temporarily offload the gems.

Sawyer asked around about any unscrupulous farmer wanting to make a quick buck and found the Grant County farmer's son, Stan Henrichs. Once again manure would provide a safe place for the stash until the heat was off, and the pearls could be concealed in sheep's wool and carted to a different port on Lake Michigan where less scrutiny was likely. The smaller Wisconsin port of Manitowoc served that purpose.

From there, it was pretty easy for Frankie to figure out how the third heist came to be. She recounted the story to Violet, Carmen, and Peggy, who were assembled at Bubble and Bake for the evening wine shift.

"Stan Henrichs was friends with Franklin Turner from the sheep auctions. Birds of a feather flock together, they say, so Stan provided Franklin's name as a guy in need of easy cash, and Sam Starr capitalized on the fledgling." Frankie paused for effect.

"Sam Starr! Don't you mean, Neill?" Peggy was first to ask.

Carmen jumped in to speculate. "If this was the third heist, Neill probably was goading his brother, because maybe he'd have enough money to buy control of the company. I'm thinking Sam Starr was probably as ruthless as Neill, and wanted to make sure he hired some guys on the inside."

Frankie smiled broadly, ready to burst. "Excellent job, Carmen. Exactly. Sawyer was loyal to the Starr family, and that included Sam. Once Sam got wind of the third heist, he contacted Sawyer, who delivered some names on a silver platter."

Violet was wide-eyed as the details tumbled out. "So, Sam hired Franklin Turner to shoot Sawyer?"

Frankie nodded. "Allegedly. With Sawyer dead, the operation was sure to go sideways. That left the door open for Sam to call the feds and turn in his brother."

Carmen stamped her foot, smirking. "What a creep to turn in his own flesh and blood. But, what about Clay's getaway plan with the others?"

Frankie was walking around the kitchen as the conversation ping-ponged back and forth. "Clay had a good plan, but he trusted the wrong people. He and Boots, or Janus, took Monty into the fold but they didn't know he was a wolf in sheep's clothing."

Carmen and Peggy exchanged eye rolls as Frankie warmed up the story with her sheep metaphor, while Violet wore a look of disgust and shock.

"Monty, or St. George, was an undercover hire by Sam, too. Monty's cousin owns Saints Shipping, hired on to transport the stolen gems from Duluth around the Great Lakes to Montreal. All four operators planned to be aboard the freighter. Once they were in Canada, the diamonds would be sold to the highest bidders, and the five would split the money and head to the hinterlands to hide."

Carmen interjected. "Wait, what about Jonesy's truck? Didn't the Turner hand say Monty was driving it the night of the shooting?"

"Yes," Frankie went on, "but he was mistaken. It turns out Monty and Franklin look very similar in low light. Jenks had seen Monty milling about, so he assumed what he saw. But, Turner was with Jonesy's sister, Regina. He always borrowed Jonesy's truck when he stepped out on his wife. He couldn't be seen in his own truck with the farm logo on the side."

"Poor Ashley Turner. I bet she'd like to disappear. And their poor kids. Even by the time school starts, this will not have blown over. Small towns have long memories. We should do something to help them if we can." Violet clearly understood what Ashley was going through, even though Ashley had more at stake than Violet.

Frankie, Carmen, and Peggy surrounded her with a comforting hug.

*   *   *

After Bubble and Bake closed for the night, Alonzo rapped on the back door where the four women were finishing cleanup duties.

Frankie motioned him inside. "We're just about to have a glass of wine from the opened tasting bottles. Come join us."

Alonzo flopped down on a kitchen stool, weary from too many long days. He waved away the wine glass and asked for a beer. "Spotted Cow if you have it."

Carmen scooted to the cooler and brought back two cold ones. She knew the look on Lon's face all too well.

He popped the top and took an indulgent drink. "Ah, that's better than wine any day. No offense, ladies." He picked up the manilla file he'd set on the counter and opened it.

"We might need a whole drawer for the Green Envy file by the time it's over, but I just brought along some loose ends for you tonight."

The women were as quiet as pew sitters, waiting.

He looked at Carmen. "You'll be happy to know that Jonesy is in the clear. He and his sister will have to answer for concealing information about a crime, but Jonesy feared his sister would get hurt, so they'll get off pretty easy. Other than Clay, the rest of your hands are in the clear, too."

He turned his attention to Violet and Frankie. "Clay is probably going to prison for a long time. Grand larceny, kidnapping, interfering with commerce, and the list goes on. His defense will be that he wanted to protect his sister, but that's not going to hold water."

Protecting someone seemed to be the common theme running through the threads of this case. Frankie and Violet exchanged questioning looks. "Protect Melanie?"

Lon paused and took another slug of brew. "Clay masterminded the rest of the scheme after Turner killed Sawyer. It wasn't part of the original arrangement, but Clay needed to clean up after the shooting. That's why he took Sawyer's personal items and hid them at the vineyard. Once he heard from Melanie about her breakup, he concocted a new game plan to cut out Neill Starr completely and disappear. He didn't know about Franklin or Monty being hired by Sam."

Frankie was ready to test her theories. "Clay also hadn't counted on Manny picking up manure the day before the fertilizer truck, accidentally getting the gems in the mix. One of the hands must have spilled the beans, and Clay must have noticed too late that the wrong pile had been collected."

Lon nodded, staring at his notes. "Oh yeah, Frankie. You should know the BB gun shooter was Monty, Sean St. George. He wanted you to steer clear from the case."

Violet asked about information on Boots. "He seemed like an easygoing, gentle soul." Violet looked bewildered and Frankie wondered if her naivete pointed to an Aunt CeCe side to her personality.

Lon spoke directly to Vi. "Boots aka Tinker aka Janus Clary is anything but gentle. He was Clay's boyhood pal and spent most of his teen years in a detention center after robbing a few old people, even beat up one of them. He learned mechanics at the center, and man, was he gifted. It was Boots who cut the brakes on the Arkansas truck, and it was Boots who left the injured men lying on the roadside after he stole their diamonds."

"And what about Sam Starr? He's certainly not squeaky clean, even if he didn't know about his brother's other heists. He knew about the third one." Carmen spoke defiantly, her sense of justice on display.

Lon shook his head and puckered his lips. "Sam's no idiot. He made a deal before turning in his brother and pointed the agents to as much evidence as he could. He'll get off scot-free or close to it. At most, he'll probably get probation and live under house arrest for a couple of years."

Everyone made faces and muttered in disgust. Frankie refilled wine glasses and opened the second Spotted Cow for Lon.

"Time for a toast to us. We're safe. The bad guys were stopped, and at least it appears the Starrs have fallen from their lofty heights." A lot of eye rolls followed on the heels of Frankie's play on words, but she just giggled.

"Let's celebrate summer and new beginnings." She raised her glass to the center and the others joined in, clinking.

To everyone's amazement, Violet raised her glass a little higher. Blue eyes twinkling shrewdly, cheeks pinked from wine, and chin jutted in defiance, she sang, "Today, I'm declaring my independence—from love."

* * *

Early the next morning, when Frankie and Violet were trotting Sonny around the O'Connor property, a warm breeze kicked up dandelion fluff, sending it swirling around the trio. Violet stopped, stared at the dancing wisps, and giggled.

"Mom, I want to tell you something, but I'm afraid you'll think I'm weird."

It was Frankie's turn to laugh. "Welcome to the weird club, sweety. I feel weird about 80% of the time."

"When I was dating Clay, these little voices inside my head kept buzzing in my ear. It's like they were trying to steer me away from him, if only I would have listened."

Frankie stopped stock-still. "Did these voices sound familiar, and did you ever visualize them?" She reached for Violet's hand and gave it a reassuring squeeze.

"Strangely enough, one sounded like Grandma Peggy and the other like Grandpa Charlie. They looked like twinkle lights. It's like one would light up and give me a message, and then the other would do the same in my other ear. Wow, it sounds even worse when I say it out loud. Maybe I'm losing it."

Frankie laughed. "You're not losing it. You're introspective and finely tuned. We all have inner voices, yours just have more personality than the average conscience, that's all." Frankie was confident she knew what became of the fireflies, and maybe she had graduated in a sense. Maybe she had found her own independence.

Epilogue

Magda called after Frankie filed her updated Green Envy article. She was surprised when she didn't receive the chewing out she expected for not getting the scoop.

"I loved the article, Frankie. Compared to the one in the *Tribune*, it was brilliant. Your local spin and extra details missing from the city paper will gain volumes of attention. I wouldn't be surprised if some big-time papers call us to ask if they can run it. Of course, you'll get the byline, probably shared with Chicago." Magda offered her full attention to the phone call for a change.

"What? You really think so?" Frankie wondered if she needed her ears checked.

"I'll keep you posted, ok? And Frankie, can you write an opinion piece for me that's different from your usual type?" Magda started shuffling papers on her desk now; she had a limited attention span and a full agenda.

"What's that supposed to mean, Magda?"

"It's summer, Frankie. Lighten the mood. Try something fresh. Maybe a human interest angle, or write about wine or bakery or sheep. I don't know, just give me a happy spin. Okay, gotta go."

No follow up questions allowed. As far as Magda was concerned, the ball was now in Frankie's court and she had better score.

Frankie Champagne presents:
My Summer Diamonds

Summer is the happening season for Wisconsin tourist towns, and as a small business owner, I wasn't looking for any distractions. But, Murder arrived as an unwelcome guest and intruded into the lives of people I love. Even as bees make honey from bitter flowers, our town has come through darkness to taste the sweetness of summer again. And in the summer sun, I have gathered some gleaming gems of the season.

Diamonds in the Rough
Difficult times remind me that none of us are fully formed and polished; it's friction that reveals the beautiful diamond. Three Deep Lakes women have added their own luster to the community. My daughter Violet set her sights on learning wine science this summer and crafted her first vintage, a luscious caramel apple mead christened Golden Desire. If you head south on I39 to Deep Lakes, stop by for the grand release of our first mead in September. We'll be celebrating this and our other vintages at a posh new country venue, Under the Stars Barn, on Turner Road, owned and operated by two sparkling women, Hannah and Ashley Turner. Stay tuned for more details.

Facets of Clover Leafs

Four-leaf clovers symbolize more than good fortune. Not only are clovers the luck of the Irish and the dazzling green of life itself, their leaves are heart-shaped. It's been awhile since I really studied four-leaf clovers, although I used to spend hours hunting them in my childhood summers. John Melton wrote the following in 1620 about the clover: "That if any man walking in the fields, find any foure-leaved grasse, he shall in a small while after find some good thing." When my daughter was gifted a four-leaf clover necklace, I couldn't conceive of any "good thing" that could come from it, but I was wrong. I realized the value of each single leaf. The quatrefoil reminds me of the four most important loves of my life: my two daughters, my mother, and my aunt CeCe. The open spaces between each heart-shaped petal means I have room in my heart for more loved ones, too.

Unexpected Four-legged Treasure

Friends come in all forms: My newest sidekick and guardian is a sheltie named Sonny. Although he's going blind in his elder dog years, his sense of smell and sound are top notch. Sonny became my loyal protector when I needed him most. He even took BB pellets on my behalf, and that's every bit as good as a bullet in my book. I now have a walking partner and a bosom buddy who holds my trust.

Hidden Treasures Among Friends

It took some digging, but I discovered that no matter how long you know someone, they can still surprise you. First, there's Aunt CeCe, who I just found out was the State Women's Softball Champion pitcher three years running in the 1960's. I would never have known this prized tidbit if she hadn't lobbed a stone at a hornet's nest 50 yards away and nabbed a thief in my orchard! What a precious jewel that woman is in our family collection.

Then there's my dear friend, Carmen. She stunned me when I saw garb in her closet that no sheep rancher/bakery boss would ever wear. I can't give you any details because she and I were working undercover at the time. Let's just say I underestimated the rebel side of this mom. By the way, Carmen is now an officer in the newly named women's group: Agri-Stars. Every one of these All-Star women lead some form of agribusiness in Whitman County.

And there's more hidden treasure in Whitman County everywhere you look: shops, restaurants, lakes, campgrounds, and Mother Nature's stunning jewels on display all around you. Come take a look for yourself before summer trades her green gems for autumn rubies.

June 30th: Carmen tapped Frankie on the shoulder as she scooted out of the pew after Sunday Mass, cheering the fact the choir was on summer break except for special days, which cut the service to 45 minutes.

"I don't know if you're going right to the shop, but could you please? I'll meet you there." Carmen brushed past her friend like a whirlwind, leaving Frankie bewildered.

Despite the early hour, Carmen was already pouring wine at the lounge bar for three guests when Frankie walked in. She opened her mouth to ask for an explanation when Jake, Rose, and Grizz turned around to greet her wearing their best smiles and clothes that looked almost appropriate for church rather than The Oasis.

"Nice to see you all again." Frankie joined Carmen on the business side of the polished walnut bar. "Rose said you'd be coming sometime for a tasting; and lucky you, you get a private one to boot." Frankie began assembling red wines from the sample cart as Carmen pulled chilled bottles from the cooler.

"We're actually here to congratulate you on your newspaper article. How exciting!" Rose flushed with pride in the name of empowerment, but Frankie didn't comprehend.

"So, you liked the Summer Diamonds piece in Point Press?" Frankie scrunched her brows together, unable to imagine why Rose would be over the moon about Frankie's personal reflections.

It was Rose's turn to look confused. "Oh, I didn't see the Point Press piece, sorry." She pulled a rolled up newspaper from her leather hobo bag, made a production of unrolling it, opening it to page two, and turning it to face Frankie. She jabbed a purple fingernail at the top, where an article on the Australian jewel heists spread across the entire top half of the *Chicago Tribune* broadsheet. The byline read: *Frankie Champagne* and *Lewis Chapman.*

Frankie stared in disbelief, mouth agape, while the others suppressed giggles, even Carmen.

Frankie peered at the date-June 29th. "How did I not know about this?" She happily skimmed the article, in awe at the large chunks of information reprinted from the original *Point Press* piece she'd written on the Deep Lakes shooting, the green diamonds found on Bountiful property, and the apprehended criminals. She beamed proudly and joined in the toast raised in her honor.

After the cheers, Grizz cleared his throat. "One more thing, Frankie." He looked warily at Carmen's sideways smirk. She could barely contain her laughter. "I'm hoping you still have Sundae, the cat Carmen told me about? If you don't mind, I'd like to bring her home with me." He paused to compose himself. "I just lost my 20-year-old tomcat, and I sure could use a new companion."

Frankie picked up on Carmen's salty vibe. "Sundae's a pretty sassy tortie, Grizz. You sure you want to sign on for that female attitude?"

Grizzle nodded as a little color rose up his cheeks. "I think I can handle a little sass." Frankie couldn't disagree. She hadn't figured Grizz for a cat lover, but thinking about Sundae being coddled by the old softy made her happy. Twice in one day, Frankie was bowled over. She couldn't wait to show the *Tribune* to her mother, Violet, and Garrett. Rejoicing inwardly, she wondered what Abe Arnold of *The Whitman Watch* would say next time he saw her. Maybe he'd be a little green with envy.

Acknowledgements

Much gratitude goes out to Larry and Kathy Becker who have been in the sheep farming business since 1980. Larry has served on both the National Lamb Committee and the National Wool Committee and is a warehouse of knowledge on most sheep-related subjects. At one point the Beckers maintained a flock of 500 ewes, but have downsized to about 75 recently as they look toward retirement.

I appreciate their patience as I asked for explanations on sheep terms I didn't know, such as pronking - a gleeful leaping around the pasture that lambs do in early summer, which makes the person witnessing this as joyful as the wooly lambs. I'm also thankful they allowed me to make a pest of myself holding lambs and barn kittens and taking photos around the farm.

I'm eternally grateful to my editor Kay Rettenmund who makes my writing better with each reading she does. I love it that she challenges me to rethink my storyline and characters, which forces me to get to know them more intimately.

Thank you to the people at Ten16 Press, an imprint of Orange Hat Publishing. I'm happy to have my home-grown Wisconsin team to work with me on this book adventure. Shannon and Lauren are the go-to women who make me feel like I'm the only author in their house as they provide guidance and answers when I need them.

Thank you Victoria Rydberg-Nania for your generous spirit, publicity lessons, and just being all-around kind and admirable. You are a dear friend to authors.

Thank you to my ARC readers for your precious time and kind feedback: Kelly Young, Marilyn Levinson/ Allison Brook, Jamie Gillespie, Kim Heniadis, and Missi Martin. Finally, thank you readers of the series. Because of you, Frankie and Carmen have lives on and off the page, and I get to play with them. Because of you, I have a second home in Deep Lakes, a splendid bakery and wine lounge, and a vineyard that calls me to enjoy our natural world. How lucky I am that we have found one another. Stay in touch.

- Joy Ann Ribar

Recipes

Rhubarb Cherry Tart

Nut Crust (Use this for other fresh fruit tarts, too)
2 cups all-purpose flour
½ cup ground walnuts
⅓ cup powdered sugar
¼ cup sugar
½ teaspoon salt
¾ cup (1½ sticks) cold unsalted butter, cut in small pieces
1 egg, beaten

In food processor, combine nuts, flour, sugars and salt. Blend thoroughly. Add pieces of cold butter and pulse until mixture resembles coarse meal. Add egg and pulse just until the dough comes together. Place on floured surface, pat it into a round disk ½ inch thick. Wrap and chill for at least 2 hours.

Roll chilled dough into about a 12 inch circle and place in a 10 inch pie plate. Press dough into bottom and up the sides.

Prick bottom with a fork. Weight the crust to keep it

from shrinking away from the edges of the pan. Bake at 425°
for 10-14 minutes until it is light brown. It will bake longer
once it's filled. Cool before filling. (If you use this for fresh
fruit toppings, bake the crust until it's brown and firm, then
cool and top with a cream cheese or custard base and fresh
fruit.)

For Warm Tart Filling:
2½ cups fresh rhubarb, sliced into 1-inch pieces
2½ cups fresh or frozen Door County or tart cherries
1 cup brown sugar
2 tablespoons + 1 teaspoon cornstarch
½ teaspoon kosher salt
½ teaspoon ground cinnamon
½ teaspoon ground ginger
½ teaspoon almond extract (or vanilla)

Combine sliced rhubarb, cherries, brown sugar,
cornstarch, salt, extract and spices in a large bowl. Mix
gently, and set aside for an hour at room temperature to
blend flavors.

Before adding filling to the pre-baked crust, drain the
juices created by letting the fruit stand. Only use about ½
cup of the juices in your tart so it doesn't get soggy.

Fill the cooled crust and bake at 400° for about 30
minutes—filling should wiggle a bit. If it doesn't look baked,
adjust the time as needed.

Rhubarb Chocolate Cake Brownies
(Thank you, Lori Burbach)

1 cup sugar
½ cup vegetable oil
2 large eggs
1 tsp vanilla
Whisk the above together in large bowl.
½ cup flour
⅓ cup cocoa
½ tsp baking powder
½ tsp salt

Stir the dry ingredients together before adding to the wet mixture.

Combine the wet and dry ingredients in the large bowl with a mixing spoon.

Fold in: 1 cup chopped rhubarb and ½ cup of mini chocolate chips.

Line an 8x8 pan with parchment. Dump the mixture and spread into the pan. Bake at 350° for 40 minutes. So good with ice cream!

Two Grandmothers Berry Cream Pie
(Thank you, Chris Lalor Kearns, for sharing
this two-family favorite recipe)

Pie Crust:

1 cup flour

⅔ cup shortening

½ teaspoon salt

Mix these together.

Shake up: ⅓ cup flour and ¼ cup water. Then add to first mixture. Roll out and press into a 9 inch pie plate. Chill about 30 minutes. Bake crust with pie weights or lined with parchment on the bottom only of the crust at 375° for about 15 minutes. Remove the parchment or weights and bake another 12-14 minutes until golden brown and baked through.

Berry Cream:

2 cups raspberries

1 cup heavy cream, whipped. When cream is thick, stir in ½ cup sugar.

Place 1½ envelopes Knox gelatin into ¼ cup of ice cold water. Let this sit until thick.

Fold the berries into the whipped cream. Stir the thick gelatin in next. Spread the mixture into the cooled pie crust. Refrigerate.

Teff Muffins à la Tess
(No electric mixer needed)

1 cup teff flour
½ cup all-purpose flour
½ cup almond flour
½ cup plus 1 tablespoon brown sugar, divided
2 teaspoons baking powder
½ teaspoon baking soda
¼ teaspoon ground cinnamon
¼ teaspoon allspice
¼ teaspoon fine sea salt
2 large eggs
¾ cup 2% milk
¼ cup of the lightest olive oil
1 apple, chopped
½ cup dried cranberries
¼ cup toasted sliced almonds

Preheat the oven to 350°F. Butter a 12-cup muffin tin or line with paper muffin liners.

In a large bowl, whisk together teff flour, all-purpose flour, almond flour, ½ cup brown sugar, baking powder, baking soda, cinnamon, allspice, and salt.

In a second bowl, whisk together eggs, milk and oil until blended.

Stir egg mixture into flour mixture until just combined.

Gently stir in apple pieces and cranberries. Spoon batter into muffin cups and sprinkle with remaining 1 tablespoon brown sugar and toasted almonds.

Bake until a toothpick inserted in the center of a muffin comes out clean, about 25 minutes.

Not-Your-Average Cake Bites
(Served at Joy's Book Launch)

Strawberry Champagne Cake Bites

(Yes, you can use a cake mix!)

1 Lemon Cake Mix (I like Duncan Hines best)

⅓ cup of light oil (I use the lightest olive oil I can find)

3 eggs

1½ cups of Prosecco or Champagne

Blend ingredients as directed on box. Bake in 9x13 pan. Cool.

While cake cools, **make wine frosting:**

2 cups powdered sugar

½ cup salted butter, softened, not melted

2 tablespoons Moscato or other white wine

1½ teaspoons vanilla extract

2 spoonfuls of strawberry jam (you can add more to taste)

Blend butter and powdered sugar, then add wine and vanilla. Stir in jam last.

Crumble up the cooled cake. Add ½ to 1 cup of wine frosting and check consistency before adding more. You should be able to form into balls without them falling apart.

Chill or freeze. Bites should feel solid before dipping them.

Dip in melted white chocolate and sprinkle if desired.

Empanada Dulces from Tia Pepita

Dough:

3 cups unbleached flour

⅓ cup sugar

Pinch of salt

8 ounces unsalted cold butter, cut into pieces

2 eggs

2-4 tablespoons cold milk

Mix the flour, sugar and salt in a food processor.

Add the butter, eggs and water and blend into a dough ball.

Knead the dough for a few minutes.

Form 2 balls, flatten into thick discs, and chill in the refrigerator.

Roll into a thin ⅛ inch sheet. Cut into 3 inch circles.

Place circles on a parchment lined sheet to fill.

Filling:

4 cups chopped fresh peaches

½ cup sugar

1 tablespoon cornstarch

1 teaspoon lemon juice

2 teaspoons fresh thyme leaves

½-¾ teaspoon allspice

Allow peach filling to marinate in the above ingredients for an hour. Drain any juices (you can use juice to make a glaze for the empanadas, thickened with powdered sugar)

Add peach filling to center of each empanada circle. Be sure you leave enough room to seal the edges. Fold in half and use fork tines to crimp edges firmly (or you can use a tart mold that has a crimper).

Chill before baking. Chilled dough bakes better, more evenly, and doesn't spread. Bake at 375° for about 20 minutes or 400° for 15 minutes until golden. Cool 3-5 minutes and remove to a wire rack. Sift powdered sugar over the top or make a thin icing from the peach juice and drizzle over the tops.

Leeky Ceiling Quiche

Make your favorite pie crust, but do not pre-bake it. Prick the bottom and sides for heat circulation.

Filling:
2 large cleaned leeks, sliced thinly into circles

Chopped garlic to taste (2-3 cloves)

2 teaspoons French thyme

¼ teaspoon culinary lavender flowers, if you can find them

French herbs (2 teaspoons): If you cannot find this mixture, it includes: dill weed, basil, chervil, oregano or tarragon, and chives. I use whatever I can find!

Sauté the above ingredients in 2 tablespoons butter over medium-low heat until tender, glistening, and aromatic. Remove from the stove and cool.

Place cooled leek mixture on the bottom of pie crust. Top with zest of one lemon.

Top with 1 cup shredded Swiss cheese and 1 cup of white cheddar or Monterey Jack cheese.

Whisk together: 1½ cups whole milk or half & half, 5 eggs, salt and pepper to taste. Pour carefully over the cheeses and leeks.

Bake at 415° for 15-20 minutes until crust edges are browned. Turn down the oven to 325° and bake for another 25-30 minutes until golden. Let sit for 10 minutes or so before cutting.

Book Club Discussion Questions

1. How did the setting of the book contribute to the mystery?

2. Who was on your list of suspects? Did you guess correctly? If so, how did you figure out the right answers?

3. Follow the clues given in the story. Which were helpful? Which led you astray?

4. Mother/Daughter relationships play an important role in this book as well as the series. Discuss the relationship between Frankie and Violet. Describe the relationship between Peggy and Frankie. How do these relationships evolve within the story?

5. Read your favorite passage from the book. How do you think the author's style adds to the narrative in this passage?

6. Discuss the head of chapter quotes. Which ones did you like? How did they contribute to the theme of the novel?

7. The author believes in life lessons and invites readers to delve more deeply in a personal way during and after reading the novel. What would you like to share about the book's message? Did you make any personal connections in the lessons offered?

8. If you lived in Deep Lakes, where would you see yourself as a community member or character?

Coming in 2022:

Deep Dire Harvest

Grapes wait for nobody. The tourist season is running full swing when Frankie's vineyard is ripe for picking, leaving her a little frazzled as she divides her time between the Bubble & Bake shop and Bountiful Fruits winery. When a dead body surfaces in nearby Blackbird Pond, it quickly becomes an albatross around Frankie's neck. The victim, a national bird expert in town for Fall Migration Days, also happens to be a cousin to Cherry and Pom, Bubble & Bake employees. The B & B crew are sure to ruffle some feathers during their sleuthing: Can they solve the murder before the guilty bird flies the coop?

About the Author

 Joy Ann Ribar lives in central Wisconsin where she writes the Deep Lakes Cozy Mystery Series, starring baker/vintner Frankie Champagne and her cohort in business and adventure, Carmen Martinez. Joy is inspired to share the beauty of Wisconsin's four distinct seasons and shed light on the state's whimsical quirks. The many hats Joy's worn in life such as news reporter, paralegal, English teacher, and administrative assistant, factor into her writing. She is a proud member of Sisters in Crime, Blackbird Writers, and Wisconsin Writers Association. Joy and her husband, John, plan to sell their house, buy an RV and travel around the U.S. spreading good cheer and hygge! Joy's first two mysteries, *Deep Dark Secrets* and *Deep Bitter Roots*, are bestsellers for Ten16 Press, a division of Orange Hat Publishing.

Sign up for email updates and see more about upcoming events at joyribar.com.
Follow Joy at: blackbirdwriters.com
Instagram: @authorjoyribar
Facebook: Joy Ann Ribar Wisconsin Author
          Blackbird Writers

If you enjoyed this book, I'd be delighted to receive a short review. An independent author thanks you kindly!
Leave a rating and review on:
Amazon.com
Goodreads.com
BookBub.com